BACKSTABBING LITTLE ASSETS

BACKSTABBING LITTLE ASSETS

BIRTH OF HEAVY METAL™ BOOK 3

MICHAEL TODD

MICHAEL ANDERLE

DISRUPTIVE IMAGINATION

JIT Readers

Kelly O'Donnell
Nicole Emens
James Caplan
Crystal Wren
John Ashmore
Peter Manis
Jeff Eaton
Paul Westman

Editor
Skyhunter Editing Team

DEDICATION

To Family, Friends and
Those Who Love
to Read.
May We All Enjoy Grace
to Live the Life We Are
Called.

CHAPTER ONE

The whole objective of power armor was to supposedly lower the impact of a massive automatic rifle. Sal agreed that it had done its job fairly well, all things considered, as he had fired on and off for the past couple of hours or so.

He remembered the time when he had shot these creatures without a power arm to stabilize the weapon for more efficient use and how sore he had been afterward. Given that, his assessment of "fairly well" meant he was simply doing some first-world complaining. Out in the middle of an alien jungle in Africa, granted, but still.

His arm still ached from having to maintain the constant firing, and each time he pulled the trigger, it only grew worse. Kennedy had mentioned something about fatigue and how doing the same thing for too long would make your body ache simply from constantly holding the unnatural position. It made sense, but what the hell was he supposed to do about that?

"This wasn't one of your best ideas!" Monroe growled

at him from where she knelt on the ground. She had emptied all the magazines for her sidearm and since she hadn't brought any extra weapons, if she wanted to help them ward their attackers off, she needed to be creative.

"Come on, Doc," Kennedy said with a grin, "we all know you're better suited for setting up traps now that you're running dry."

"Pun intended?" Sal asked and reloaded his rifle quickly as two panthers pounced from the trees, their lips peeled back in a snarl. These creatures were smaller than usual but had an odd shape to their venomous fangs, which Sal took a picture of before he eliminated them.

"Fuck yeah." Kennedy laughed and fell back quickly behind him when her own mag ran out. He covered her while she reloaded.

"It's still a dumb fucking idea," Monroe said and shook her head. The new suit they'd purchased for her was lighter, smoother, and included top-of-the-line scientific software. In addition, it was nimble enough to allow for easier tactile dexterity when she conducted experiments. It was a suit fully designed for a specialist and wasn't easily adapted to a gunner's role.

"Hey, it's old-school," he said defensively. "Old-school has all the best ideas. You should know that by now."

"Not to bother you or anything but we have angry animals over here you might want to focus on instead of chit chat," Kennedy said and sounded annoyed.

"Right." Sal nodded and moved ahead to cover her as she once again needed to reload. He tapped the trigger and his gun kicked painfully once more. The slugs struck home in another two of the panthers, exploded their skulls, and felled them with a heavy thud.

"Shit." He hissed with annoyance. "I should have tried to clip it."

"Stop fucking around," Madigan remonstrated. "When you're too busy trying to wound them instead of killing them, they'll end up killing you. So shut up and kill shit." She activated one of the new weapons functions on her suit. A small, shoulder-mounted launcher jutted from the plate and fired a small projectile which rocketed into a pack of hyenas and unleashed a firestorm of carnage.

"Classy," Sal said and shook his head. As much as he detested the brutality of it, he couldn't say it didn't look as cool as fuck.

"Well, you can take the man out of the lab but not the test tube out of his ass," Kennedy said with a grin as the launcher retracted into her suit.

"Hey now," Courtney said and pulled herself up from what she was working on. "I think if that was what he liked doing, he would have brought it up with us by now."

This was why he shouldn't be physically involved with his business partners, especially when it meant trips into the Zoo with both of them. He had moved past the fear of a shot in the back but now, he had to deal with the snide comments and the double entendres that flew as fast as the bullets.

He liked to be the one to hand out those little gems, damn it. Since he was still relatively new to all this, he simply didn't have the mental dexterity to keep up with them while he fought for his life at the same time. Maybe multi-tasking was a particularly feminine attribute, after all.

Sal simply muttered and shook his head as he examined the steel trap Monroe had worked on. "I thought...the rules—"

"Yeah, rules are to keep personal and professional lives separate," Kennedy said through their private comm connection. "I guess you'll have to spank her when we get back."

"Wha— Damn it, Kennedy," he snapped before he turned to the scientist. "Are you finished setting the trap up yet?"

"Yep, all done." She made a gesture of wiping her hands clean. "Your stupid traps are set and ready."

"They're not stupid," he protested. "There's a GPS marker on each of them with a trigger that will alert us if the traps are activated while we are in here. We'll disable them when we leave so no one gets the benefit of our ideas but this way, we can bring more live specimens back to the base. Need I remind either of you of the kind of money we get when we bring live specimens in? Maybe in the form of our nice little complex?"

"Show off," Kennedy said. "But it looks like we're in the clear for the moment."

"And one of our traps just went off," Sal said and grinned victoriously. "What were you saying about stupid traps again?"

"Your traps are still stupid." Monroe shrugged. "Even if they do work. Even a broken watch is right twice a day."

"Clock," he corrected as they moved toward the trap in

question. "Digital watches are wrong every second of the day."

"Nitpicker," Kennedy accused and shook her head. It was nice that even though they bickered constantly, they were still able to keep things mostly professional and at least part of their minds on the job. She took point quickly and handed the other woman her spare sidearm while he brought up the rear.

The sounds of gunfire and snatches of comm conversations, shredded by the interference around them, could be heard as they gradually moved closer to where the trap had been triggered.

"It looks like we've run into another squad," Sal said. "Should we go ahead and give them a helping hand?"

"Do you think they'll pay us for the trouble?" Kennedy asked.

"I doubt it." Monroe rolled her shoulders and eased her pack into a more comfortable position. "They'll be really grateful and buy us a couple of rounds at the base, but other than that, in terms of actual monetary compensation? No, I don't think so."

A moment of silence fell as they proceeded cautiously through the tough, dark terrain.

"We'll help the useless bastards anyway, won't we?" Kennedy asked and sounded resigned to their inevitable goodwill actions.

"Well, we are out here often," Sal rationalized, "and if we were in the kind of trouble where we needed help, wouldn't we want those useless bastards to come to our aid too?"

Madigan rolled her eyes. "Ugh, fine. We'll help them out of trouble. But I still don't think they'll jump to return the favor if we are up shit creek with no paddle."

Sal looked at her and tilted his head with a small grin. "Come on. Up shit creek without a paddle?"

"I know, I know," she said and shook her head. "I heard it too."

They reached the place where the trap had been set and looked around.

"Where'd you leave the damn trap, Monroe?" Kennedy asked.

"You guys asked me to make them hard to see," the specialist pointed out. "That's what I did. It's right over there."

She pointed a little to Kennedy's left. The woman turned and looked where the cage rested above a woven mass of roots rather than on the ground itself. It had, in fact, been triggered and a smaller reptile was captive inside. The creature had four legs and a long, whip-like tail that now wrapped around the steel bars.

"I wonder what they'll pay for this little guy?" she asked thoughtfully. "What do you think we should call him?"

"Two very irrelevant questions," Sal said. He tensed instantly and took a few steps back. "It's calm now, but if you move any closer, it'll be agitated. And you don't want to agitate that one."

"Why not?" she asked. "It's not like he'll be able to break through the bars or anything."

As if it could understand what she had said, the reptile immediately acted to prove her wrong. Round flaps unfurled from under its jaw and fanned upward around its face, which made it look far bigger than it was. The bottom half of its jaw parted down the middle and a pair of fleshy blue jets spurted a foul-smelling liquid at the bars. The fluid dissolved the metal in seconds and created a hole large enough for the reptile to squeeze through. Once it was out, it rose onto its two hind legs and raced away into the underbrush.

"You had to go and jinx it, didn't you?" Monroe asked and rolled her eyes at the other woman.

Kennedy shrugged. "I don't believe in jinxes."

Sal tried to slap his face with his palm but was prevented from doing so by the helmet he wore. "This is why we end up in so many fights. Some people who shall remain nameless simply have no respect."

"You're nothing but a pair of babies," Kennedy retorted and checked her weapon again. "Now, do you guys want to give me the whole speech about how jinxes are real or do you want to come along and help some useless bastards out of a mess they probably caused all by themselves?"

He shook his head. While he was a rational man, it was very clear from everything around them that there was a ton of shit out there they still didn't understand. He couldn't say for a fact that jinxes were real, but he couldn't say they weren't either. It seemed to be only good sense to keep all his bases covered one way or another.

Madigan obviously didn't feel the same way and he had no inclination to run her through the science of what he thought. They lapsed into silence and set off in the direction in which the gunfire could still be heard. It was more intense now and the barrage of firepower was impossible to miss. They pushed in deeper and prepped their weapons as they walked.

Eventually, they moved in close enough to hear the chatter with more clarity, and Kennedy pinged her location in the comm channel before she spoke into it.

"Unidentified team, this is Team Heavy Metal," she said. "It sounds like you folks could use a little backup there, over."

"Roger that, Heavy Metal," a man's voice responded immediately. "We have ourselves in some trouble. If you're in our area, we would really appreciate your support. Over."

"We are in your area," she said, "and we're moving toward you, heading northeast. Try not to shoot us. Over."

"Understood, Heavy Metal," he replied. "Out."

The three of them broke cover and navigated through the animal corpses the beleaguered team had left for a full minute before they reached them. Although the sound of gunfire had now ceased, what they found was a handful of stragglers. They had encountered a couple of people in suits sprawled on the ground during their advance, but given that they had been left behind, Sal could only assume they were already dead. The torn and gashed appearance of their armor confirmed the assumption.

The team was two down with five left standing but a couple of them looked like they needed medical attention.

"What's the situation?" Kennedy asked and took control.

"I'm Sergeant Jeffords," the man who had replied over

the comms said. "You have no idea how much we appreciate your help. Is it only the three of you?"

"Yeah, we work freelance out here," she told him.

"This is a dangerous place for smaller groups," he said with a furtive look around him. "The critters swarm more often lately, and many more teams have gone missing out there."

"Yep," she replied with a nod. "We've been careful, though, and come out here with larger teams. We broke away a short while ago since we had company business to take care of out here. We were actually on the way to catch up with them when we heard the battle."

"We really appreciate it, Sergeant Kennedy."

"It's not sergeant anymore," she pointed out.

"Once a Marine, always a Marine," Jeffords responded. "Besides, we all know you're among the best around here."

"It looks like the critters have had their fill," Sal said, although he tried not to make it sound like the circle-jerk of military-based compliments these discussions could end up as. "They've backed away for good. We didn't see any on our way in here."

"That said," Monroe interjected, "there's no guarantee they won't come back for another attempt. We should probably get you boys back to the base."

"Agreed." The man nodded. They paused for a moment to tag the bodies for recovery and retrieve the dog tags before the two teams headed back the way they'd come. Conversation was almost non-existent as most of the energy was used to help the wounded. They made good time despite the constraints and under five hours later, with the sun only about halfway down to the horizon, they reached the outskirts of the Zoo. A quick glance confirmed that the jungle edged closer and closer to the Staging Area on the Zoo side of the wall, and Sal didn't much care for that.

They mounted the six-wheeled JLTV and set off toward the base.

CHAPTER TWO

"What was our haul today?" Sal asked as Kennedy and Monroe joined him in the common area of their compound. It was a place meant for at least two dozen people, so it felt rather empty with only the three of them. He knew there would be complaints about the lack of space if they added more personnel but when he saw a place as empty as this, it only served to remind him of the dangers they would face outside.

"I have it right here," Kennedy said. She took a seat in one of the loungers and kicked her feet up. Her hair was still wet from a shower which had failed to clean the grease stains she'd acquired when she'd repaired the minor damage their suits had taken.

She had dedicated a fair amount of time to learn how to work on them, which kept their repair expenses at a minimum. The haul that had enabled them to purchase the property had rapidly been whittled away. There was still some of it left, but Sal had decided to put it into a buffer fund rather than spend it too quickly.

Which meant they once again relied on their day-to-day income to keep up with official expenses as well as personal money.

Monroe stepped in, also damp from the shower with her towel still wrapped around her head. She dropped onto a couch and tucked her legs under her.

"Well, the Pita sets we brought in accounted for a little over forty-five thousand," Kennedy said. "That plus the research grants, which were thirteen. The team we helped out referred us to the commandant, so we might see some pay from that, but it probably won't come in this week."

"All in all, it's not bad for a half-day's work," Courtney said with a smile and looked pleased.

"Not bad at all," Sal agreed. "Even so, I thought about what the sergeant said in there. What was his name again?"

"Jeffords." Kennedy tilted her head as she waited for him to speak. "What did he say?"

"About how the job has become more dangerous." He leaned back in his lounger. "The animals now swarm more, attack more, and grow more aggressive with each passing day. It has definitely become more and more dangerous to go out there with only the three of us. We might want to think about signing more people on, preferably gunners."

"I don't think we can afford that," Kennedy said and shook her head firmly. "Not if you intend to keep that million and a half locked away for a rainy day."

"Why not?" Monroe asked. "Look around. We have nothing but space."

"It's about more than space," the other woman replied tersely. "They'll want a cut. With the amount of money needed to run the generators and fill the vehicles, our profit margin has taken a hit. Add one more person with all the supplies, salary—can we afford that?"

"Well, like Courtney said, we have more than enough space," Sal said after he'd considered the question for a moment. "Everyone and their grandma knows how expensive it is to live in the base if you aren't on the government's payroll. Anyone who wants to work for themselves would be able to take a pay cut if they come out here. They'll have a place to live, supplies, and a team to work with that gets them into the Zoo regularly. I think we can afford that."

"Yep," Kennedy said with a slight edge to her tone. "Look for a mercenary who's willing to take a pay cut. Good luck with that."

"Thanks," he said with a grin.

"I was sarcastic." She rolled her eyes.

"I know." He chuckled. "I merely decided to assume you were optimistic."

Courtney laughed as Madigan shook her head.

"Speaking of personal expenses," he continued once it was clear that particular conversation was over, "I say we head out and get a little something to drink."

"That's the smartest thing you've said all day," Kennedy said.

Summer in Russia needed to be filmed and put in all the movies and TV series to make sure everyone remembered exactly how bad it was to stereotype. Of course, everyone knew what winter was like. There were movies, anecdotes, and all the garbage about how an army should never invade Russia in winter, but to be fair, those people had a point.

They merely forgot why people invaded Russia in the first place. It had to be the kind of people who enjoyed the sun and the opportunity to acquire a good tan. It grew hot enough in some places that you could fry eggs on the sand of several lake beaches. If you liked the sun, come to Russia in the summer.

He didn't like sun. Sometimes, he thought that was the only reason he'd taken the job of computer programming. There were a number of reasons, of course, one being that he liked an office job where he didn't have to answer phones or serve people. It was a reason he often forgot until the moment he stepped outside and felt the humid and dense heat that came with the summertime in St. Petersburg.

He hated dead drops, he hated going out in places where there were too many people, and he definitely didn't like the fact that he only did this in his free time. As much as he disliked the places where his job took him, it felt that he somehow made a difference. More of a difference than managing the security firewall in some corporation or another, anyway.

He dropped the SD card into a small trash bin and walked quickly away from it with his hands tucked into his pockets and his hoodie lowered against the glaring sun that wouldn't set for a couple more hours.

As he made his way back to his car, his phone buzzed. He slipped into the driver's seat before he retrieved it.

Thirty-five thousand Euros had been added to his online bank account, and a message confirmed the payment.

Appreciated. Keep up the good work. Pay same as always. Info on the metal extracted and processed from the Zoo will see payment bonused by twenty percent.

The man shrugged. There wasn't much information on any metal extracted from the Zoo but at this point, very little would surprise him about that place. He messaged a *will do* and replaced his phone in his pocket. It was a burner, but he preferred to destroy his pieces somewhere safe.

Either way, he had enough money to pick up a new one before he went home.

Sal leaned back in his seat. It wasn't an easy thing to do given that the bar stools didn't have much in the way of backs. Still, he managed it by keeping his hands on the bar top and used the motion to stretch and groan gently.

"Okay," he said finally, "I'm sorry the whitepaper doesn't have the information you need, but I can't simply put anything in there that isn't supported by cold, hard evidence."

"Look," repeated the man dressed in a suit with a decidedly lawyer-like look about him, "my client doesn't mind having facts in the whitepaper. But with certain indications from the views as they are, there are certain details that must be emphasized, even if the investigation into those details is still ongoing. Merely a mention. That's all he wants."

"I can add the studies of how these critters produce the acid from their own systems, but it will have to include all the studies we've done on the reptiles," Sal said. There was a fully scientific name for the little beasts, but it was over ten syllables long and he wasn't sure he would be able to pronounce it correctly. He was a perfectionist when it came to things like that.

"So what?" A third voice entered the conversation, which originated from a man a few stools down. "Did you get paid to do other kids' homework in high school too? Simply hearing you guys talk about the same bullshit over and over makes me want to blow my brains all over this damn bar."

"I'd take it as a kindness if you didn't," said the bartender, a new girl with the look of former military.

Sal glanced around as he wondered who the man had spoken to and then realized the obvious. "Oh, he's talking to me?"

"Yeah, I'm talking to you, you useless lab geek," the man muttered and moved to where he and the lawyer were talking and draped his arm over the shoulders of the latter. "I bet you needed the girls to protect you too. What in the hell are you talking to this little priss for anyway?"

It took the lawyer a few seconds to realize that the last sentence was directed at him. "Because this man is the best at what he does."

"Best?" the man scoffed and shook his head. "At what? Poking needles? Crossing T's and dotting I's? Please, if this guy's the best at anything, I know I can do it better than him." He turned and addressed the rest of the bar. "Write me some papers? Check. Shoot a gun? Double check. Pay me the big bucks, baby, and I'll do anything you need."

Sal didn't want to make a sexual innuendo about this man, but he had asked to be made fun of. Either way, he was about a foot taller and sported almost fifty pounds more muscle than Sal. As much as he'd progressed, he wasn't sure he could take a man like this on, no matter how drunk he was.

But he really was asking for it.

"Well, that's a mighty high claim," a woman's voice drawled from behind him. Fingers traced up his back and sent chills up and down his spine. Madigan only drawled when she was half-drunk and in the mood to mock someone.

"You know I can back that claim up," the man said with a grin. "All night long."

"Oh, is that right?" She tilted her head and perched her chin on Sal's shoulder. "I happen to know that this man right here can out-drink you all night long, so that's one thing you'll never be better at than him."

"Fuck that." The man growled and leaned in closer. "How much are you willing to bet that you're wrong about that?"

"What I have between my legs is what I have to bet," she all but purred. "No way will I give you any money."

"I'll take it," he said with a grin. "I'll be sure to ruin you for all other men, too."

"Well, Sal here has already done that for me," Kennedy said with a grin and ran her fingers up and down Sal's neck. "And if he drinks like he fucks, I don't think you'll have the chance anyway."

The man looked flustered but nodded quickly and sat on the stool next to him with a determined expression.

Sal turned to face Madigan, but she pressed her lips to his before he could say anything.

"What the fuck have you gotten me into?" he asked once she pulled away.

"As much trouble as I can," she whispered and kissed the tip of his nose. "You have been licking Madie, right?"

"Yeah, but—oh," he said when he suddenly realized that she meant the blue goop he extracted from his flowering plant called Madie. "Yes. Yes, I have."

"Then you have nothing to worry about," she said with a grin. She kissed him on the lips again before she turned him to where the bartender had already poured a couple of shots of the new Russian vodka into two glasses.

"The rules are," the man said and eyed the clear liquid in his glass, "no regurgitation, no pausing, and no falling asleep. Loser pays the bill and winner has a nice long night of plowing the sergeant."

"May the best man win," Sal said with a nod, picked his glass up, and raised it to the group that had already assembled to watch the contest. He downed it in a single gulp.

He shook his head. There was no way he would ever learn to like this stuff, but if it meant he could put an arrogant bastard in his place, he could tolerate it for the moment. He simply wasn't sure how effectively the goop would prepare his body to process this much alcohol.

Five shots later, Courtney slipped into the bar and immediately wondered what all the commotion was about. Too many people milled around for her to have a clear view, and when she saw Madigan seated at an empty table, sipping from a beer glass, she decided the easiest way to find out was to ask her.

"What's going on?" she asked as she plopped beside her.

"Oh, Sal and some asshole have a bet about who can drink the most," the woman explained and grinned over the rim of her glass.

"Oh?" she asked with real curiosity. "What does the winner get?"

"A night with me," her companion replied. She tilted her head coyly and a sneaky smile played on her lips.

"What? That doesn't seem like you—oh," Courtney said as the penny dropped. "And when Sal wins…"

"I guess I'll have to deliver unto him his winnings," Madigan said and took another sip of her drink.

"You sly bitch," she responded, although she didn't really mean it as an insult. "I want to be you when I grow up. That's some devious shit."

"It comes from being in the military," the woman responded with a chuckle. "If you aren't cheating, you aren't trying. You simply cheat the other side, is all."

Their conversation was cut off by a roar from the crowd that surrounded the bar.

"Fifteen," Sal said with a grin. "You're looking a little tipsy there, friend."

"Bullshit," the man slurred but he grasped the bar top to keep from falling over. "I can do this all fucking night."

"Suit yourself," he said with a shrug. "I don't have all night, though, so…bartender?" The woman turned to them with a fresh bottle of vodka in her hand. "Do you mind lining up five glasses for us?"

She nodded with a smirk, placed ten glasses deftly on

the bar, and filled them quickly without spilling a single drop.

He felt a little woozy but given the amount of alcohol they had consumed, he wondered why he wasn't on the floor already. Maybe Madigan was right about what the goop could do for the processing speed of his liver.

"You have as many as you can," he said with a smile once the bartender had finished filling the glasses.

"No, you go first," the man muttered and his face looked flushed. "I'm not stupid. The first man on the floor loses."

Sal shrugged. He felt more than a little arrogant. Maybe it was the booze or maybe it was the fact that both Madigan and Courtney watched him with real interest. He took the first glass and tossed the contents down his throat, flipped it, and slammed it down. Three glasses later, there wasn't so much as a drop of vodka on the bar top. He took care to let his tongue flick into the last glass to make sure he'd taken every drop of the spirit before it joined the rest.

The crowd cheered wildly when he put it down, but his challenger stared at him with wide eyes. The man turned to where Madigan was seated.

She grinned and mouthed the words "like he fucks" to him. He gulped and steeled himself visibly before he took his first shot glass.

After his third, he had already splashed more than the equivalent of a full glass on the bar top. He paused halfway through glass number four, slid out of his seat, and spilled the rest of the vodka as he sank to the floor with a groan.

The crowd cheered again as Sal picked up the man's final and still untouched glass and raised it to the crowd.

"To drinking like you fuck!" he said and slurred a few words before he threw his head back and let the burning liquid slide down his throat. A flurry of hands patted his shoulder and he pointed at the man at his feet. "The bill's on him."

The bartender grinned and winked as he turned and worked hard to walk in a straight line toward Madigan's table. When he stopped beside her, he bowed dramatically.

"Your ride awaits, milady," he said in a bad British accent and offered his hand. She grinned, finished her beer, and slid her hand in his. He guided her out of the bar and managed to not trip on the way.

Once they were outside, though, his bravado faded quickly as he stumbled and fought to keep his balance.

"Wait," she said with a challenging grin. "So you don't drink like you fuck?"

"I'm not sure," he said, vaguely aware of the fact that he most likely looked as though he fought to both stay conscious and on his feet. "I've only ever fucked to twelve, myself. I'd have to see if I can get you to twenty-one."

"I'm fairly certain I'll need to lick Madie myself if that ever happens," she said with a grin and helped him to their vehicle. "I've drunk a fair amount, but something tells me it's probably best if I drive us home."

"Good call." Sal slurred his words. "Wait, how will Courtney get to the compound?"

"We brought both JLTVs, remember?" Madigan started the engine and pulled out of the lot. He simply nodded, leaned back, and fumbled awkwardly with his seatbelt before he finally managed to secure it.

It wasn't long before they were at the compound and in the apartment Madigan had claimed for her own.

She slipped into the bathroom to freshen up. From the state he was in, there was a fifty-fifty chance that he might not be awake when she returned to the bedroom. Still, she stripped completely because there was that fifty percent chance that he might be awake.

True to form, Sal was asleep on her bed by the time she emerged from the bathroom.

"Oh, well." She dumped her clothes on her office chair and crossed to the bed to press a light kiss to his lips. "I guess you'll have to claim your winnings some other time."

There was no point in getting dressed again. She helped him into a more comfortable position and turned the lights off, climbed into bed, and pulled her covers over them. A little regretful, she curled up behind him, pressed herself against him, and closed her eyes.

CHAPTER THREE

"Wait, so you need a mechanic?"

Sal nodded and leaned back in his seat. It was almost painfully hard to focus. He didn't like to drink as much as he had the night before. Aside from the matter of the horrible burn, the hangover the next day merely added insult to injury. By rights, he should have remembered little about what happened after he finished the twenty-first shot. Surprisingly, he did remember the ride home and that he'd managed to drop onto Madigan's bed, but that was the limit of his recall.

As it turned out, maybe having her drive them to the compound was a bad idea. Getting up the next morning was tough when his head screamed bloody murder and light became a continuous source of agony—which was worse when your compound was in the middle of the friggin' desert.

They had realized somewhere along the way that the shocks were shot to hell. All of them. When you dealt with a six-wheeler, that was a nightmare. They'd had the vehicles looked at before they'd added them to the price of the compound and there hadn't been a problem with the shocks. They were meant to traverse rough terrain. Of course, they were also meant to be driven carefully but, as his sore back and ass could attest, nothing of the sort had happened.

He would make sure to bring up the reckless driving with Kennedy when he got back. Again.

"You'd get some sweet deals if you put your machines in the shop here," the mechanic—a young man who went by the name Higgs for some reason—said with a chuckle. "What do you guys want a dedicated mechanic for?"

"Well, we don't really want a mechanic," Sal said and drummed his fingers on the desktop. "I mean...we do, but we also need someone who can fix our suits too, hopefully while we're in the Zoo. We want someone with that kind of experience."

"Oh," the kid said and scratched his head thoughtfully. "You won't find that many around here. Maybe Gutierrez, who went into the Zoo a few times before joining up here."

Sal leaned forward in his seat and immediately regretted it as his head pounded harder. "That's all very well, but how good is he with the mechanical stuff? Beyond the JLTVs and vehicles, how much technical knowledge does he have with the suits and stuff?"

"Him?" Higgs said and straightened from the leaning posture he'd held for most of the conversation. "Oh, yeah, him. I guess he's good with the suits, wouldn't you say, Hammy?"

"Huh?" One of the other mechanics, apparently named Hammy, looked up.

"You know—Gutierrez," the younger man clarified. "He's good with the suits, right? You'd recommend the guy to repair them in a fix, right?"

"Him?" Hammy asked, frowned in thought for a moment, then nodded. "Oh yes, Gutierrez is the guy I'd call to fix suits and the like on the go. Yes, I'd definitely call him."

Sal narrowed his eyes. "Okay, you two are acting weird. Do you have any contact information for this Gutierrez?"

"No phone or anything, and I don't think we should give out home addresses," Higgs said with a shrug. "But you'll find him working out at the gym right about now."

"Right. Thanks, guys." He pushed himself out of his seat. It was a pain because he really didn't feel like going to a gym right now, not in the state he was in. But the reality was that if he intended to contact this guy, it might as well be now. He could live with his hangover getting worse in order to meet this potential new member of their squad.

"We'll let you know when the vehicle is ready for you to pick up," the kid said with a grin. "It should only be a couple of days."

"Hey, Sal." Top, the guy in charge of the gym, greeted him cheerfully when he pushed his way inside. "I haven't seen you in a while. I thought you had a place to work out at your new compound or whatever."

"We do," Sal said. "Sorry, I didn't mean to replace you, but I don't really like working out anyway, and especially not when I have to commute for a few hours every day to get to the gym."

"Hey, no hard feelings." Top raised his hand in a dismissive gesture. "So, what are you here for, big guy?"

"Hah, not that big yet," he said and unconsciously flexed his arms a little. "No, I'm here to steal one of your regulars —maybe offer him a job at the compound."

"Oh, which one?"

"Uh…Gutierrez?" he said and watched the man's reaction carefully. He still couldn't be sure the mechanics hadn't screwed with him because their odd behavior suggested they knew things he didn't. "I was told he would be working out around now and thought I might catch him and have a couple of words before he goes to work."

"Him? Oh, him," the man said and nodded. "Gutierrez does seem like the right kind of person, but only if you offer…him the right stuff. He has had a ton of offers over the past couple of months and always turned them down. Anyway, you'll probably find him over on the squat machine at this time."

"Right…thanks," Sal said. Everyone acted strange about this. He wasn't sure what he was supposed to expect from this Gutierrez, but some odd scenarios now played out in his head as he moved to the squat machines. The place was deserted except for a young blonde woman dressed in a tank top and yoga pants.

Sal suddenly remembered that nothing had happened the night before with Kennedy, and the realization made his head pound a little harder. There didn't seem to be any guys around, though. Was he having second thoughts about bringing a guy onto the crew? Sure, but he wasn't married to Courtney and Madigan, and all things considered, he was the last person who could claim any moral grounds when it came to jealousy. They'd simply have to figure it all out.

The woman finished her set and turned to look suspiciously at him. "Can I help you?"

"Uh, yeah," he said. He wondered if she thought he'd been staring and looked away quickly. "I'm looking for Gutierrez. He was supposed to be working out around here."

"I'm Gutierrez," she said and leaned on the machine she'd been working on. "SPC Amanda Gutierrez, and I can tell you there isn't any guy by that name around here. So, how can I help you?"

"You're Gutierrez?" he asked. "You work in the chop shop?"

"That's me," she said and now looked annoyed.

"Oh...oh!" Sal said once the penny dropped. "Fuck... yeah, now I realize why everyone's acted so weirdly when I asked about you. The guys at the chop shop said you were a guy—well, I assumed it and they played along. I guess they thought it would be funny."

She smirked. "It is a little when I see you floundering like that. But it's less funny to know that the boys at the shop tried to play it themselves without cluing me in."

"Right." He shook his head and winced at the quick stab of pain. As first interviews went, this hadn't gone very well, but if things went bad, what exactly did he have to lose? "Anyway, I'm sorry for the misunderstanding. I'm Sal. Sal Jacobs."

"Nice to meet you, Sal, Sal Jacobs," she said with a grin,

took his hand, and shook it firmly. "I hear no military rank or doctor at the start of that name, and you don't look like the skeevy lawyer types I've seen around here before. What can I do for you?"

"Well, I know I didn't make the best first impression," he said and decided to steer into the slide, as the metaphor went. "I started a company out here called Heavy Metal, and we recently purchased a small compound just outside the base. We're in need of someone who can make hands-on repairs to both vehicles and armored suits while out in the Zoo. I talked to Higgs and he said you were the... woman for the job."

Sal drew a business card from his pocket that they'd had printed a couple of weeks before. Gutierrez took it and studied it closely.

"Look, Jacobs," she said, "you're not one of these military jerk-offs or the pompous doctor types, which is a plus for you in my book, but you don't have what I like to play with. Besides, I'm not really looking for a job right now."

Sal was tempted to make a bet on that, but he decided not to. From the way she talked, he could safely assume that she had to deal with a long list of assholes, all things considered. He didn't want to be included on that list.

"No problem," he said with a smile. "But think about it. I have a job for you that might work if you plan to stay around the Zoo in the near future. We have a compound, so I'm easy to reach. Let me know if you change your mind."

She nodded and raised the card in acknowledgment as he turned and walked away. As he did so, he passed another soldier headed toward the squat machines, and he heard Gutierrez call him over.

"Hey, Perez," she said, "what do you know about this Salinger Jacobs?"

He slowed and tried to listen unobtrusively. It wasn't often that he heard what people said about him behind his back, after all.

"Sal Jacobs?" Perez asked. "Oh, yeah, I made a run with him into the Zoo once. He's young but knows what he's doing. The dude's got a pair of titanium *cojones*."

"Is that so?"

"Yeah, he goes into the Zoo way more often than most other freelancer teams," the man continued. "He's got...you know Sergeant Kennedy? Yeah, she's on his team too, and I hear they have a full-time specialist working with them now. Oh, yeah, he put Corporal Brandon to sleep over a drinking game yesterday. Once the guy was down, Jacobs took the guy's last shot and downed it himself. They call themselves...uh, Heavy Metal or something like that. It's a fun team and they seem to make a pile of money. They have some trade secrets they only share with the teams that go into the Zoo with them."

"Is that all?" Gutierrez asked.

Perez shrugged and walked toward the squat machines again.

"Okay, thanks." She returned to her own workout. "Remember to keep your back straight this time, *coño*. You don't want to have to call a medic again because you can't do leg day properly."

Sal kept walking and couldn't prevent the smirk that

crept over his face. He'd always assumed his reputation was much worse than that. A man could have a worse rep than having titanium *cajones*.

CHAPTER FOUR

Sal held his beer and stared at it as the droplets of condensation started to form. He'd hydrated all day, but his sense of taste was still influenced by the vodka he'd had the night before. It wasn't necessarily a bad thing, but his stomach roiled as he looked at the pale gold of the beer in his glass and watched while the foam dissipated from the top. He could drink without getting drunk too quickly, but now, he simply didn't want to try it.

Instead, he drew a deep breath and looked at the pictures of the jobs that were posted on the board.

A couple of people would make deep runs, but that wasn't what he was looking for at the moment. They had recently completed some deeper runs, and he didn't want to get them too involved too soon. Even between the three of them, there was the risk of burning out too quickly. Also, as they'd made massive investments into the area, he didn't want to risk something like that.

He rubbed his temples, picked his beer up again, and took it to the bar. *Keep hydrating*, he thought to himself and returned with a tall glass of iced water and a jug of the same. *This feeling has to pass eventually, right?* He hoped so, anyway.

Once again, he focused his attention on the board and one job in particular looked interesting. It seemed to be a quick research job that needed specialists as well as gunners.

His phone buzzed and vibrated against his leg.

"Oh, for the days when you could make phones stay in one fucking place." He growled with irritation as he pulled it out of his pocket.

"Hey, Sal," Kennedy said over the sound of a vehicle's engine, "how are you feeling?"

"I can still taste sounds," he replied and rubbed absently at his temples. "But only the bad ones like nails on a chalkboard."

"Fun times." She laughed. "How goes the job hunt?"

"I found one that calls for help on retrieving company equipment. Suit computers and hard drives, that kind of thing."

"And they'll pay for this?" Kennedy asked.

"Oh yeah, and full price too," he replied. "Although, since it's only a couple of days, it won't actually end up being that much on its own. The reason it caught my eye is because it'll pass close to the leg we found and we'll be able to pick up the GPS signal, which is still in place."

"Oh, right. I almost forgot about that. Look, my armor will be ready tonight, so if they leave in the morning, I won't even need to rent."

"That's perfect." He chuckled. "I'll text you the details and we'll talk about it when I get to the compound."

"That sounds good," she responded. "I'm headed back myself, so I'll see you there."

"Wait, did you take our JLTV?" Sal asked. "The one I parked outside the bar?"

"Oh, no. The guys at the shop sent me a message that we can bill them to rent a vehicle while we have one in the shop," Kennedy said. "It's an incentive to make sure they don't overcharge us or keep our vehicle longer than they have to."

"Oh...awesome," he said. "They didn't say anything about that to me."

"That's probably because I have boobs," she retorted with a chuckle.

"Right. How could I forget?"

"Well, I'll give you a reminder when you get to the compound," she replied and left him speechless for a split second before she laughed and hung up. He kept his phone pressed to his ear for a long moment as he struggled to move his mind out of the gutter her comment had left it in.

Courtney checked her laptop. It wasn't like her to be this anxious about something, but as the dedicated specialist of their little team, it felt like it was her job to make sure all the whitepapers went through without a problem. Sal had done the alterations to the one on the acid-spitting lizards no one could remember the ridiculously long name for and she had edited it before sending it in.

She was good at this but it wasn't only about her experience. The simple truth was that she actually enjoyed being out there. Did she want to be at the top of her field? Sure. Did she want some kind of recognition for what she'd done so far in the form of a Nobel prize or a research grant or something like that? Of course, but none of that mattered as long as she did something she really cared about. Especially if it was with someone whom she really cared about.

Someones, rather.

That thought prompted her to recall the conversation she'd had with Sal about wanting to impress her father. It was still true, as much as she hated to admit it. She wanted out of her father's shadow, and in order to do that, she had to make sure that what she put out there was as amazing as what he had done, if not more so. She was competitive and damned if she didn't get that from the man himself.

Once the payment cleared for the whitepaper, she shut the browser down and opened a writing document. She paused when she was asked to name it. It would have to be a working title for a rough draft, she knew. Courtney tilted her head and typed *Everything You Wanted to Know About the Zoo but Were Afraid to Ask – by Dr. Courtney Monroe.*

She smirked and nodded. That would be the kind of thing that would get her noticed.

Before she could start, though, her concentration was broken when the doorbell rang. Of course, the compound didn't have an actual door, but there was a doorbell, apparently. When she checked the camera that covered the front entrance, she saw a JLTV parked outside.

"Um...hello," she said into the mic. "How can I help you?"

"Hi," a woman's voice responded. "I'm Specialist Amanda Gutierrez. Is this the Heavy Metal compound?"

"Uh...yes, it is," she confirmed.

"Salinger Jacobs gave me his card and said that he was interested in having me work for him," Amanda replied. "I thought I'd come and check to see if he was serious about the offer."

"Oh, okay. Come on in." She pressed the button that opened the gate into the compound and the vehicle eased inside.

Once the unexpected visitor was indoors and had turned down the offer for something to drink, Courtney led her into the meeting room. As they walked, she couldn't help but admire the woman Sal had found. She knew he had something of an appetite, but she never thought she'd have to fend off someone who looked like that.

Her blue eyes and curly blonde hair contrasted perfectly with deeply tanned skin and a body that had considerable work put into it and—with all the Hispanic emphasis on the curves. She didn't seem the kind to put in that much work simply for appearances, though. The woman looked like the perfect cross of a Latina beauty and a sexy tomboy encased in combat fatigues.

Well, that's fucking great, Courtney thought acidly.

"So what kind of work did Sal...Jacobs say you would do around here?" she asked when she had difficulty deciding how to handle the situation.

"He said he needs someone to cover repairs," Amanda said with a nod. "Not only the mechanic stuff. I could stay in the shop for that, but he said there's a need for someone to go into the Zoo for repairs while on the job, and since I know how to work as a gunner in there too... I'm sick of being stuck in the garage, you know?"

"Well, if you call that a reason," she said under her breath.

"What was that?" the woman asked.

"Oh, that's a good reason," she added quickly, louder this time. "I know what you're talking about, at least in part. So, you're good with suits, huh?"

"Oh, yeah. I got my degree in mechanical engineering and Boulos has called me in a couple of times to help him fix the suits. Okay, more than a couple of times. All the time, to be honest. I spend more time at the armory than at the shop."

Courtney looked at her phone, which had buzzed with a new message. It was from Madigan.

Sal said there might be a new recruit showing up at the compound for an interview.

"Sorry, I have to take this," she said to explain why she moved away quickly and tapped her phone's keypad.

She's here now. Did Sal tell you he's recruiting a total hottie? she replied, took a picture surreptitiously of the woman who sat on their couch, and sent it with the message.

Not a problem, Madigan replied almost instantly. *I'm already close but hire her if you can. It's the best thing we can do.*

Monroe rolled her eyes but thankfully, her gaze on the camera that covered the entrance was rewarded with the sight of Kennedy rolling into the compound. It wasn't long before she came into the room where the two women were seated.

"Gutierrez!" Madigan called as she entered the room. "It's really good to see you, girl!"

"Kennedy!" Amanda responded with the same enthusiasm. She grinned and stood to shake the other woman's hand. "I heard you'd gone all corporate on us."

"Well, you know us greedy Fortune Five-Hundred types," Madigan said with a grin.

"Is that why you're looking to hire more people?" Gutierrez asked.

"We're bringing in more vehicles and suits and stuff, and we could really use someone who has the company's interests at heart working on them," she explained. She walked to the fridge and pulled a beer out. "Could I interest you in something to drink?"

"No thanks." Amanda smiled and winked at Courtney. "I have to drive back to the base."

"Everyone knows how treacherous those long drives can be at night," Madigan said with a grin.

"Tell that to the shocks on your vehicle," the woman retorted.

"Smartass."

"What was that?"

"Oh, nothing," Kennedy amended quickly. "Let's talk about the job. I don't know how much you make at the shop, but I can tell you now that the basic salary won't be that high. You'll have food, board, supplies, and some drinking money. You do get a bonus with the jobs you do, though, and you can take a few side jobs on top of that. Jacobs wants everyone to work out here without the overbearing presence of the assholes who run the base."

"Right, about Jacobs," Amanda said and narrowed her

eyes. "I caught him staring at the ladies when he came by. He's young so he gets a pass for the wandering eyes, but I want to make sure sleeping with him isn't a prerequisite for this job."

Courtney and Kennedy shared a quick look, and the woman laughed. "You're kidding me. Both of you are sleeping with him? He's a fucking kid. How does that work?"

"For a kid, he has a surprising amount of stamina," Madigan said, and Monroe blushed furiously. "That, coupled with a young man's enthusiasm and adventurous nature, it's...a ton of fun."

"But not necessary for the job, right?" the woman pressed. "Because that's a deal-breaker."

"No," Courtney said. "It's definitely not required."

"Cool. I've wanted to strike out on my own for a while, and it would be nice to have some structure behind that. I'm in, but I need to close...shit, everything with the base first. I'd guess with their amount of red tape, it'll take at least a couple of days."

"Good call." Kennedy shook the woman's hand once more. "It'll be great to have you on board, *chica*."

"No," the armorer said and shook her head firmly. "Sorry, but you can't pull off *chica*."

"Right. I thought I'd try. Drive safe now."

"You know I won't," Amanda replied.

"Then what's the point of not drinking?"

"Can you imagine me driving while drunk?" she asked in response.

"That's a good point." They shared a laugh.

Once their visitor had cleared the compound, Courtney turned to face Madigan.

"Are you serious?" she asked and shook her head. "What's he doing—running around and hiring all the hottest women in the base? Is that it?"

"So you think I'm one of the hottest women in the base?" her companion asked. "That's so sweet."

"Oh, shut it. You know what I mean," she snapped. "Come on. You saw her, right? She wore baggy fatigues and she was still a jaw-dropper. Can you imagine if we put her in a dress?"

"She doesn't like dresses," Kennedy replied. "You won't ever see her in one, I guarantee that. Besides, you have nothing to worry about. As hot as Sal is, there's nothing about him that interests her."

"Thanks for trying to make me feel better but now, I'm starting to think you're blind."

"I'm serious, Courtney," the other woman said with a laugh. "She bats for our team."

Monroe stared at her for a moment, not sure what she was talking about.

"Amanda Gutierrez is gay," she said when she saw the need to spell it out as clearly as she could.

"Oh...oh!" her companion exclaimed as she finally understood what she was talking about. "Well...that's okay. Nice even. Heavy Metal should be an equal opportunity place for people of all genders and sexualities."

"Now you're getting it," Madigan said with a grin.

CHAPTER FIVE

"Are you sure Courtney was okay with being left behind?" Sal asked as they trudged through the dense jungle. Even with power armor, it had become grueling. The goop seemed to draw water from deep underground, and it turned the jungle into more of a swamp in places. It was only a matter of time before massive crocodiles became a concern, Sal realized and shook his head. He really didn't need that particular image in his head right now.

"Dr. Monroe?" Kennedy asked and slipped into the use of her professional name. He wasn't sure if that was deliberate or not, but it niggled at him. "She seemed fine to me and said she had a batch of whitepapers to look at and write. I'd say she seemed as happy as a clam. Besides, we didn't need two specialists on this run. Why do you ask?"

"She seemed a little...snippy with me this morning before we left," he explained and maintained as wide a line of sight as possible. He didn't want any giant crocodiles to sneak up on him.

"Oh, that's probably only a little hostility left over from when she met SPC Gutierrez," she said with a nod.

"She was mad about that?" he asked. "Well okay, sure, I'd be lying if I said she wasn't hot."

"You know Gutierrez is gay, right?" she asked.

"Yep." Sal nodded. "She made that perfectly clear when we first met. Courtney knows too, right?"

"Of course. I told her."

"Oh, that's good."

"You were staring, weren't you?" she queried with a grin.

"Did she tell you that?" He asked, tilting his head.

"Oh yeah," she replied with a chuckle. "She wanted to make it perfectly clear that she wouldn't sleep with you to get the job."

"Shit," he responded. "I know, I shouldn't have stared at all and it was a trashy move on my part, but she was in yoga pants and doing squats. My eyes kind of gravitated. I apologized right after."

"Hey, there's no need to justify yourself to me, Jacobs," Kennedy said with a laugh. "I've never had a taste for the ladies myself, but even I can see she has an ass that would not quit under any circumstances."

Sal tried to keep his mind focused. He did remember that but didn't think it was appropriate to even think about it, all things considered. She was a prospective employee and not interested in him in the slightest, so he really needed to simply not think about it, period.

"Can we change the subject?" he asked and turned away so his companion couldn't see his face was a bright red.

"Sure." She chuckled.

"So you're sure Monroe's okay?" he asked again.

"Yeah, she needs to work out some personal issues, is all," Kennedy assured him. "She'll be fine."

"Good." He dropped into a crouch. "Because I think I found something."

She joined him and her bright gaze identified what he pointed at. With the ground now a clay-like mud, it was difficult to miss the footprints left behind despite the darkness.

Even better, the clay left a clear imprint of the boots.

"There has to be at least a dozen of them," she estimated. "Maybe more. It looks like bounty hunters or poachers. That's interesting. I thought there was a report about their camp being completely annihilated."

"And it shows," Sal pointed out. "Look at these boot prints. This is power armor and scrapped suits from the look of things. These guys have to be one of the poorer equipped teams I've seen in the Zoo in a long time."

"Hey, they have numbers. I think they can make up for it," she responded easily.

"Come on, we have top-of-the-line equipment. We can totally handle these assholes," he said with a grin. "I've never known you to back down from a fight."

"Yeah, remember the last time I didn't back down from a fight where we were outnumbered by bounty hunters?" she asked. "Remember how I was shot in the leg and you had to help drag me out of the Zoo's version of a lynch mob?"

"Well, yeah," he conceded. "But think about how much we've learned since then."

"Like not attacking groups of bounty hunters that outnumber us?" she asked.

"Well, besides that," he retorted. "Come on, we need to at least find out what they're up to. They wouldn't have come in here unless they were after something specific. Besides, they have headed off in the direction we're going in anyway, so…yeah."

She shook her head but sighed. "Fine. But if I get shot again, I will hold you personally responsible."

"That's…not fair at all," he said but he shrugged. "Fine, hold me responsible all you like. Let's go."

They followed in the direction of the footsteps. The deeper they went, the more it seemed like the numbers of the men they pursued had grown.

"I'm nervous here, Sal," Kennedy said and peered at the prints. "We need backup. There have to be at least twenty guys in this team. It doesn't matter how badly armed they are. They'll be able to pin us down and eliminate us without too much trouble."

"Yeah, I get that," he agreed with a nod. "Let's fall back and maybe coordinate with the guys who gave us the ride and track these assholes—"

He blinked when the sound of a gunshot blasted his ears before his noise filters could kick in. Sal spun to see Kennedy's smoking weapon.

"What the hell?" he asked, but his question was answered when a man fell from behind a tree. He was dressed in a suit of armor that was mostly welded pieces of scrap.

"Oh, crap," he muttered.

She nodded and swung her gun in an arc when they heard shouts and more gunshots from around them.

Sal raised his weapon. He was more used to fighting creatures that didn't shoot back, which was a problem now that he had to adjust to the need to hide behind cover. Kennedy knew what she was doing, though, and pushed him behind a trunk before she ducked behind one herself.

"Do you have any idea how many assholes we have to deal with here?" she asked when she'd opened a secure comm line between them.

"You mean besides me?"

"Now is really not the time for a self-pity party, Jacobs!" she snapped and stepped out briefly to lay down covering fire before she ducked back.

"I count twenty-three," he replied as he slid to the other side and returned fire, then moved out of sight once more.

"Shit," she exclaimed and reloaded her gun with a scowl. "This isn't a defensible position, Jacobs."

"Should we fall back?" he suggested.

"Yeah, that sounds good."

He moved to fire at the men who now closed in on them and she retreated about thirty paces before he ran out.

"I'm out!" he called.

"I'll cover you!" she yelled in response and he fell back. He let his suit reload his rifle automatically as he jogged to where his partner had taken cover. The bounty hunters moved closer relentlessly and he wasn't sure if they had wounded any of them in the shooting.

"We need to do something," she whispered as he dropped beside her.

"Do you have any ideas?" he asked.

"Okay, we do have the smoke grenades that are standard issue these days," Kennedy said.

"And if these guys have heat-seekers like the missiles on your shoulder?" he asked.

"Come on. Their suits would have been considered old-fashioned during the Civil War," she said with a smirk.

"Are you willing to risk your life on that assumption?"

"You make a good point. So, do you have a plan?"

"Kind of, but I don't think you'll like it." Sal peeked over the fallen trunk they hunkered behind. The bounty hunters now approached more cautiously. He estimated there were fewer of them than before—maybe eighteen—but still too many to handle without help.

"Tell me and I'll decide how I like it," she said and directed a few shots at a couple of younger-looking men who had broken cover and tried to sprint forward to their position. They dropped in mid-stride, holes clearly visible in their haphazardly constructed suits.

"Well, my idea is that we use the jungle to our advantage," he explained. "Since we've been here the most over the past couple of months, it only makes sense, right?" At her look of interest, he proceeded to lay his plan out for her.

"You're right," Kennedy agreed. "I don't like it. But it's the best plan we have right now. How many of them are still out there?"

Sal peered cautiously over the log and used the opportunity to take a couple of shots after he'd done a quick headcount.

"Sixteen," he said as he ducked down again.

"Fan-fucking-tastic," she snarked. "Cover me."

He laid down a solid volley of slugs at their attackers as she crawled from behind the log, changed direction, and scuttled behind one of the massive trees. She activated her heat-vision and the little missile launcher emerged from her shoulder pad. Instead of targeting the men who continued to fire on them, she aimed upward into one of the trees where a group of the simians watched the fight. They seemed to realize they were in danger the moment the small missile launched and rocketed towards them. Most escaped but some were caught in the blast that shredded a few branches. By sheer luck, one of the bounty hunters was caught under the falling branches. The scream they heard from him indicated that while the branch didn't kill him, it did break something.

The monkeys, understandably angry that their haven was destroyed, attacked the man quickly and ripped into his armor and the flesh beneath.

"Fifteen," Sal tallied and didn't bother to waste any bullets on the wounded man as the sounds of angry roars and the yip and chatter of hyenas drew closer. Drawn by more than simply the sound of gunfire and explosions, these animals seemed to converge when any of their fellow Zoo creatures were attacked. That was what he had counted on.

The bounty hunters realized the danger they were in too late as two panthers bounded from between the trees. One dropped and three bullet holes appeared on its body, but the second pounced on one of the men. Its claws held him captive on the ground as the venom-tipped fangs sank into his neck. The man screamed, but it quickly turned into a bloody gurgle.

Fourteen.

Bullets riddled its corpse even after the panther collapsed, but the sounds of hyenas grew louder. The animals were close enough to draw attention to the rear of the group where a couple of the men were snatched by the legs and dragged off. They yelled frantically for help that wouldn't come.

Twelve.

The Heavy Metal teammates emerged from their cover as the bounty hunters now seemed less concerned to remain hidden and more worried about the animals that descended on them en masse.

The renegades were quickly reminded of their mistake when three of them fell to the bullets that punched easily through their armor. A call from the apparent leader—or the leader of the men who were left—was enough to push them under cover, but not before some of the scorpion-tailed locusts dragged a couple more of the men away.

Seven.

"Now," Sal instructed. Kennedy retrieved two of the smoke grenades from her belt and tossed one to where the animals attacked the remainder of the bounty hunters. She dropped the second one where they stood. Thick, billowy gray clouds released into the jungle almost immediately. The two switched to heat vision on their HUDs. While it wouldn't tell them where the locusts were, the rest of the animals and bounty hunters were all easily visible.

Cover was no longer needed so they prioritized the need to remove the bounty hunters from the game. One by one, the men fell until only three remained alive. The smoke had begun to dissipate, and the few creatures that didn't detest the smoke enough to run away were quickly gunned down as well.

"Well, it was a shitty plan," Kennedy said as she manually reloaded her rifle, "but hot damn, it actually worked."

"If it worked, it wasn't a shitty plan," Sal argued. "Why are you reloading like that?"

"I have mud in the mechanism," she explained and attempted to shake the dirt clear. When she had no response from the reloading mechanism, she kept at it with her hands.

"Yeah, they'll need to come up with something to help with all the mud," he said.

"Well, unless you intend to spring for new suits for all of us, I think we'll have to improvise a solution on our own," she responded, finally ready for combat again. "It's a good thing we have a new mechanic on our team now, right?"

He nodded. It was a good point.

CHAPTER SIX

S al dropped into a crouch beside the man who had seemed to be in charge of the bounty hunters and tugged at his suit. Even the leaders of this team had shitty armor. It was amazing that they'd managed to convince so many people to join this ultimately doomed expedition. Then again, they were in a part of the world that was notorious for its extreme poverty, so there was no shortage of willing and desperate men who would put their lives on the line for extra cash.

He actually felt bad that they'd eliminated them and even worse about his attempt to find out what they had been after. He looked beneath the man's armor and eventually found an actual paper map that had been folded and hidden under his shirt.

It was a map of the Zoo, he realized, and was marked off in lines of latitude and longitude. That would have made it easier to navigate without a need to rely on the usual landmarks that constantly changed in the area. Sal studied it quickly and noted a couple of red x's that marked locations in the area.

"What do you think this is?" he asked and showed Kennedy the map.

"Huh…hold on," she responded and brought up the imaging from her altered satellite phone that was able to detect the clusters of Pita plants. She directed it to his HUD and he compared it to the map.

"Well, that explains what the markings are," he said after a moment, his head tilted in thought. "They only have three of the clusters so it's not a great map, but these three are only off by a couple of hundred meters. It would seem they had some good intel."

She nodded. "Do you think someone else figured out that whole radio frequency resonance thing we use to track the plants ?"

He nodded. "It would appear so. Either way, we should probably consider selling the tracking software to the highest bidder the next chance we get."

"Agreed." Kennedy scowled. "I'm not happy that we have to give up our little edge, though."

"If we don't act quickly, we still won't have our edge and we won't have a payout from selling it either," he pointed out.

"Yep." She nodded. "I say we bring it up with the rest of our team when we get back. You know, company decision and all that."

"Good call," Sal agreed. "In the meantime, it's only a couple of hours until sunset. I think we should use what little daylight we have left to put as much distance between us and all these bodies and find a place to set up camp."

"That's also a good call," she said with a grin.

They looted the bodies and took samples from the dead animals before they pressed forward and headed deeper into the Zoo. Thankfully, one of the Pita plants marked on the map was almost on top of the GPS marker they'd placed on the leg which they'd picked up once in range. It wasn't a great thing to do, but it was something they felt they had to do. Instinct told him the armor held secrets he needed to unravel.

He grasped his gun tighter, unsettled by the feeling that they were being watched. It was a common sensation out there in the Zoo. Humans were intruders, and any animals that wouldn't attack them on sight certainly had a good deal of hostility for the two-legged monsters in suits of armor. He could only expect that the monkeys up in the tree branches wouldn't feel happy about their comrades being blown up—a good enough reason to call the wrath of the jungle down on them.

If the truth be told, he wasn't too happy about it either and it honestly annoyed him how easily these decisions came now. Back in the beginning, he would have attacked the creatures only if it meant saving his own life as a last resort, but now, he sacrificed them as a tactical move? It made his stomach churn.

Of course, he knew what Kennedy would have to say about it. At least he still had a stomach capable of churning. That was the idea when going into a place like this. Survive and thrive at all costs. The only problem was, it was the Zoo that did the surviving and thriving better than any of them, which only made it more and more dangerous to continue with these runs. A time would come when they would need bigger and better weapons to even set foot in there, much less loot the flowers. He didn't like it. Even so, it seemed like things would change whether he liked it or not, so he would simply have to change with the times too.

He was changing with the times, he realized. That was the problem.

Sal shook the feeling off. Kennedy had berated him enough times about how this attitude would be the death of him to make him trust her on it. If he hesitated, he died. If he had these thoughts while in the middle of a firefight, he wouldn't be there afterward, wondering if he'd done the right thing.

Survival. That was the point.

The sun set slowly, but there wasn't much of a visible change around them. The tiny spotlights that seeped through the trees disappeared and were replaced with the blue twinkles that appeared on the trunks now that there wasn't anything else to contest their claim on the visual spectrum. It didn't do much to light their surroundings, but the starlight appearance of the tiny blue spots of goop that glowed from beneath the tree bark sure as hell made the sight of the world around them more interesting as they set up a camp.

The duo kept their suits on, not wanting to be caught unawares should anything come across them. They set up the motion sensors and a couple of heating plates to prepare their meals.

He still wasn't tired of the rations, even though they tasted rehashed and there were only five variations of the same meal. On principle, he refused to forget the days he had spent pining after better food back in the day. It tasted like it had been frozen and dried, but it was still good food, at least in comparison to his pre-Zoo meals.

Never forget your past. Grow from it. He'd seen the quote on social media but wasn't sure where it came from or even if it mattered. All that was important was that the stale ration food still tasted great.

The night passed quickly as the two of them alternated to keep watch. The scenery changed very little as morning came. He might have missed it altogether had their HUDs not alerted them to the time.

"I still can't fucking sleep in these suits," Kennedy complained and pushed herself from the hard jungle floor.

"Well, we meet up with the team for a ride back to the base later today," Sal told her, "so you shouldn't get used to this."

"Believe me," she said and chewed on pieces of dried meat as they packed the camp up again, "what I'll get used to is a nice, soft bed."

Sal grinned. "Yeah, I know what you mean. Let's hurry. You probably don't want to walk all the way back to the base either, which is what will happen if we're not there when they need to go. After we stole that other team's JLTV, they aren't too understanding about our strange schedules."

She nodded. "That's a good point. Let's get a move on, Jacobs."

"I was...it was my idea first," he grumbled playfully, which made her laugh as they moved deeper into the jungle once more. The location that had been marked off on the map was only a couple of kilometers away, and even in the tough terrain, they made good time. Soon, they approached an area where the foliage gave way as it usually did and allowed the Pita plants to receive a good portion of sunlight. Even the thick, mucky ground changed quickly into something firmer and more manageable.

He crouched suddenly and she stopped alongside him.

"Look—grass," he said.

"You've never seen grass before?" she asked. "Even if this stuff is blue."

"That means it's not using chlorophyll as an energy source," he explained with a grin. "At least, not any kind we know about. Give me a sec. I'll collect a couple of samples."

"Take your time," she said. "I think we may be here a while anyway."

"What do you mean?" he asked as he looked up. He'd expected to see the usual cluster of dense bushes with the bright blue flowers that were so coveted around the world. There weren't as many as he'd hoped for but it was a good patch—although he couldn't see how it would take an especially long time to collect the blossoms.

"No, not those. We have another problem," she said and pointed to something bright and shining on one of the lower branches of a tree that grew close to the Pitas. He focused with a frown and soon identified the familiar shape of a leg encased in metal armor.

"Oh, fuck."

"How long has it been since you climbed trees, Jacobs?" Kennedy asked.

"I've never climbed trees," he confessed. "I was too busy trying to discover what string theory was."

"What is string theory?"

"It's a theory in physics that deals with a theoretical

framework in which the point-like particles…" he started but paused when she looked oddly at him. Her response indicated that she'd posed the question as a joke and didn't actually expect an answer. "No one's really sure, but it used to have scientists really excited for some reason."

"Anyway," she said, "how do you propose we get up there? I don't see how we'll we retrieve that leg if we don't climb."

"Well, I do have less experience," Sal said, "but my armor is much lighter than yours. Unless you feel the need to strip down?"

"I only striptease when we're not in a jungle full of creatures that want us dead," Kennedy said with a grin.

"Big fat bummer." He shrugged his pack off and lowered it gently to the ground. "Wish me luck—and watch my back."

"Well, that's asking way too much," she responded. "I can multitask as much as the next guy, but to wish you luck while I watch your back is…and he's ignoring me."

He shook his head with a chuckle. While he could never ignore what she had to say, he could piss her off if he made her think he was. It always got her to talk more, and that could be a win-win—most times. At other times, he could simply tune out her yelling at him until she calmed.

Sal pushed himself up the trunk, careful to avoid the smaller branches. Had he climbed trees as a child? Of course, although not as much as the other kids, but at least he knew enough to rely on the trunk and only use the branches for leverage. He made slow progress but he wouldn't fall anytime soon.

"Could you pick up the pace?" she demanded over their

comm when he was five meters up. "It's not like we could be swarmed by angry hybrid animals at any second or anything."

"Don't break my concentration," he snapped. "Besides, I'm almost at the branch."

He gripped the trunk between his legs, which left his arms free to pull up on the branches that grew thicker the higher he climbed. The leg was wedged between two limbs in a way that indicated either that someone had put the damn thing there intentionally, or the plant had grown over the time it had taken them to get to it and simply taken the leg with it.

It wasn't clear which was the least likely scenario. All he cared about was that he was now close enough to the branch to be able to pull it down. With his legs wound around the trunk, the position wasn't big on dignity but it did the job. If it worked, it wasn't stupid as the old Internet adage went.

He felt the trunk move and groan under his weight. Even though his armor was lighter than Kennedy's, it added a solid hundred kilos or so to his overall weight. As high as he was, he was sure the trunk would definitely take strain. He tugged faster and yanked harder in an attempt to retrieve the leg before the whole tree collapsed.

"Jacobs, get out of there!" Kennedy yelled. He looked away from what he was doing and in that moment of distraction, he leaned too far back and the tree bent alarmingly. With a loud and reverberating snap and splinters that seemed to explode around him like shrapnel, he plummeted with a tree trunk still between his legs.

His partner wouldn't let him live this down. That was his last thought before he struck the ground.

The armor absorbed most of the impact of the landing, but the weight of the tree on his chest knocked the breath from his lungs. A loud crack from inside his suit triggered the prognostic software, which quickly detected a problem.

He had bigger issues, though. His head pounded as he suddenly realized he had an unimpeded view of the sky. There was no sun directly above him, which meant it was still morning, but it was all he could do to not fall asleep while he lay there helpless. The massive trunk slowly squeezed the resistance out of his armor and ribcage.

A loud creak from the wood as it strained under pressure drew his attention to Kennedy, who put the full strength of her power armor behind her attempt to shove the tree off him. After what sounded like a groan from the wood, the pressure suddenly lessened and finally lifted. He sucked in a long breath of the recycled and filtered air from his suit and leaned to the side as a powerful cough wracked him. It hurt his ribs, his stomach, his...everywhere, honestly, and he felt that it had little to nothing to do with the actual cough so much as what had caused it in the first place.

"Are you all right?" she asked once he seemed to recover.

"It was only...what, a five-meter drop?" he said and tried to put on a brave face. "That's nothing to an experienced climber like me. Well, quasi...I've been up a couple of trees. But I've never had one fall on me."

"What can I say?" she asked. "You've put on weight. There's no going back now."

"Hah!" Sal grunted. "Fake laugh, hiding real pain, both metaphorical and physical. Oh, shit, that fucking hurt."

"I'm sorry," she said with an empathetic smile. "Although if you want to look on the bright side, you did bring the leg with you on your way down."

"I'd celebrate, except I think I have a concussion, a couple of broken ribs, and a bruised pelvis, so I'll leave the cheerleading to you."

"Why did you climb the tree like that anyway?" she asked.

"I tried to distribute my weight so it wouldn't fall," he explained. "A ton of good that did."

"Well, as much as I empathize and would like to give you all the time you need, that tree not only damaged you but some of the Pita plants as well. I don't know if that will rile the monsters, but I'd rather not stick around to find out. Let's get the leg, collect as many flowers as we safely can, and head to where we can get a ride home to decent medical care, what do you say?"

Sal nodded, glad she'd made little effort to tease him for his climbing skills or lack thereof. He disengaged from his power arm and fumbled in his pack for the tools he needed to collect the flowers before they left for the Staging Area.

Some fifteen minutes later, no animals had appeared to attack them as a result of the destruction and he wondered if they had worried over nothing.

"Okay, we've picked this patch clean of the fucking flowers," Kennedy said. "Let's take our leg and get the fuck out of here. I don't trust this silence and the apparent contentment of the jungle despite the fact that we felled that damn tree and crushed a good number of plants. It doesn't seem realistic."

"Agreed." Sal chuckled. "Let's get going."

He moved to where the leg was still entangled in the branches. As he came closer and tried to dislodge it, he realized there was something different about it. Wiring and mechanics and other pieces of metal had jutted out from it when they'd last seen it. More importantly, chunks had been missing from where they had taken a couple of samples.

They were all gone. It looked as though the piece had been intentionally plucked clean like the jungle had tried to absorb everything one piece at a time.

"That's creepy," he muttered. Something about it seemed to sound a warning, a feeling in his gut that told him to leave it alone or to simply take samples like they had last time. They had the flowers and a couple of samples would be more than enough to continue his research, as limited as it had been. He wasn't a geologist or a metallurgist, so he was far from the expert who was needed to study this.

Sal shook the feeling off. It was time to be aggressive and assertive, dammit. What did he have to fear about it anyway?

He tugged the piece clear and shook the plant residue off before he shoved it into his pack. It was still heavy but much lighter than it had been, which made sense.

As he turned to head toward where Kennedy waited for him, movement caught his attention out the corner of his eye. He looked in that direction but didn't see anything at first. Whatever it had been was lost in the shadows of where the trees closed the sunlight out again. He thought perhaps he'd imagined it but then realized something that made him want to make use of the waste disposal unit of his suit.

What startled him wasn't an absence of movement. Rather, it was that it was so large, it seemed like it was in one long, continuous motion. He gulped and glanced at his partner when he saw four huge eyes that caught a hint of sunlight and reflected it fully.

"Oh, fuck!" he shouted. "Get back! Get back n—" His warning was interrupted when a long tail flicked out from the shadows and lashed toward him.

"Down!" Kennedy shouted, and he ducked barely in time to avoid having his head severed. Something sharp on the tail latched onto the shoulder of his power arm, though, swept him off his feet, and yanked him toward the jungle.

Not this shit again.

He crashed hard into Kennedy and they pounded into a nearby tree. The impact was hard enough to shake enough leaves free that it looked like it had suddenly begun to snow brown and green. He groaned. A couple more ribs had pulverized, and pain surged through him. He moaned again, rolled off her, and dragged his gun out from where he'd stashed it in his pack.

The mutant that had attacked them was out in the open now and looked at him with four eyes that were each about half the size of his head. It was a reptile—or so it seemed from the long, forked tongue that flicked out from its mouth and scaly skin that glowed a soft mixture of green and silver in the sunlight. It also had six legs, each of which ended in three toes, which finished in huge, sharp claws.

As if in challenge, the creature opened its mouth to reveal a row of dagger-long fangs. Even from a distance of about ten meters, he could smell the stink of death on its breath. It watched him and its tail slithered right and left like it dared him to make the first move.

The fact that the reptile was the size of a Clydesdale gave him serious pause, though.

"What the fuck is that?" Kennedy asked as she regained her feet and drew her gun.

"I don't know," he whispered, "but I don't think it likes us very much."

"Thank you, Captain Obvious." She raised her weapon cautiously.

Sal nodded and didn't bother to answer as he leveled his rifle at the monster. As much as he felt it would only attack if they moved again, he knew they couldn't continue this stare-off with the massive creature forever. They would have to move, and it would use its tail to cut them in half.

"Please tell me you're recording this," his partner whispered.

"Oh, you know it," he responded and clenched his jaw. "I only hope we get this footage along with a massive keep-out sign."

"That may be the smartest thing you've ever said," she whispered with a grin.

"You move first," he said. "I'll cover you. When it gets close, you cover me. Does that sound like a plan?"

"Another dumb plan," she retorted. "But again, it's not like we have any better options."

"Unfortunately, you're right about that. We move in three...two...one...go!"

Kennedy sprinted to the left, still heading south where they would be able to rendezvous with the rest of the team that had dropped them off. That was assuming, of course, that this monster hadn't already eaten them.

As she moved, the creature darted forward at an impossible speed—way too fast for something that large, although Sal had come to expect the impossible from the Zoo and the creatures it created. He made no assumptions, not anymore, but it was still fascinating—except not so much when it could take your head off in one bite.

As it serpentined toward his partner, he moved in a different direction—not quite opposite but away from her as he opened fire on it. He'd flicked the weapon to auto before he squeezed the trigger.

The bullets sank into the scales, but he could also see they hadn't gone too deep. It clearly hurt, as the creature emitted a hissed roar that was quickly picked up and filtered out by the sound filters in his suit. It still hurt worse than the gunshots, he realized as the mutant turned to him and ceased its advance on his partner.

Sal had only a moment to register its attack before he flung himself to the ground. The tail, three times again as long as the rest of the body, whipped into the trees, circled the trunk of one of them, and narrowly avoided taking his head off again.

As it withdrew, something like the teeth marks of a saw

were visible on the wood and almost felled the tree with one stroke.

"What the fuck!" he shouted to no one in particular as he sprinted to where it now headed toward Kennedy again with another ferocious roar. She directed a barrage of fire at the beast, but it seemed her bullets did no damage either. It was almost on top of her now, and she ran and fired at the same time. The reptile slithered between the trees and somehow navigated the forest easily despite its size.

"Hey! Over here, you giant fucking fossil!" he called and released another fusillade at it. Body strikes did no damage and only made its anger worse, but it pulled away from her and snaked rapidly in his direction. It looked like a huge serpent in the darkness of the jungle, the four eyes frighteningly visible. They glowed and reflected what little light there was as it powered toward him.

It was all he could do to not react like a deer caught in the headlights. He sprinted forward again and ran despite the agony that defined his body at that moment. While the goop did have an effect and healed him much faster than was humanly possible, it wasn't instant. The broken ribs would heal in a week instead of six to twelve.

That was assuming he made it out of there alive, he suddenly realized as the scent of death and decay surrounded him.

Something caught on his foot from behind and tripped him. The gyro in his suit prevented his fall the first time. The second time was much more difficult to avoid as one of the creature's feet with the massive claws dug brutally into his back and shoved him to the jungle floor. The claws sliced through his armor like it was made of paper mache.

Thankfully, while the weight of the creature pressed down on his body and made his ribs and lungs scream in agony, the claws didn't cut into his abdomen. Something pinched in his shoulder and arm, but aside from that—

At that moment, Sal looked up and the massive jaw descended slowly toward him. Well, far be it from him to judge a massive reptile that liked to play with its food, but he really wanted it to be over quickly.

The fangs lowered on him with surprising gentleness. For something that easily weighed a bajillion tons, it still felt like he was being licked by the world's largest housecat. The reptile tore his pack off and the entire mechanism that attached it to his suit. The pack ripped open and he narrowed his eyes as the creature picked something up. It was shiny and looked very much like a leg.

Wait, was all this about that piece of armor?

He felt the pressure on his chest increase when suddenly, something loud sounded right next to his ear. It wasn't one of the hissed, high-pitched roars he'd heard earlier. This sounded suspiciously like a gunshot.

A gunshot?

Sal looked up again as the pressure suddenly lifted from his chest. His ears rang, along with a horde of other messages sent to his brain by his abused nervous system. Someone lifted him—this time by the collar of his suit— with actual fingers. He wavered on his feet as he stared at Kennedy.

"How do you feel?" she asked.

"I've been better," he gasped and winced as his lungs pressed painfully against his broken ribs.

"Too bad. Let's get going." She reached down, lifted the

ruined pack, and stuffed everything that had spilled out into it—including the piece of leg armor—before she pushed it into his chest.

Normally, he would have taken it without even a flinch. This time, though, he stumbled a few steps, his fall prevented when he dropped onto the collapsed corpse of the monster that had squeezed the life out of him only moments before. He looked at it in bemusement. Three of the four eyes were shut and the fourth sported a massive, still-smoking hole where the eyeball should have been.

He gritted his teeth and tried not to hurl, although he wasn't sure if it was from the smell, the sight, or the sensation that his body was about to fall to pieces. Or maybe a combination of all three. He was usually much sturdier about this, but he felt like he couldn't take another step before he dropped and fell asleep. Forever.

With a determined grimace, he pulled himself to his feet and struggled to remain upright despite his effort and determination.

At the moment in which he knew he would faceplant on the ground again, Kennedy slid her shoulder beneath his to support him.

"Thanks," Sal gasped.

"No problem." She grunted and adjusted his weight. "You're the one with all our loot so it's the least I can do. I do need to get paid, after all."

"Right," he said. "This is a purely selfish action on your part. I understand."

"Absolutely," she agreed as they picked up the pace. "Totally selfish. By the way, has this armor held up under pressure or what?"

He glanced at her armor and saw the same teeth marks on the metal as he'd seen on the tree after the monster's tail had lashed it. The teeth had peeled the metal off to expose the circuitry beneath.

"Yep," he muttered and tried to keep his breaths shallow. "It looks like we already have more than enough work for Gutierrez when we get back. She'll be so happy."

Kennedy chuckled. "What the fuck was that monster supposed to be?"

"And why did it want the leg of armor we retrieved?" he asked.

"Oh, yeah, I noticed that it tried to take it before I pumped a couple of bullets into its eye socket," she said. "Is it an animal that likes shiny things or this particular shiny thing?"

"It seemed like that leg was what it was after in the first place," he said as he struggled to keep his body in forward motion. "Maybe it has something to do with this new metal it's made of?"

"Maybe," she conceded. "Come on, buddy, you're lagging. Focus on running and we'll be out of this fucking jungle."

He nodded. This was the kind of thing that could be thought about once they were out of danger and he no longer had a hard time sucking in air.

CHAPTER SEVEN

Morning came too early for Madigan's liking. It had been a rough trip out of the Zoo, especially since she had to get Sal out. She'd almost carried him toward the end and they barely managed to reach the JLTVs in time to get a ride back to the base. Sal had dipped in and out of consciousness during the whole trip. His suit was supposed to have rudimentary first aid capabilities that protected his open wounds from infection. From the way he had breathed, at least neither of his lungs had been punctured by the broken ribs, but that was the only good news. He'd been sluggish and passed out periodically as they traveled.

The team that drove them back didn't even bother to stop at the commandant's office but went directly to the hospital to drop him off at an emergency room. Once they peeled the armor off him, she realized the extent of his injuries. His entire torso was bruised to a dark purple interspersed with splotches of bright red where the bruises had been punctured and blood had spilled under his skin. Livid, painful cuts were etched into his shoulder and arms. There were more injuries, including a concussion, but they were less of a priority.

He had saved her life, she realized as the doctors wheeled him into an operating room. Well, no less than she had saved his, of course, but it wasn't a competition. Neither would have made it out of the Zoo without the other.

Courtney arrived at the hospital barely minutes after Sal was taken away.

"What's happening?" she asked and sounded flustered. "Is Sal okay? Will he make it?"

"He's in surgery now," she responded and began to remove her armor piece by piece.

"What happened?" the other woman repeated. Kennedy didn't reply but retrieved the memory stick from Sal's armor and handed it to her. She plugged it into her phone quickly and scrolled through the recorded videos until she reached the one in question.

"What the fuck?" Monroe gasped as she stared at the video he had recorded.

"Yeah," she muttered. "It...attacked us from the shadows. We barely made it out. It seemed like it tried to take the leg of armor. Like it wanted to keep the metal that it's made of? I don't know. It all happened so fast. We ran for our lives and then I shot it and it died."

"You guys didn't happen to get any samples, right?" the woman asked.

"Nope, I was too worried about getting Sal back alive," she replied, annoyed. "Look, I need to pick something up at the compound. Can you please call Gutierrez and let her know that if she wants extra work before she signs any contracts, we could really use her help to put our suits together again?"

Her companion nodded, properly admonished, as Kennedy shrugged free of the last of her armor and walked away. She scrambled into the JLTV that Courtney had brought and drove away.

Monroe dialed quickly, the video she had seen still vivid in her head. She only hoped she still had the armorer's number right.

"Well, I'm sorry I cared enough about you to get as much of the goop as I could lay my hands on," Kennedy muttered.

"Look, it's not that I don't appreciate that, okay?" he said. His voice still carried something of a whine from the tubes that had been in his throat. "I really do. Believe me. And I also appreciate the trouble you went through to help me."

She smiled and pressed her fist gently to his shoulder. "I knew you could use a little more Madie than usual," she said, her eyes averted.

"It's not only that," he went on, uncomfortable with the personal direction this conversation had taken. "I know you practically—and sometimes literally—carried me out of the Zoo, and...you saved my life back there."

She nodded but deliberately said no more so as to not compromise her status as a badass.

"But for next time, when you...milk Madie—"

"Oh, God," she muttered and rolled her eyes.

"I know, I know," he said quickly. "But when you get the goop out, you need to leave at least half of what the flower made still in, otherwise it wilts and dies. It takes a while for new flowers to bloom, so it means we won't have any of the blue stuff for a while, is all. I'm not criticizing you or anything. It's only a heads-up if you need to milk—withdraw more of the goop in the future."

She smirked and stroked his cheek gently. "You know you saved my life in there too, right?"

"Well, I think I did considerably less than you," he returned with a smile. "So, let's say we both needed each other to get out of that place alive. Again."

"You more than me." She covered the statement with a cough.

"What was that?" he asked.

"Oh, nothing—a bit of a cold." Kennedy chuckled. "Get some rest. Just because you recover quicker doesn't mean I'll let you push the limits, Sal."

"Yeah, I know," he said with a smile. "How does the armor look?"

"Oh, I put Gutierrez to work on that." She grinned. "She was really impressed with how much damage it absorbed while we got out of the place alive ourselves. Of course, I say impressed, but it's probably not a good thing."

"Yeah, let's try not to run into any more of those big… fucking monster things," Sal said.

"I gave Courtney your recordings as well as my own statement on what the critter is capable of," Madigan said. "She didn't believe everything I told her, but she's already writing a whitepaper about it. It'll actually be featured. A ton of people will pay to know what the new alpha predator of the Zoo is."

"I'd contest you there," he said, "but even those big dinosaur replicas wouldn't be a match against something like that. I…" He paused and closed his eyes. She noted that his hands shook while he talked about it and that he clenched them quickly into fists.

"Are you okay?" she asked.

"Yeah." He opened his hand and wiped it over his face. "The doc said there might be some trouble with nerve damage. It'll probably all go away as I heal."

He sounded less confident than she would have liked, but she breezed past it. If he wanted to talk about the traumatic experience he'd had with the monster in the Zoo, she was probably not the one to talk about it with. Her advice would more than likely range from "Yeah, that's tough," to "Get over it, you pussy," and she knew for a fact that neither would help when someone suffered from something real.

She took his hand gently as Courtney and Gutierrez stepped through the door of his hospital room.

"Well, I talked to the docs here," Monroe said. "The price of your treatment is astronomical, so I took it out of the money from the sets of flowers you guys brought back. He said it should have been much worse, but you have impressive recovery powers stocked in that body of yours, Salinger Jacobs. You'll have to let me study that in person someday."

"Someday," he agreed as she hugged him as gently as she could over the hospital bed.

"Well, I won't hug you," Amanda said with a chuckle,

"but I'm really glad you're fighting back. I looked into the amount of stress the armor was put under while the critter pressed on you, and you have no right to be alive right now. You're a lucky man."

"Lucky." He grinned. "Yep, that's me. Lucky as hell."

"Anyway, it should be a little while before the suits are ready to go again," the mechanic continued. "They took a nasty beating out there. The both of you. There will be a ton of welding, and the price of the spare parts needed came out of the sets you brought in too. I'm afraid it brings the overall profits of your trip into the Zoo down to almost zero."

"Not really," Courtney said with a smile. "Of course, the flowers paid for all this, but we still have people bidding for the whitepaper on the monster you two faced, so that should pay dividends in the near future. That, plus the samples you collected...not a bad trip. Financially, I mean," she added quickly. "I'm not...not talking about all this."

"Okay, okay," Kennedy interjected. "Sal needs his rest. I need to have a quick chat with him before he goes back to his beauty sleep."

Sal smirked as Courtney and Amanda made their exits, the two already talking like they were almost fast friends. His face assumed a somber expression once the door closed and Madigan turned to face him.

"You didn't tell them?" he asked.

"Tell them what?"

"About the papers we recovered from the bounty hunters. The map we took off their bodies that matched our own reports exactly."

"Almost exactly," she muttered defensively.

"You know what I mean, Madigan," he said in a warning tone. "Deflecting won't make this conversation not happen."

She sighed and shook her head. "I didn't feel I could tell them without you present. Not only do I not know the science behind the tracking system you set up, but we also don't know who might have used it and why they haven't made their findings public yet. Or why they use third and fourth-rate mercs to make the run for them."

"You're right." He sighed and shifted to find a more comfortable position. "We need to find out who's using the tech before we actually put it on the market. Otherwise, they'll underbid us and we'll lose everything."

Kennedy nodded, even though the marketing problem presented hadn't even occurred to her at all. She usually left that kind of bullshit to Sal and Courtney. It was her job to get them in and out of that fucking place alive and in one piece.

"We need someone new," she finally said. "Someone who can trace that kind of thing to a source for us to pin down."

"A hacker?" he asked.

"You're too smart to think it'll be as simple as that, but yeah, in essence," she mused and sat in one of the chairs that flanked the bed. "Someone who can track the signal we know and find out who else is using it."

"Do you have anyone in mind?"

"I don't," she said with a shrug. "I don't really think we need more people on our team. We can't keep supplying food and board to the folk who join us. Eventually, we will run out of room. Besides, what kind of idiot would leave the comfort of their parents' basement to come out here and put their lives on the line against monsters of alien descent?"

"It's not like they'd actually go into the Zoo," he reasoned. "For some guys, they don't need to be in the jungle itself, merely near it. Imagine the reputation a hacker would have simply living near the Zoo."

Madigan nodded. "That is a good point. I know a couple of people on the Russian side who might know people who might meet our purposes."

"It shouldn't be hard to find a criminal hacker who wouldn't mind moving out here where oversight is minimal and Internet speed is optimal," he said. "The kind of guys who need to get very, very far away where no one can find them."

"That is practical, I'll admit," she conceded. "But do you really think you'd be able to trust someone with that kind of history? Trust them with your life, I mean."

"I guess not." He sighed again as he adjusted his pillows with a small grimace of pain. "It's exactly like you to ruin a great idea and perfect opportunity with a strong, healthy dose of self-preservation."

"I keep your dumb ass alive, Sal," she said with a grin. "That's my job. It's what I signed up for and damned if I'm not good at what I do."

"The very fucking best," he agreed with a chuckle.

"Look," Madigan said. She pushed out of her seat and ran her fingers through his hair. "Gregor on the Russian base owes us a couple of favors. I'll ask him to throw a net out and see if he can't catch us something. In the meantime, you get some rest and recover, you hear?"

"Will do, boss," he said and his eyes had already drifted shut.

He knew they wouldn't let him out of this place easily. They liked having experienced, underpaid boots on the ground, and they used it whenever they could. They twisted elected officials' arms and those officials made generals tell colonels like him to stay where he fucking was and not move an inch.

What Anderson had seen and the scathing report he'd sent on Pegasus' use of mercenaries who were more than willing to kill people who were on their side of this conflict of man versus nature had essentially guaranteed his exile. He should have known they wouldn't let him back on US soil until they all had their stories squared away.

Why couldn't he simply lie like the rest of them?

It wasn't in his DNA, of course. He couldn't do it. It would very likely get him killed, but that didn't mean he had to change a goddamn thing.

The colonel sat on the desk chair they'd sent to make his stay more comfortable. Once the orders came through that he would remain there—in this construction site that had long since been surpassed by the wall's construction and yet had still been converted into a covert operation base—they had made sure to send in some new amenities to make his stay more comfortable. A supply of coffee, real beds, and office chairs and desks had arrived, all to make sure the people who operated out of there and tested the new sets of armor could do so in as much comfort as was possible.

Anderson would miss his son playing in the soccer finals. He blamed Pegasus for that.

"Fucking bullshit," he exclaimed for what felt like the thousandth time since he'd landed in this infernal desert. He leaned back in his seat as the Pegasus logo spun on the screen of his tablet while he waited for a call from the man who had set all this up.

Finally, the logo disappeared, replaced by the face of Carlson, the Pegasus CEO—a man with neatly combed white hair in a New York high rise.

"Colonel Anderson, nice to see you again," the caller said with a practiced smile.

"Mr. Carlson," he replied, his tone intentionally cool.

"I hope all the armor testing has kept to schedule?" the man asked. He'd noted the icy greeting but maintained his own civil tone.

"Well, as long as your horde of thugs in armor runs through everyone they meet with maximum prejudice, we'll continue on your timetable," Anderson replied. "Although there are still problems with the Friend and Foe Recognition software—apparently."

"Of course," Carlson said. "I've read the reports at length. Our engineers will do everything they can. They are working around the clock to fix the issue."

"You might find the problem is human error, not mechanical."

"Nonsense," the CEO cut in quickly. "Our engineers are not to blame for the malfunction. It's a very complex coding issue. I've been assured it'll be fixed before the next battery of tests starts."

The colonel smirked. The man knew what he was talking about. Anderson's own report had been very vociferous as to his doubts that the errors involving the FOF software were strictly mechanical, but Carlson made sure it wasn't admitted to on tape. They would simply redact that when they submitted the report to the Pentagon.

"Good news, though," the CEO went on. "The Mark-Ones of our suits are being shipped out as we speak. There's been considerable demand for them around the globe, mostly in jungle areas. Venezuela, Vietnam, Brazil, places like that. We were sold out before we even started production. Good work on that, by the way. We'll make sure you get a bonus for all your hard work."

If they thought they could buy him off with a consulting bonus, they would have another think coming. Anderson gritted his teeth but nodded.

"We should be getting the Mark-Twos out in short order as well," he continued. "We're a profit-run business, after all, in a profit-friendly country, and we intend to keep it that way. I'll update you if anything new comes across my desk. Until then, I hope you keep up the good work over there. Carlson out, as you military guys like to say."

The screen went dead for a minute before it returned to the rotating Pegasus logo. The colonel rubbed his temples and leaned back in his seat again.

"Fucking asshole," he finally snarked at the aluminum roof of his little hut. "When the world goes to shit and some Zoo creature is munching on your intestines, you can remember all the profit you made for your company, you insufferable ass."

He was fairly certain they'd sent bugs with the new desks and chairs to make sure they maintained a good eye on proceedings. It didn't worry him. In fact, he really hoped they'd caught what he said, he realized as he pushed to his feet and made his way outside.

CHAPTER EIGHT

Over the past couple of months, it had become easier and quicker to get transport to the Russian sector. The US had opened the area to other nations as the amount of money made attracted more and more insistence from across the globe that they be allowed to participate. The Chinese were setting a base up in their sector to the southeast, while the French were already making inroads with their development in the southwest. The British were already firmly entrenched to the west of the US sector, and apparently, had made a deal with the Germans.

It would make the Zoo far more crowded, and Madigan wasn't sure it was a good thing. The reason the jungle had gone to shit in the first place was because of an unexpected arrival of fresh meat, and what people were doing seemed like much the same deal but with extra steps. She'd seen the goop take something and twist it, and she didn't want to see what it had in mind for the various humans who had gone missing in there.

This was all so far over her head that she wasn't sure why she worried about it, but the thought nagged constantly in the back of her mind over the seven-hour-long drive from the base to the Russian sector.

Heavy Metal still had a couple of standing invitations there since their last visit had been the culmination of a Zoo trip during which she and Sal had bailed a squad of theirs out—a squad that included the son of the base's commandant. It meant that although she would arrive as the sun began to set, she knew there would be a place for her to crash should she need to spend the night.

Even so, that wasn't her first choice. If the truth be told, she would much prefer to head back to check on how Sal was doing than spend the night in a hastily prepared apartment. She shook her head and leaned back in the seat of the truck that roared across the surprisingly smooth roads that had been built to provide easier transportation between the bases. Absently, she wondered how much the companies that had been given these building contracts had profited. She knew for a fact that labor out there was dirt cheap, so they had to know there were upsides to building contracts out in the middle of fucking nowhere.

Once she reached the base, it was quick work to find where most of the men there hung out. Russians had a reputation for drinking, and while it wasn't unwarranted, she wondered if people thought excessive drinking was an exclusively Russian characteristic. Many other people liked to drink but perhaps the Russians were simply better at it than the rest of the world.

She arrived at the bar, which was far more rustic than the

one at the US base. Mark's Pub was surrounded by a ridiculous amount of hype based on its claim to be a gastro-pub or something of the like. This one had a bar, a bartender, and as much space as could be made for as many patrons as possible.

Which suited her fine, she realized, as she very soon found herself at a table with a glass of something frothy in front of her. Across from her sat Gregor, the man they'd found stranded in the Zoo about a month before. He owed his life to her, Sal, and Courtney, so he was always happy to help. For a price, of course, but the price was always with the friends and family discount.

"So, what can Gregor do for the mighty Sergeant Kennedy on this night?" he asked, clearly happy to be on the giving end of a favor this time.

She smirked. "Well, the sergeant who isn't a sergeant anymore might need your help to find a certain someone with a certain set of skills. The kind that aren't in high demand around here."

"So, I would guess you don't need someone who can use a gun?" he asked with a grin.

"Well, it's never a bad talent to have," Kennedy replied with a smirk. "But I'd prefer that their talents be more centered around computers and technology."

"Ah, you need IT guy to handle computer security, is that it?" he asked with a knowing tap on his nose.

"In a way." She took a quick sip of her drink to give her time to think about how she could word this. "Although I'd like to think his defense was more along the lines of offense. Do you know what I mean?"

The Russian raised an eyebrow and nodded slowly. "I

think I do. And more importantly, I think I know someone who is exactly what you will need."

"Oh?" she asked and leaned forward, all ears.

"Yes, this...person, who shall remain nameless," he said to emphasize that their conversation might not be as private as they would prefer. "They might be in need of disappearing, if you take my meaning?"

Kennedy raised an eyebrow. "I won't kill anyone, if that's what you think."

"What?" Gregor leaned away. "It hurts that you think me capable to ask such a thing. No, I mean this person might need to get away from certain problems that might have come during a time when they might have worked for the FSB."

She tried not to roll her eyes. To get a straight answer out of these guys would be damn near impossible, but she still needed their help. She wasn't sure whom she could trust with someone from the States, and with people like Gregor who owed her their lives, she had expected to feel safer. Still, with the implications of his beating around the proverbial bush, she might have been wrong to think that. Besides, it was probably not the best idea to get on the bad side of the Russian secret service.

Kennedy took a deep breath. In for a penny, in for a pound, right? She didn't want to have to resort to bullshit like this, but if he left her no other choice, she might as well make the most of it.

"What kind of trouble would this...hypothetical person need to escape from?" she asked with a sigh.

"The kind that would require them to disappear," Gregor continued. "New name, new location, somewhere with place to live and good Internet connection where they can lie low until the heat dies down, yes?"

Well, hot damn, Sal was right. All they had to do was find a place where people could live cheaply and they would come. Maybe a hacker in trouble with the Russian government wasn't quite what she'd had in mind at the time but things changed.

"I don't suppose you'd have any clue what kind of mess this guy is in, right?" She assumed it was a guy. They generally were.

"I was left unaware of details," Gregor said and shrugged. "But as I heard it told, you are as good as those you worked for. This one's handler in the FSB had...how do you say it? Gotten handsy with the wrong person and when it came to light, the hacker was burned as well. So as long as you, me, or him do not admit to anything, no one would contest if word were to come out that he died in the Zoo, yes?"

Kennedy nodded and sipped slowly from her glass. "It's very risky, I think."

"Life in the Zoo lacks guarantees," he said with a shrug. "You could die tomorrow and this wouldn't be your problem anymore, yes? He's a typical hacker—sleeps on computers and has wet dreams of hacking the NSA, but he never screwed his employers over. For someone of his qualities, that has to mean something. Test him and see for yourself."

She shook her head and put down her glass. "Well, I suppose I can give this guy a chance. Email me the pick-up details, and we'll handle him once he's appropriately dead."

Her phone rang and interrupted the conversation. She retrieved it and glanced at the screen. It was Sal.

"I have to take this," she said, stood, and moved away quickly for a couple of minutes. When she returned, she looked rather concerned.

"I need to head back." She frowned. "Sorry to cut this visit short."

"When boss calls, you must answer," Gregor said with a grin. He stood and hugged her tightly. "Everyone understands this."

"You still owe me, Gregor," she said and patted him on the cheek as she moved away. "Remember that. Hooking me up with a potential employee doesn't cover saving your life."

"That depends on what I must do to hook you up with this employee," he said. "But this can be discussed later. Have safe trip."

With most of the night spent either waiting for another van to the US base or riding in it, Kennedy didn't get much sleep. While the smooth roads and the dull roar of engines could lull anyone to sleep, she spent most of the time anxious about what Sal had called to talk to her about.

Of course, she was sorry to hear that Courtney's father had passed away and she knew that as the woman's only friends out there, it was the least they could do to fly to the States for the funeral. And it wasn't like Kennedy didn't want to be back in civilization again.

She simply wasn't sure how well she would handle

being back. Before her transfer to the Zoo, she'd been stationed in Afghanistan and hadn't been home in almost five years now. She'd butted heads before she'd shipped out and so much preferred to be out there and risk her life for money instead of going back home.

Then again, she wouldn't actually return home since her family all considered California to be the geographical equivalent of blasphemy.

Still, it was close enough to bring all those feelings of anxiety and unworthiness to the forefront of her mind and they wouldn't go away, no matter how hard she tried.

Which meant that when they finally pulled into the base less than an hour after sunrise, she was pissed, tired, and hungry. There was no way she would get any sleep now unless she got fucked, and with Sal still in the hospital, that wouldn't happen.

A distant second choice, then, would be to have a drink, some food, and try to sleep a little of this anxiety off before she attempted to find a plane that would get them halfway across the world in time for the funeral.

She stepped out of the vehicle and made sure to tell the men that the money for the ride had already been transferred. Technically, they were supposed to be free, but it was always a good idea to be sure they were well compensated for their efforts. It never hurt to try to make more friends in a place where enemies weren't hard to find.

Kennedy scowled at the sun as it began to climb in the sky as she walked the terrifying three blocks to where the bar was still open, even though most of its usual clientele would be absent.

She strolled in, shook her head, and blinked rapidly to

adapt to the darkness inside. A waitress who looked as tired as she felt came up and asked what she needed for the morning.

"Steak, dirty rice, fries, and a beer," she replied, her tone a little surly. "And put it on the corporate bill."

The waitress smiled, winked, and tapped the stylus on the pad she used to take orders. The corporate bill was something she'd come up with although Sal had been a part of it. She'd argued that since they spent so much time at the bar to find work, it was only fair that she put her drinks on the company's bill. He'd agreed, although he'd been drunk at the time, and they'd set it up. It was technically billable hours which were deductible according to US tax law, so he created the account for her to use while she conducted business there. Anything he couldn't deduct month to month was taken from her salary.

Was it an honest arrangement? Probably not, and there were likely a horde of lawyers who would jump them for fraud if they were in the US. Thankfully, very few lawyers were out there, and the ones who were fished for a much bigger catch than low-level tax evasion.

They would have to clean their act up when they returned to the States, though, Kennedy realized as she sat. The beer arrived well in advance of her meal and more than half was already gone before the food was set before her.

She had almost finished her meal when someone sat on the opposite side of the table. Madigan didn't look up. She hadn't had much to eat all night and the whole day yesterday, so damned if she would look up from her food to talk someone out of even an attempt at conversation.

"Seat's taken, pal," she snapped around a mouthful of fries as she dug into the medium-rare slab of meat of suspicious origin.

"I have a bone to pick with you," a man's voice said.

Madigan looked up briefly from her food but continued to eat and spoke around her current mouthful. "Yeah, well, get in fucking line, pal. I'm not drunk enough to deal with any bones that need picking. Who the fuck are you, anyway?"

"Brandon."

"You say that like it's supposed to mean something," she said. She shook her head and took a sip of her beer. "Brandon. You sound like a fucking jock who gets defeated by a nerd in a made-for-TV movie."

"Corporal Brandon," the man said belligerently as he leaned forward on the table top, "and I was the one you and your little boytoy embarrassed here in the bar not that long ago."

She smirked. "Oh, right, now I remember. You got in deeper than you could swim, passed out, and pissed yourself. I wasn't around for that last part so I'm assuming, of course."

He glowered in return. "Well, I hear you guys like to cheat people out of their hard-earned money and that you try to poach the best for cheap labor at your new company. Now normally, I wouldn't bother with someone with your rep, but seeing how you operate, I think I should be bothered. Your boy is simply a kid in over his head who thinks he can game the system. I almost don't blame him, since you're clearly the dumbass who likes to hide behind kids to do your dirty work."

Kennedy looked at him now and narrowed her eyes. It was difficult to tell in the lighting how drunk he was, but she had to assume he'd been there all night. Most likely, he'd been unable to return to his unit after the stories about how he'd lost a drinking match to a twenty-two-year-old specialist had made the rounds.

"I don't have to explain jack or fucking shit to a dumbass who can't hold his booze," she said with a chuckle. "Get off my table or there'll be trouble."

A couple of the guys who sat at tables in the back stood when they heard the altercation. She was there regularly enough to know they were usually bouncers and were supposed to be off duty. Of course, that didn't mean they would sit around while a fight brewed.

"What's the matter, honey?" Brandon asked, reached arrogantly across the table to pick up one of the fries from her plate, and ate it with a smug expression. "You're not so tough without your boy around to back up your big talk, huh?"

The two bouncers moved toward the door when they heard that last sentence. They knew what would happen and only wanted to make sure no company property was broken in the inevitable ruckus.

"Touch my food again," she said coldly, "and the stories that'll make the rounds this time will be about how you had your ass kicked by a woman. One hell of a woman, of course, but I think the sexist fucks you call your team will still hold that shit against you."

The corporal sneered and she resisted the temptation to roll her eyes. Guys like this were too fucking predictable —drunk and with bruised egos who needed to assert themselves over what they saw as the weaker sex. To attempt to teach him a lesson would be a waste of time since nothing would be learned but sometimes, that didn't matter.

The man's hand stretched toward her plate again in the sluggish, slow movements of someone who had abused their liver all night. Madigan attacked with the speed of someone who had hoped for a fight.

She caught his fore and middle fingers, twisted savagely, and grinned at a crack that confirmed both had popped out of their sockets. Brandon fell and clutched his hand. His mouth opened but no sound emerged since the sudden agony had sucked the breath out of him. He began to push to his feet in an effort to escape her wrath. Stupidly, he probably hadn't consider that she could move around the table to continue the fight.

The bouncers opened the door a split second before the man was unceremoniously tossed out. They didn't need to lift a finger themselves except that she would have ruined the door with Brandon's head. That would come out of their paychecks, whether they were off duty or on.

The corporal scrambled to his feet and stumbled as he tried to staunch the blood that flowed copiously from his nose before he collapsed once more. He probably had a concussion, she thought coolly as she stepped out of the bar herself.

"Some dipshits never learn." One of the bouncers chuckled as she stepped past him.

"Are you talking about me or him?" she asked.

"Him," the man said and laughed. "As for you, you're around here so often I wonder why the boss don't hire you as a bouncer and save all of us some time and money."

Madigan smirked. "You'd best call an ambulance for this dumbass."

"Don't break him too bad," the bouncer said, and both men stepped inside. She had essentially finished her meal and damned if a fight wouldn't relax her. It wasn't as good as a great fuck but it was way better than only a meal and a beer, she mused.

Brandon pushed himself onto his hands and knees. He mouthed something at her but she couldn't make it out. Quite honestly, she didn't much care to, either. Instead, she hammered her boot into the side of his head.

He dropped without a sound and a few seconds later, quiet snores indicated that she hadn't killed him.

Small mercies. The paperwork would have been insane and she would have probably had to pass on the trip to the US.

"Sweet dreams, asshole," she muttered and marched away to find her apartment for a nice, long nap.

Carlson studied the latest report from the Zoo with a deep frown. While they had managed to get the suit production to pay for the exorbitant expenses, it didn't change the fact that the project hemorrhaged almost as much money as it made. He had a board meeting in less than two weeks and he wanted to be able to explain the situation without the risk that the investors would jump down his throat over how much money was invested in a product that was already on the market.

Did he need to worry about this? Probably not, he

decided. His vice president—some kid barely out of Harvard whose father was on the board—could take care of it. He could also handle the damned fallout from the amount of money it drained from the coffers.

But it was his pet project. He'd started it from the research and development stage and followed it all the way, and damned if he would allow a trust-fund-dependent frat boy to take credit for it when it did eventually come together. This would be his legacy. It was his retirement plan, and he wanted his name stamped on it. Without doubt, it would change the world, and the name people would put to that change was Robert Carlson, CEO of Pegasus.

That said, fires had started that would be difficult to explain to a group of assholes who hadn't been around from the beginning, and he wanted them out before he had to address the board. If all was well and good on the bottom line, all would be well and good when the time came to sign off on company expenditures.

Carlson leaned back in his ergonomic seat—commissioned by his second ex-wife back when the hag had wanted to try her hand at making them. The woman had absolutely no business sense but damned if her chairs hadn't turned out well. He'd ordered half a dozen after he was forced to bail her company out and kept them in reserve for when he needed them.

He tapped the call button on his screen and it went dark for a moment as a secure comm line was created and tunneled to the office he now contacted in Barcelona.

"Rodrigo," he said with a chuckle. "How's the Mediterranean lifestyle treating you, my friend?"

"I can't complain," said the tanned, good-looking man on the other side of the call. "Sunlight and fresh sea air are precisely what the doctor ordered. What can I do for you, Robert?"

"Well, what I have in mind for you is considerable sunlight but far less fresh sea air." He gave him a sly smile. "I take it you've been updated on the Zoo situation?"

"Of course." His contact nodded and his tone turned serious. He was the owner of the company that had provided the mercenary pilots for their new armor. There had been complaints about the men, of course—mostly from that idiot Anderson—but so far, they had been worth every single penny.

And there had been a satisfying number of pennies.

"I've been updated by our contacts in Morocco that someone else has looked into the metal we've extracted," the CEO said and rocked on the chair. "I don't need to remind you that we don't need any competition before we have it locked up."

"Of course not," Rodrigo agreed.

"I'm not worried about accidents." Carlson waved away the concerns he could already see in his friend's eyes. "Six thousand people and their families all depend on the solutions we come up with. Don't kill anyone if you don't have to, but if it comes down to it, we'll mark them down as... necessary losses. The cost of doing business, understood?"

"Of course." The man laughed coldly. "Although it should be noted that I strongly suspect there will need to be more than a few...happy accidents, shall we say?"

"You're my fucking Bob Ross, Rodrigo. But get it done."

"Will do, boss," the man said before he terminated the connection.

Carlson didn't like being hung up on. He preferred to reserve the pleasure for himself, but in this day and age, it wasn't worth it to squabble over such petty things. He shrugged and leaned back far enough in his seat that he could look at the ceiling.

These were some damned good chairs.

CHAPTER NINE

"So, the doctors were happy to let you simply walk out?" Madigan asked.

"Well, not happy, obviously." Sal chuckled. "You know, they wanted to run a string of other tests. People apparently don't recover from concussions so quickly, and they said they need scans and blood screens to make sure it wasn't a false positive."

She smirked. "I guess you didn't want to tell them you suspect your improved recovery comes from imbibing blue goop from a plant you pulled from the Zoo, right?"

"How would you even begin to explain that to someone anyway?" he asked with a shrug. "Without giving away company secrets, of course."

"Wait, so only your concussion is better?" she asked and glanced away from the road for a second. "What about your broken ribs and bruised bones? The lacerations?"

"Everything is well on the way to being completely healed." He nodded. "Although I think the trauma to the brain heals faster than broken bones and lacerated muscles. That makes sense since concussions tend to take a couple of weeks, while bones and muscles take a couple of months."

"That's really not the point, Sal," she protested as she pulled the JLTV into the compound. "Are you sure you're in a safe condition to travel? I'm sure Courtney would understand if you pulled out. You did almost die and go through the digestive tract of a massive lizard."

Sal shrugged. "The concussion symptoms have all disappeared. I'm good to go, although I do need to be a little sedate when it comes to rushing through airports."

"Rushing through airports?" she asked with a raised eyebrow as they stepped out of the vehicle. "Bitch, please. I scored us direct flights to SoCal."

"Bitch?" he repeated and tilted his head in challenge. "SoCal? Hi, I'm looking for my friend with occasional benefits, Madigan Kennedy. Have you seen her around?"

She grinned and shook her head. "Okay, serious faces. Our friend's dad just died. We need to be supportive."

He nodded and his expression shifted to something more somber as they moved into the building.

"Hey, sweetie," she said to Courtney in a soft voice he had never heard her use before. "How are you feeling?"

The woman looked like she had been crying as she stood from the couch, approached them, and wrapped Kennedy in a hug first before she moved to Sal.

"I'm so sorry," he said softly as he pulled her close and stroked her hair gently.

"I was working on a project I wanted to show him, you know?" she said, her voice hoarse. "I don't generally believe in stuff like that, but it was so weird. I was writing up some memoirs—kind of like he did when he was my age—when the call came. I've been away from him for so long I almost forgot he was human. I built him up so much in my head I almost didn't believe it."

Sal nodded. He didn't quite understand something like that, but that didn't mean he couldn't be supportive. He smiled as Kennedy sandwiched Courtney between them.

"I got us a flight to Los Angeles tonight," Madigan said softly. "We should get there in time for the memorial."

"Thanks, Madie," Monroe said softly and shifted to hug her too. It was something of a touching moment, he realized. Sure, they all knew each other and were all friends individually, but this was the first time they were all friends together, the three of them.

The moment lasted longer than he thought it would, but it came to an end when the buzzer announced that someone was outside the compound.

"Well, that'll be Gutierrez," he said as they broke the hug awkwardly. "I told her we'd be headed out for a couple of days. Since she already signed off with the base and is officially on our payroll, she agreed to stay at the compound."

They stepped out of the building to greet the armorer, who had arrived with the JLTV he had left at the shop.

"Hey," Sal said with a smile. "Thanks for coming. We really appreciate you keeping an eye on the place while we're gone."

"I should thank you," Gutierrez said with a chuckle. "Having the place to myself for a while to get all my stuff moved in has to be the best deal I've had in a while."

He smirked and handed her the access pads to each of the buildings. "Either way, thanks."

"Do you really trust me enough to take care of this place in your absence?" she asked.

"With my life, and more importantly, with that of my teammates out in the Zoo." He smiled. "This is all simply stuff. I think you can handle it. Besides, our choices were you or leaving it open to attack from whatever the fuck might come out of the Zoo, right?"

The woman smirked. "Well, you know how to make a girl feel accepted in a new working environment. You all fly safe, you hear?"

"Will do," he said and held his hand out. She took it and shook firmly.

Their bags packed, they headed into the base to catch the flight to the States. Kennedy glanced down from the road as her phone buzzed for attention. Sal had chosen to drive and Courtney was seated in the back.

"What's that?" he asked, his attention focused ahead.

"I got a message back from Gregor," she said with a sigh. "I told him we wanted to give our prospective member a test to see if he was everything we needed."

"What kind of test?" Monroe asked.

"I asked him to dig into who might be exporting the metal from the Zoo," Madigan replied. "We know the armor manufacturers are getting it from inside, but we've hit a stone wall on who is actually digging it out. It's not from the US base and we're certain it's not the Russians. It might be the new sectors that have sprung up all over the damn place, but they're too recent to have sent it out for the suit we got our hands on."

"Well…leg, anyway," he said. He didn't really want to think about what they'd gone through to get that leg, but there were benefits from that little trip inside. They now had far more material to test the new alloy that had gone into these space-age suits. He still wasn't the right man to research it, which was why he had kept most of it saved for someone with the proper experience and tools to take apart.

There was also the fact that there were a number of people who wanted an exclusive on the whitepaper of the big, four-eyed bastard, so silver linings abounded. He smirked. While he'd never needed glasses thick enough to earn that nickname, it still didn't stop kids calling him four-eyes back in the day.

But the tables had turned and now, he was out there, risking his life for money. Maybe they hadn't turned all that much, he mused.

"I'd be willing to bet they used the US base when we were the only game in town," Kennedy said with a chuckle. "Which means there have to be shipping records or something with details as to how they moved it out. Bureaucrats love them their paperwork, so there has to be something we can use."

"Not to be a killjoy or anything," Courtney interjected, "but why do we care about this? Why the need to poke this particular hornet's nest?"

Sal shrugged. "Because we're a curious bunch." He peered into the distance. "Besides, if someone is pulling any covert operations they want to keep secret around here, it's best that we know who they are, if only so we know who to avoid from this point forward. This kind of shit means a threat we don't know about. With the Zoo, where most threats are stuff we don't know about and probably haven't seen before, we don't need any new ones."

She raised an eyebrow and shrugged. "Yeah, I guess that makes sense. Although if there are covert operations, you might want to keep in mind that any investigation we make into them would put us on their radar. Which means they might come after us anyway."

"In that case, we would definitely be better off if we knew who they were," Kennedy pointed out. "Anyway, our prospective applicant received the message and we should hear from him in the next couple of days."

"Which lets us focus on what we're going to the States for," he said and glanced at Courtney from the rearview mirror.

She didn't answer but squeezed his shoulder gently to acknowledge his support.

Rodrigo stepped out of his limo and adjusted his suit carefully before he walked toward the building that housed the offices where he'd worked over the past couple of months. Unlike most stereotypes, he really didn't like working in a location with this much sunlight and warm weather. He'd grown up on a tiny beach town in Tenerife, and over those years, he'd had more than enough sunlight and beaches to last him the rest of his life. It was why he'd joined the army—to get away from that dead-end place.

That said, when he stepped into the air-conditioned offices that had been bought by Pegasus for him to operate from, he had to admit there were worse places to be. While in the Foreign Legion, he'd worked out of tiny little tents in the middle of Syria and he still considered that the worst office he'd ever had. Anything else was an improvement.

One of his aides jogged in close and handed him a ringing cellphone. It was an old flip phone with no GPS tracking and absolutely no attachments. He would drop it in the furnace in the basement of the building after he'd completed this call.

"This is Rodrigo," he said softly into the mouthpiece once his aide was out of sight. "I'm told you're someone with connections in the Zoo. No, I don't care what kind of connections. I simply need boots on the ground. Your bill will be paid in cash—half now and half once the job is done. If you're captured, there will be no ties to me or my employers, do you understand?"

He paused and rolled his eyes. Mercs could be such divas sometimes. If they were paid as much as they demanded, they had to know they would absolutely be left to hang high and dry if they failed in their mission.

"No ties," he repeated. "Go out into the Zoo, see what you can do, and call me back. You know the number. Expect the money to arrive within the hour."

As always, he didn't wait for a response but killed the connection quickly and flipped the phone shut. With a smile, he took a moment as he marched to the elevators that would carry him to the basement to remember how cool flip phones used to be. He couldn't help it but he still felt they were cool, which was why, when he bought burners, he always chose those. What was the point of being filthy rich if you couldn't indulge in the small pleasures?

CHAPTER TEN

It had been a while since Sal had needed to dress up. He'd had a moment to head to where Caltech had put his belongings into storage and dug out his old suit, only to find it didn't fit anymore. Surprisingly, he'd put on almost fifteen pounds of muscle which made it tight around the chest, shoulders, and arms.

That meant a rush to find a shop where he could get a tailor-made suit in time for the service. The flight, as loud and uncomfortable as it had been, had landed them in California in record time and allowed them a couple of days to settle in before they had a funeral to attend.

It was great to have the money to be able to buy your own tailor-made suit. They weren't rolling in dough, of course, so it wouldn't be the most expensive suit ever. Still, it was more costly than anything else he wore that wasn't armor specifically designed for the Zoo.

The service was, as expected, something of a somber occasion, with more than a hundred people in attendance. Most were academics in the man's peer group, but there were more business executives and lawyers than Sal had expected. Apparently, he hadn't only been a scientist but something of a businessman as well.

Courtney found herself engulfed in the logistics of the funeral and businesses. She was the only daughter, so while her mother had taken care of most of the service, Courtney was still required to sign off on many of the papers for businesses in the family.

Which meant Sal and Madigan didn't see much of her during the couple of days they were in Los Angeles.

Once the funeral was over, he noted that she looked exhausted. More so than any time he'd seen her when they came back from the Zoo, which was telling. Maybe his mind had exaggerated, but it still concerned him.

He hated that he could only stand on the sidelines. Somewhere along the way, he had changed and become a take-action kind of guy. When someone was in trouble, he'd grown accustomed to being the one who could help. Instead, he had to stand back and watch everything grind his friend down and there was nothing he could do but provide moral support. It frustrated him beyond anything.

Kennedy looked as though she felt the same way, and after the funeral was over and everyone headed off to the reception, she took the time to give Courtney a long, tight hug.

"Will you go to the reception?" she asked when they drew apart. "Or do you think you can get some rest? No offense, but you look like you need it."

"None taken," the other woman said softly. "I do feel like I could sleep for about a week now. But we still have the will reading to attend."

"We?" Sal asked. "That's not a family-only kind of thing?"

"Of course," she said with a small, sad smile. "And you two are family. If I have to sit through an hour of legal paperwork, you know I'll need both of you to help me through it."

"That's emotional blackmail," he said with a smile and tugged her into his arms to hold her close for a moment. "But we'll forgive it this time."

"Thanks," she said, pressed her face into his chest, and remained there for a few seconds before a limo pulled up to drive them to her dad's lawyer's office.

Sure enough, it was a long session, stuffed to over-flowing with lawyers, Courtney's mother, and a few other family members. The woman didn't seem happy to see her daughter there and barely even gave her two friends a glance. She seemed like the type who had enjoyed a some-what comfortable life over the years. He didn't know enough about her to know what kind of person she was, but her cool treatment of his friend was enough to make him dislike her.

As it turned out, Courtney's father had fought cancer for the past few months and kept it a secret from everyone but his doctors until the very end. Even so, he'd had enough presence of mind to write a will and have it nota-rized before his last days.

The lawyer had gradually explained the full extent of the estate owned by the deceased, which came as a real surprise to Sal. Most academics were the kind of people who had their brains in the clouds and needed research grants and other, more business-minded people to keep

MICHAEL TODD & MICHAEL ANDERLE

them from going broke. This wasn't one of those cases. He only knew the man's name from a couple of papers he'd published in his field, and yet it seemed he had somehow inherited a significant amount of old money. He'd had investments across the board, which included a couple of companies Sal recognized as having ties to the Zoo. All paid out handsome dividends on his significant shares.

Most of it went to Courtney. It explained the cold shoulder she received from her mother, even if it still caused him to bristle protectively. Anyone who wanted money more than they loved their children was trashy to begin with. He'd heard of the kind of family disputes that ended in feuds that lasted years. Even so, the old woman was left with enough to continue living a relatively comfortable life as well as a house and other investments that provided a good income for her.

Sal shook his head, draped an arm over Courtney's shoulders, and rubbed her neck gently. She turned to him and smiled, leaned her head into his chest for a moment, then straightened once more.

Once all the details were clarified, most of the family and lawyers began to take their leave but her father's attorney came to them and placed a hand on Courtney's arm.

"Excuse me, Miss Monroe?" he said and tilted his head to show as much sympathy as he could without explicitly voicing it.

"Yes?" she said and turned.

"There is one more item we need to discuss, but I was instructed to deliver it to you personally and in private, away from prying ears," he said in a soft voice to ensure he wouldn't be overheard.

Monroe shrugged. Sal and Madigan stood aside to give her space with the lawyer, who withdrew a handwritten letter from his desk and handed it to her.

She made it through the first few lines before her hand came up to her mouth and tears ran down her cheeks. Her head lowered and her shoulders sagged, and her friends both stepped beside her.

"Do you want me to read it for you, sweetie?" Madigan asked softly.

Courtney nodded as Sal stroked her hair.

Madigan nodded. "Okay..." She cleared her throat. "Dear Ceecee, I know things haven't been as good between us as we would have liked. Either way, since I don't think I'll have the chance to say this to you in person, I want to make sure you know you have been in my thoughts these last few months."

She drew a deep breath before she continued. "We both know I've never been the best at personal conversations. I've tried to come up with something to say to you, but I've written this letter in case I chicken out. I want you to know that I admire you. Sure, science in a lab is interesting and judging the academic efforts of others is equally rewarding, but you should know that I really wish I had your grit and determination. And the kind of will that puts you at the forefront of your field, no matter how dangerous it is or how much it wants to kill you. I wish I'd taken the time to get to know you, not only because I wish some of that courage could have rubbed off on me but also because the knowledge that I could have been a better father to you hurts worse than these tumors in my lungs. You're everything I wish I was and more, and the fact that you achieved everything with so little input from me shows how much of your mother you have in you."

Sal looked up when Kennedy's voice broke. She'd never struck him as the emotional type, but he realized it was a touching letter and even he had tears running down his cheeks. He'd had a healthy relationship with his parents, so it hurt him that someone he cared about lacked that something. He also realized that he was the distant one in their present relationship.

It wasn't a pleasant thought.

"I wish I had the time to get to know you better," Madigan continued. "To get to know the scientist and the woman you've become. I know you'll do amazing things. With all the love in the world, Dad."

She folded the letter and took a deep breath. A few tears brimmed in her eyes too, which was another first for him. He wondered if she had the same moment of horrifying introspection as he'd had only seconds before.

"Thank you, Madie," Courtney whispered as the other woman handed the letter back to her.

"Anytime, sweetie," she replied and threaded her fingers through her friend's hair. "And anything else you need."

"I think I need a drink. I know they say you can't drown your sorrows, but it doesn't mean I shouldn't give it the old college try, right?"

Sal nodded. It probably wasn't the healthiest decision right now but drinking your sorrows away for the night seemed like the best of any number of bad options. At least he and Madigan could be there for her if things went off the rails, right?

That was assuming they weren't the ones who went off the rails first, he thought with a small smile.

"Thank you so much, Mr. Silverton," Courtney said and shook the lawyer's hand.

"It's Isaac, and you already know that," the man replied with a warm smile. "And you have my number, so call me any time of the day or night if you need anything, okay?"

"I'll try to keep all my calls to business hours." She smiled.

Courtney turned and Sal wrapped his arms around her. The suit made movement a little stiff but less so than he remembered with his others. One of the benefits of putting money into the process, he supposed.

Madigan hugged them both tightly. "Let's go drink our body weight. I know a nice little place right next to our hotel."

CHAPTER ELEVEN

I t was nothing like the bar at the base. With Sal's limited experience of the bar scene, he wasn't sure if that was a good or bad thing. There were more young people and, amazingly, they were even louder than a horde of soldiers who had either just come out of life-threatening situations or were about to head into them.

Kennedy brought three glasses of beer as the other two held their table—a difficult task, given how full the venue was.

The first few seconds felt awkward and he wondered if perhaps a drink in the comfort of their hotel rooms might not have been a better option.

"To Dr. Monroe," Madigan said and finally broke the silence. "I don't know much about him, but I do know he raised one hell of a fantastic daughter."

"Hear, hear," Sal said and raised his glass to clink it gently against both women's before they all took a long draught. It had been that kind of day and they deserved to be a little tipsy. It wasn't like they had to drive anywhere.

"I'm still struggling to process it," Courtney said after a few seconds. "He was always such an academic. I'm not sure if you know what I'm talking about, Madie, but Sal does—all stuffy and judgmental even when they try to be nice. Cold shoulders and silent treatments were all he knew how to do. And now that I know that he actually liked what I did? Followed it? Admired it? I knew he got me the job out there in the first place, but I always assumed it was because he wanted me out of his hair."

"I don't mean to step all over your moment," Madigan said, "but...come on, you know I don't like being called Madie, right?"

Courtney looked at the woman like she was about to break down, but after a few seconds of suspense, she grinned broadly and turned to Sal. "You owe me twenty bucks."

He laughed and shook his head.

The other woman looked at the two of them with narrowed eyes. "What...what did I miss?"

"I noticed that she called you Madie at the compound," he said, "so while you snoozed on the plane, we made a bet about how long it would be before you called her on it. I had it as a week or longer, and she had it at less. Three days means I owe her twenty bucks."

She leaned back in her seat and looked annoyed. "You will both go to hell. I tried to be nice to her since her dad died, and you made bets?"

"Well...just because it's a sad time doesn't mean I can't make some money," Courtney said and leaned in to kiss Madigan on the cheek. "Don't be mad. It's done wonders to keep my spirits up."

"You're still an asshole," her friend retorted but her features softened, which indicated that she would probably forgive her after a couple more drinks.

It would take her longer to forgive him, though, he realized quickly.

He was about to say something to help move the process along when three young, muscular young men stepped in. They looked like they were rather more comfortable with the bar scene than Sal, Kennedy, or Courtney were.

"I forgot how many jocks are around here," he said with a grimace of distaste. "There are a number of colleges in this area that focus more on their football teams than on the academic departments."

"Aww," Kennedy said and tilted her head with mock sympathy. "Was young Sal bullied by the big strong jocks?"

Sal snorted. "Please, no one bullies a teenager in college. That said, I was always a little jealous that these guys got away with so much simply because they could throw or catch a ball well or...block, or something. I don't watch much football. Anyway, I had to attend all the classes and keep my scores at the top five percent in every subject to maintain my scholarships. These guys didn't even have to show up to class, only practice."

"Well, admitting it's a problem is the first step," Courtney said and swallowed the last sip from her glass before she placed it on the table.

"I guess the next round is on me?" he asked and pushed to his feet.

"Don't think getting drinks here will count toward repayment of what you owe me, Jacobs," Monroe called, a little louder than she probably intended, but a broad grin played on her lips. He decided not to call her on it and simply patted her cheek gently before he gathered the empty glasses.

"Three more," he said once he reached the counter. The bartender nodded.

"Thirty-six dollars," the man said and left Sal to pay with a card while he slid the three glasses under the taps.

"Fuck." Drinks were far more expensive than they were at the base, which was bullshit since the supply-demand ratio had to be much sharper there than here. He shook his head, swiped his card quickly, and watched as the taps filled their glasses slowly.

"Hey," a feminine voice called from his left, "I haven't seen you around here. Are you new in town?"

He turned to identify the speaker and frowned at a couple of college co-eds who studied him like he was a slab of rare steak.

"Ah...yeah," he replied. "I'm a local who got back after a long absence."

"I can tell," the second girl said. She immediately moved in closer and ran her hand over his arm. He'd left his jacket hanging on his chair and pulled the sleeves of his white shirt up to his elbows. A little surprised, he looked at the touch. He really wasn't used to being hit on in a bar. Given that he'd never hit on anyone himself, he was lost as to what the appropriate response should be. His time on the Internet suggested he should tell them he had a girlfriend.

"Yeah, that is a sweet tan, even for Cali," the first woman said and laughed at an annoyingly high pitch. "Where were you?"

"North Africa," he said and studied the confusion in their faces as they tried to determine if the exotic nature of where he'd acquired his tan was a good or a bad thing. "Look, I'm taken and my party's waiting for me."

"Come on, honey," the second girl said with a giggle. "You can always use more company. Especially when we're the new company."

Ah. Gold diggers. They'd seen the suit and assumed he was loaded. They weren't wrong, but they had to know he probably had no desire to buy any additional drinks, especially as it seemed they were there with company already.

Madigan looked up from her conversation with Courtney and saw what Sal was tangled with. She kicked the other woman under the table.

"What...oh," Monroe said with a chuckle when she looked in the direction in which her companion tilted her head. "Poor guy."

"He looks about three seconds away from saying something really stupid," Kennedy said. "And I don't think I have the energy to fight off a couple of preppy sorority girls. Do you think you can help him?"

"Come on, Madie," Courtney said and winked as she stood. She barely avoided a slap to the head. "With that kind of girl, you simply need a little subtlety and panache."

"You know I don't do subtle, Ceecee," the woman retorted.

"Watch and learn." She chuckled and sashayed to the bar as the bartender put their drinks on the counter. Sal hadn't seen the glasses. He was uncomfortably flushed and too distracted over the brazen conversation with the two co-eds.

"Hey, baby," Monroe murmured, which marked the first time she had ever called him that. "Are these girls bothering you?"

The two younger women backed away when they saw her, and she decided to emphasize her point. She leaned in and placed a light kiss on his neck. Her gaze held the two the whole time.

"No," he said, even more bemused and conscious that he now blushed an even deeper shade of red. "No, they were just leaving."

They took the hint and backed away quickly as she helped him carry their drinks to the table.

"You owe me big time," she said with a laugh. "You looked like you were about to stutter your way into having those two follow you around for the rest of the weekend."

He chuckled. "I'm not used to being hit on, especially not here. I think I intended to tell them I had a boyfriend."

Madigan, who had taken a sip of her beer at that moment, immediately stopped and snorted loudly. "Oh... fuck, beer out of nose... Totally worth it, though."

Monroe laughed with equal amusement. "Well, I have to say, that would have sent those two running faster than I did."

Sal grinned and shook his head. "Yeah. I don't think I'll ever be good at this kind of thing."

"It comes with having a big brain like yours," Kennedy said while she dabbed her mouth with a paper napkin. "You start overthinking and end up forgetting to talk. Okay, I think we have that resolved while you're in a combat situation—for the most part, anyway—but it still haunts you when talking to the fairer sex."

"Yeah, yeah, I get it," he muttered and swigged his beer. "Can we move the conversation on?"

"No, I think we need to delve deeper into your psyche there, Salinger," Courtney said.

He grinned and shook his head. Over time, he had grown accustomed to the way they talked to him. He didn't mind, though, not when it came to them because he knew they had his best interests at heart.

It wasn't like he couldn't show his face around there anymore. The story about how he'd fought with Kennedy and lost had spread to most of the base, but the fact that she was something of a kickass had already been well known. So instead of a wimp who lost a fight to a girl, he was the dumbass who picked a fight with someone who was clearly more experienced than he was. He'd only been around the Zoo for a couple of months as his battalion was part of the rotation that the army had put in place.

It still stung when he entered the bar and there was an almost collective silence when everyone saw him. None of his teammates were around, which meant he would probably drink on his own for the moment.

A few comments and snickers were tossed behind his back, but at least they kept it among themselves. He would have to throw a punch at anyone who brought the subject up to his face, but as he was fresh out of the hospital, he didn't think he could carry a full-on brawl.

Besides, getting into two fights in as many days would probably have him banned from the premises, and drinking at home was much sadder than drinking alone at a bar.

Brandon made it to one of the seats in the corner and waited patiently for the bartender to see him and bring his drink. His beer arrived as someone took the seat next to him.

"Corporal Alfonso Brandon, right?" the man asked.

He didn't look up from the frothy glass in front of him. "Who's asking?"

"Someone who has a proposition you might be interested in."

The corporal turned to see who had spoken. It was a man in an expensive suit with an equally expensive haircut. A newcomer to the Zoo, he realized, who stuck out like a sore thumb. He had a faint accent, but not enough of one to confirm where the man was from, only that he wasn't American.

"Sorry, pal, I already have a job," he snapped and turned away. Hopefully, the man would take the hint and leave. He wasn't in the mood to deal with someone who tried to poach him.

"Believe me, I am aware of that," the man said with a chuckle. "What I want would not replace your current employment but would rather be more...extracurricular. I need someone—or a few someones—and would pay a small amount to simply be pointed in the right direction. And even more for...let's say more comprehensive help."

Brandon looked up from his glass and narrowed his eyes. In the darkness of the current lighting, it was difficult to read the man beside him. That said, he could certainly do with the extra cash. He had a couple of gambling debts back home that needed attention once his tour was over.

"What do you need a guy like me for?" he asked, still wary.

"Well, I'm new around here," the man explained, "and the Zoo is more unpredictable than I expected. Sure, I could buy armor and go out with other teams, but if I can find someone to do that for me, it would save me time and effort as well as money."

The corporal sipped slowly as he studied his companion. "How much time, effort, and money would I save you?"

"That would be entirely up to you, corporal," the stranger said and glanced around quickly. "Although it should be noted that what I'll ask you to do won't be entirely...within the realm of morality, if you take my meaning."

Brandon wasn't the kind of guy to turn his nose up at money that could be earned in a less than moral fashion but had a feeling the man beside him knew that. He'd probably already done his homework and cherry-picked him.

He smirked and shook his head. "I have the feeling you already know that won't be much of a problem."

Sal dropped onto his bed. When the reservations had been made, he hadn't known what accommodation would be required so he simply requested a room each for the three of them. So far, Courtney had spent most nights in her family's home, which was the case tonight as well, and Kennedy had spent every night in his room.

She insisted that rooms for all three of them hadn't been a bad idea since they all needed space for their individual belongings, even if the beds weren't used.

"We could always sleep in your room instead of mine," he said as she flopped on the queen-sized bed next to him.

"Why would we do that?" She turned onto her stomach to look at him.

"Well, it seems that whenever we sleep together, it's always in my room," he pointed out and stroked her hair gently.

She smiled and leaned into his hand. "Well, yeah…but it's not so surprising. I'm generally the one who initiates our time together, which means I always come to you for sex."

"As nice an ego boost as that is," he said, "I think I should initiate more in the future."

"You won't have any argument from me," she replied with a chuckle. She pulled him closer and pressed a kiss to his lips.

Sal grinned and shifted to prolong the kiss. "You know, I have a dream—"

"It's called a wet dream, Sal." She grinned, sat, and wrapped her arms around her knees.

"Ouch," he replied. "There's no need to be nasty. No, I think that since we're in California now anyway, and… Well, Courtney said she'll be busy handling her family's business for the moment. There was an exhibition in San Francisco to display the new suits of armor that will go on the market next year. Some of the companies are based there and since we have a very complete sample, we might be able to look around and find out who's already making armor with this new metal."

Madigan narrowed her eyes.

"Plus, we get to look at all the new sets of armor and weapons that will be used in the near future," he added with a grin.

"How romantic," she said with a chuckle. "You sure know how to get a gun bunny all hot and bothered."

"Gun bunny, huh?" He smirked.

"That name does not leave the bedroom," she warned and leaned closer to him. "Although you can feel free to make frequent use of it within those restrictions."

"Noted," Sal said, wrapped his arm around her shoulder, and pulled her against him. "We still have contacts with those development companies. We could call them tomorrow, get an appointment and hire a car, appeal to your...bunny-ness, and maybe do a little research while we're out there."

"It sounds like a plan to me," she consented with a smile. "It'll have to be tomorrow, though."

"Agreed."

CHAPTER TWELVE

Tales of Heavy Metal's work to help develop software for Zoo-based suits had spread among the development companies. In addition, the word was they'd recently received a massive influx of funds when they brought back the first live specimen from the jungle and therefore had money to spend.

Sal made sure to manage expectations and told the people whom they called that they weren't looking to buy any new hardware immediately but wanted to research what would be available next year. The stories about how they intended to increase their numbers meant that any company-wide purchase would be hefty and they would be able to pay the lofty prices for top-of-the-line material.

Four companies were contacted, one of which he recognized. Pegasus had won the impromptu auction they'd run for Shuri, the panther cub they'd brought back from the Zoo. He'd never heard much from them thereafter, although Kennedy had visited the containment unit where they maintained an open study on her and told him the tiny thing had grown by leaps and bounds and her fangs had already come in. They made playing with her difficult, but that didn't stop his partner.

"Dr. Jacobs," someone said as they entered the flashy building. "Sergeant Kennedy. So nice of you to join us this afternoon."

Sal looked at the man who almost jogged closer to talk to them. After two meetings with a couple of other companies without any success, he began to feel he knew the type of person whom they would talk to. Mid-level sales reps were always the same—mid-range suits, clean and bright, and surgery-enhanced smiles to make them as welcoming as possible.

Heavy Metal wasn't important enough to have the attention of any of the CEOs or vice presidents, which was kind of the idea, he mused. Their primary purpose was to find who used the new metal discovered in the Zoo, which in turn would give them a lead as to who they should look for to find the source. He definitely didn't want anyone to think they were anything but a couple of Zoo-runners in need of new suits.

"He's not a doctor," Kennedy was quick to say as she was the first to shake the sales rep's hand.

"And she's not a sergeant," he countered.

"Right," the man said and looked confused. "Well, my name is Andrew Murphy. I'm junior vice president of sales here in the Pegasus San Francisco branch, and I'll give the two of you a view of what we'll have on sale next year."

"Nice to meet you, Mr. Murphy," Sal said with a smile and shook his hand firmly. "Things have become increasingly hairy in the Zoo lately, and we've been hard-pressed to keep up with it. I've actually recently returned from a visit in there where we ran into a giant lizard that almost had me for lunch, so you could say we're very motivated toward safety."

"And we're more than happy to accommodate you," Murphy responded with a practiced smile as he guided them to the elevator.

Some fifteen minutes later, they made the rounds through the research and development facility that was housed in the building, which was the combat armor developers' answer to Silicon Valley.

Sal kept his eyes peeled for any sign of cutting-edge metallurgy, but so far, all they saw was a group of former military engineers who designed weapons and vehicles for use in the Zoo. He noticed a couple of designs for JLTVs similar to the ones he'd seen the Russians use. These showed that they were miles and miles ahead in terms of vehicle development but otherwise, nothing of real value caught his attention.

He suppressed his disappointment and continued to chat amiably with their host until they reached the section where Pegasus developed armor. On a basic level, he had little interest since he didn't know much about the suits in general. That job fell to Kennedy, who was like a kid in a candy shop. She asked about specs and release dates as they moved forward and almost completely forgot about him, and he hung back a little. This was deliberate, not because he wasn't interested in what they had to talk about —which, of course, he wasn't—but because he was more interested in what he could find when he wasn't babysat by a sales rep.

After a cursory look to confirm that he was unobserved, Sal came to a stop beside one of the models that had been put up for display. The confidential tag on a folder in front of it meant the display was not meant for them, but he retrieved his phone surreptitiously and took a couple of pictures of the design. He slid the device into his pocket quickly when he heard footsteps returning from the direction in which the other two had gone. What he had done was probably illegal, but as long as Murphy thought they were clients and there weren't any cameras around, he would probably get away with it.

"You should have checked for cameras first, idiot," Sal murmured and scanned the area as quickly and as subtly as he could. Thankfully, there was no sign of any security hardware. He was aware that no obvious indications didn't mean there weren't any, but he was smart. While he couldn't talk to women who hit on him, what he could do was bullshit his way out of trouble.

It was part of his charm, really.

"How soon until this baby hits the market?" he asked. Murphy tried to keep his fake smile in place as he scrambled to get the file out of sight and motioned for someone to wheel the display out.

"Oh, this is still in the hardware development stage," the man said but his façade had cracked ever so slightly. "It should be another two or three years since they still have considerable kinks to resolve."

A couple of aides moved into view and received a few harsh words whispered at them by their boss as they moved the one-fourth-sized model out of the room.

"It's not that we are worried about the two of you,"

Murphy said and quickly assumed his role as salesman once everything was squared away. "It's simply that with all the patent laws out there changing, we don't want to give one of our bigwigs a coronary by leaving a project in progress out for anyone to see and make copies of."

"Absolutely," Sal said with a nod. "We completely understand." He didn't, but when it came to salesmen like this, there was no point in saying otherwise. They liked to explain things to people whom they thought knew less than them about something. Talking was what they were paid to do, and if they got too deep into it, he knew they would hear about the man's high school football team in short order.

All he wanted to do now was get out of the building.

"Well, Mr. Murphy," he said and shook the man's hand again as they reached the lobby once more. "We had another visit scheduled to one of your rivals this afternoon, but with the prices you mentioned, I don't think we'll attend that visit. This is a competitive place to work with, I'll say that."

The man looked inordinately proud of himself as he shook their hands. "Well, you should probably visit them anyway. If they can give you better pricing, be sure to give me a call. I'll see what I can do for you."

Sal held his broad and friendly smile for so long that his face began to hurt. It disappeared quickly as they stepped out of the building. Kennedy followed his lead and kept in step with him until they were out of earshot.

"We're not visiting the last company?" Kennedy asked. "I was kind of looking forward to that."

"Sorry," he said and meant it, but he handed his phone to her. "But I think we saw all we needed to see here."

He unlocked the device and guided her to the pictures he'd taken of the suit.

"Does that look familiar?" he asked.

"Well, the design is very similar," she conceded and tilted her head as she studied the image. "But there's a reason for that. Sometimes, designs are developed in different locations simply because they're the best."

"That's not what caught my eye," he said and zoomed the picture in on an area on the display that showed a layered framework of the inner workings of the power armor technology as well as the wiring.

"That…" Kennedy started and as her voice trailed off, he continued for her.

"That's a shot for shot remake of the piece of armor we have," he told her. "Of course, all the wiring's gone and what's left is the armor, but you can see the slots the whole thing is based on, and…that's it. Unless Pegasus stole the designs, the leg we have is theirs."

"Shit," she muttered and shook her head.

"And what's worse," Sal continued as they opted to walk in the bright, sunny San Francisco afternoon to where they'd parked the town car that had been hired for them. "What's worse is that Pegasus put out the five-point-two million for Shuri. It means that, whatever games we play here, we're already on their radar."

She nodded and lowered her head for a moment. He knew her well enough by now to know that this was what she looked like when she considered her options. Their options. There were many things he was good at, but this was far out of his league. He was worried it might be out of her league as well.

"Have you heard from Courtney yet?" he asked once the silence had dragged on long enough for it to be awkward.

"Yeah," she replied. "She's tied up with the lawyer all day but said she'd meet us at the hotel restaurant for dinner."

"Okay, good." He nodded. "Because I think we'll have to break it to her that we might have to head back to the Zoo."

"Do you think she'll be okay to leave all her family businesses unattended?" Kennedy asked.

"Probably not," Sal said, "but with all the trouble we could potentially be in, I'm inclined to wonder whether the decision to leave Gutierrez alone to deal with whatever fallout comes from this is a good idea."

"Speaking of fallout…" she said and moved the conversation forward. "These guys make this armor with this new-fangled metal and are obviously testing it since we found what I assume was a failed test in the form of a human leg. So why hasn't there been any talk in the military channels about it? What are they trying to hide? And what would they be capable of if we get caught too close to their turf?"

They were all good questions to which he had no answers. From the way she turned to look in the direction from which they had come, she didn't seem to have any answers either or believe that he did.

CHAPTER THIRTEEN

In this day and age, there was almost no reason to actually go out and fish. Games were available if you wanted to enjoy the experience and supermarkets provided a guaranteed haul with far less time and effort.

But nothing in the world replaced the sensation of sitting beside a lake for hours on end with poles in hand, shooting the breeze with your best friend while snagging a couple of lookers to put on the grill for dinner.

That was the idea Bill had used to entice his friend Jim, which led to a five-hour drive that started at six in the morning. They took another hour to find and set up their preferred location, which meant it was almost midday by the time they finally sat down to fish. By then, the heat was almost unbearable.

The Arkansas summer proved to be far hotter than anyone had thought it would be. That, in turn, enticed a horde of mosquitos and other insects to be the veritable plague they were anywhere else in the world. The insect zapper could only eliminate so many, and the now disgruntled friends sat in the rising temperature and tried to make an hour last forever.

Even so, neither man complained. Conversation between them was considerably less than there would have been had the temperatures been more pleasant. As Bill's head lolled back and his eyes closed as obvious evidence that he needed a nap, Jim drew his phone from his pocket.

It wasn't the latest model but it was still serviceable, even in this day and age. Surprisingly, he still had damned good cell service out there in the middle of nowhere. He could remember that his dad regularly complained about the lack of service out in the countryside, but those days were firmly in the past. No one could live without a constant lifeline to the Internet these days, and that was provided in abundance.

Bill snapped his head up with a loud snort when he heard the roar that issued from the phone's speakers. He leaned across in his seat to see what his friend was watching, and Jim mirrored the movement to accommodate him.

"What's that?" Bill asked.

"It's a new app I got my hands on," he replied and looked a little smug. "Called ZooTube. It has all the latest footage people pick up from that crazy place in the middle of the Sahara. You know, where the—"

"Oh, yeah," his friend interjected and his voice rasped faintly as the after-effect of his short snooze. The footage they currently watched was fairly dark but it provided its fair share of action and movement. Men in heavy armor called orders on a radio as a massive reptile stepped into view.

"Oh...that's an ugly sumbitch," Jim said with a deep chuckle. "That there is a face only a mother could love."

"Hell, if I was mother to a critter like that, I'd wash it down the crapper." Bill laughed. "Is any of this stuff real? CGI's getting reasonably good. Look at that. There must be five inches on those teeth. No way that's real."

"Well, the site owners say it's all very real," Jim responded and tapped the screen to start the next video. "These are selected off the science databases of the places they use to study the critters in there."

"Nah, that's bullshit," the other man protested and drew back to settle comfortably in his seat. "Ain't nothing getting that big and they only studying them."

"These guys are shooting back, sonny," he said and turned the screen for his friend to have another look. "Them's bringing back the videos when they survive the encounter. I suppose it could still be CGI but come on. You have to admit it would be cool to have rifles and take shots at a couple of those bugs."

"Oh, yeah," his companion agreed. "Killing critters that aren't covered by some environmental law or other? You know I'm there."

Jim chuckled. "You know, I think maybe the fish ain't biting today. I blame you for getting me into this. If we don't catch anything, you buy the beers. And dinner. I told Stacey we'd get dinner for tonight and damned if I'll pay for this debacle out of my pocket."

"Fair 'nuff." Billy growled irritably and fiddled with his fishing rod. "The day's young, though. You might want to hold off on your declarations of doom for another couple of hours. Fishes are lazy this time of day."

Brandon looked up from the piece of metal he toyed with when he heard some of the mechanics shout greetings to someone. He'd told them he was looking for scrap to work with, but the truth was that he'd waited for someone to arrive.

Someone who was a new addition to Salinger Jacobs and Madigan Kennedy's little company. She was new enough that she might lack loyalty to the brand while she'd still been around long enough to know the goings and comings of the place. Word around the base was that Jacobs, Kennedy, and Monroe were all on leave of absence to take care of the death of a relative, which meant the whole operation was currently under the watchful eye of the one and only Amanda Gutierrez.

And guess who now stepped through the door of the shop where she used to work? It truly was weird how things worked out in his favor.

"Hey—Gutierrez, right?" Brandon called breezily and turned away from the useless scrap he'd looked at to jog to where she stood at the front desk.

She looked at him like he had spilled strawberry jam all over himself and tilted her head in query. "Yeah, that's me. Who's asking?"

"Corporal Brandon." The look of recognition was all he needed to see to know she knew precisely who he was.

"Right," she said with a smirk. "Aren't you the guy who—"

"Yep, that was me—both times," he said and tried to fake a smile, although he failed miserably. Just because he had to play nice to get his big payout didn't mean he needed to take the kind of abuse he'd suffered over the past couple of days from someone he barely knew.

At a push, he was even willing to say he'd deserved what he'd received on both occasions, but he hoped it wouldn't come to that. He really wanted to be able to walk away from this with his dignity somewhat intact.

"How can I help you, Corporal?" Gutierrez asked and cocked her head to the side with obvious impatience.

"I heard from these guys that they'd let one of their best mechanics walk away," Brandon said, determined to play the brown-nosing card as hard as he could. "After having my ass handed to me by the Heavy Metal guys twice now, I wondered if I might not have something to learn from them. When I heard they were hiring, I thought I might try to get in on their action, as it were."

The woman didn't look entirely convinced by his story, but she shrugged in an off-hand way. "Look, I haven't been around long enough for Jacobs or Kennedy to trust me when it comes to hiring decisions, but if you like, I could put in a good word for you. Although, from the way they've laid it out, I don't think they need another gunner on their crew."

"Yeah?" he asked and leaned casually against the front desk. "What kind of skills might they be looking for?"

"I'm not sure," she said and shrugged once more. "Being only a gunner doesn't cut it for them and I see the logic of it. They like them some multi-taskers. I heard Jacobs was looking for a geologist or metallurgy expert to inspect a piece of armor or something they pulled out on salvage on a trip that got him all banged up. Other than that, I'm not really sure."

"Well, I failed chemistry in high school, so I don't think I would be what they needed there," Brandon said and had to work hard not to show his excitement.

"Shocker," Gutierrez said with a chuckle. "But yeah, if you like, I can give you a heads-up if they need another gunner to join the crew."

"Thanks, I appreciate that." He took her proffered hand, shook it firmly, and made his way out of the shop. Once he was far enough away to not be overheard, he retrieved an ancient flip phone from his pocket and pressed the only number that had been saved into the registry. It rang a couple of times before someone picked up.

"What can I do for you?" said the odd, accented voice.

"Nice to hear from you, too," Brandon responded cheerfully. "My weekend was great, thanks for asking. How about yours?"

"Corporal Brandon," the suit said and definitely sounded irritated, "if I wanted to hear you go on about your day, I would have called you myself. Since you called me, I can only assume it was for a reason. What might that be?" After a long pause, he sighed and continued. "I spent my weekend in the French Base of operations. It's not as relaxing as it sounds."

"See?" Brandon asked with a grin. "Who says we can't be civil?"

"Indeed," the man said. "Now, how can I help you?"

"I discovered something interesting," the corporal said. "Have you heard of a small startup around here called Heavy Metal?"

"I certainly have."

"Well, I had a chat with their chief engineer." He embellished his story only slightly. "She tells me they've looked around for someone to inspect a nifty piece of armor they brought out of the Zoo in their last run. It's apparently something they would need a geologist or metallurgist to examine. I don't know about you, but that sounds like exactly the kind of thing you wanted to know about."

A long moment of silence on the other end of the line finally ended with a long sigh. "Yes, it could be. Or it could be a wild goose chase. Either way, if it's the best lead you have, you might as well dig deeper."

"Oh no," he responded. "I don't work for free, my friend. You said you'd pay for my information and I expect to be paid before I take on any more work for you."

"I've already wired money to your account, Corporal. You have no need for anxiety about that." The suit sounded annoyed again. "If you were to find something that proves to be what we are looking for, I'd like you to handle it in as final a way as you can and bring evidence to support your action. That includes dealing with any potential witnesses. I assume that won't be a problem?"

"Pay me enough, and you'll find there's not much I won't do," Brandon assured him. "Until then, you know my safe word, right?"

"I don't know you well enough for that kind of joke to be appreciated," his contact said coldly. "Have a nice day, Corporal, and good luck."

"How else would you be able to get passage to the Zoo so easily and on such short notice?" Sal asked over the rumble of the massive plane's engines.

"So your assumption is that the guy must have a crush on me?" Madigan asked, her head inclined in a definite challenge.

"It would make sense," he said as he thought out loud. "You are very crush-on-able. There are five, maybe six guys in charge of getting personnel in and out of the Zoo on these delivery flights. You talked to the same guy who got us to the States in the first place, and he was waiting and eager to get you on the first flight over."

"That, or simply because it's summer and all the trades are finished, so these planes are really empty and they can use the fare?" she pointed out.

"And that explains why the guy said the Zoo missed you?"

Yeah, that was a little weird," Madigan admitted with a laugh. "And you're right, I am very crush-on-able."

He shrugged. "You have to give me the brains on this one."

"Yeah, you're a regular Casanova," she retorted and her sarcastic streak showed its colors.

Sal grinned in response, but when the silence continued, she pulled her phone from her pocket. The satellite connection they'd paid for when they moved to the compound kept them connected no matter where they were.

They paid a damned fortune for it, but one of the upsides was that the connection would be with them anywhere they went in the world. He still wasn't sure if it was worth it but would have to wait and see. They'd signed on for the three-year contract the previous owners had reneged on, and while it had cost a fortune, it was only about half of what they would have paid otherwise. Madigan had laid out the details of what a deal they would get out of it, but he hadn't really paid attention. His loss in the end, but he acknowledged that she had a better business sense in certain things than he did.

"It looks like our hacker friend got back to us," she said softly.

He unbuckled his belt and leaned in closer.

"Clearly, the guy decided to go above and beyond," she continued. "He's sent us proof of his skills by hacking into the US base's database and sending me our files. There's one on each of us, including Gutierrez— Huh, how did they know about that mole on my ass?"

"It might be something in your medical file," Sal mused. "Something your doctors might have checked on in case it was a melanoma or something like that?"

"Oh, right, I remember now." She snorted. "Who gets a melanoma on their ass, anyway?"

"Chronic sunbathers," he said quickly, "and...maybe nudists?"

"Enough about me, let's talk about you," she said and her face lit up as she opened Sal's file. "So...hmmm, not much here except for the background check the dudes who did research on potential candidates ran... Your credit score was terrible."

"Why do you think I chose to stick it out in the Zoo?" he asked with a grin. "To have animals that constantly try to kill you is all well and good but having to manage on an almost unpaid internship was truly terrifying. And I had it fairly easy compared to others. My student loans were essentially laughable since I got my bachelor's and my master's on scholarships. Even so, things were miserable."

"How in the hell did you go to school for only seven years?" Madigan asked and leaned back in her seat to regard him with an expression close to disbelief. "And how did you not get a single grade below A minus?"

"Hello?" He made a face. "Hi, I'm Salinger Jacobs, certified prodigy and genius. Nice to meet you."

"It's amazing that you want me to suck your dick given that you do it so often yourself," she retorted with a grin.

"Enough about us," he said. "Although you might want to keep those files on Courtney and Gutierrez for later study."

She looked at the empty seat to her left. "It's still sad that she couldn't join us. But I suppose it's a good thing that she'll be able to resolve things with her family without having to deal with massive, flesh-eating monsters at the same time, right?"

He smirked and looked pensive. "Yeah. I hope she does okay, though. And maybe she'll be able to stick it out there and open a Heavy Metal branch in Los Angeles."

Madigan smiled but had already moved on from the personal files they had been sent to the data the hacker had collected. This was what she'd actually asked the guy to look into for them.

"Holy shit," she muttered and handed him the phone. He took it quickly and studied the information.

"That's a damn thorough investigation," Sal said. "There's nothing here about who paid for the research, though. Everything is signed off by the State Department and the Pentagon like it's all supposed to be military research."

"Well, if it were military research, we wouldn't see it on a private company's display floor, right?" she asked.

"Well, you would if they were contracted by the government themselves," he reasoned. "They would be involved with any number of different government activities, so I don't see why they wouldn't have been able to get all kinds of stuff. Given that they currently fund much of the activity in the Zoo, I'd be surprised if they weren't the ones to conduct the test that ended with our friend losing his leg."

"Which means they already run covert operations in the Zoo area." Madigan sighed. "If that isn't fucking fantastic."

The moment in which they wondered how fucked they were passed after a couple of seconds and he continued his study of the data that had been sent to them.

"Well, the fact remains that this hacker is really good at his job," he said finally as he handed her phone back.

"Agreed." She nodded and tapped a message to Gregor that they were good to proceed with the man as soon as possible, then slid the device into her pocket.

CHAPTER FOURTEEN

It wasn't usually the Pentagon's problem to deal with environmental disasters. That kind of issue was generally relegated to the people who would protest in front of the Pentagon when they themselves were the ones who usually caused the disasters. Well, them and the politicians who wanted their votes while on a campaign trail.

That said, this was probably the first time this much money had been both put into and made on an environmental disaster, and it was certainly the largest and most public disaster of all time. This paradoxical truth necessitated a think-tank and a whole task force dedicated to determining exactly how they could finally put a stop to all of it.

The first idea that had emerged came about even before there was a think-tank. To put a wall around the massive jungle that had sprouted so virulently in the Sahara had been one of the most blunt-force ideas in history and—surprise, surprise—it simply hadn't met expectations. The Zoo grew relentlessly and spread out of control.

This completely baffled the scientists who had studied the goop before it had been sent there, and construction on the second wall began as a result. Unfortunately, evidence suggested that this might be outstripped even before it was complete, given the speed and evolution of the jungle they sought to contain.

New ideas were needed. No one was certain what would happen should the goop reach a major population center, but the general consensus was that it wouldn't be good. They already had horrifying examples of how the Zoo treated the people who headed into it more or less prepared. It was unthinkable to even consider the carnage that would result if it assimilated locations with women and children who had absolutely no training or equipment to deal with it.

The US government wasn't ready to admit how colossal their fuck-up had been. To order evacuations in the cities in the affected areas would, in effect, be a tacit confession. Besides, there were also many problems with that, mostly diplomatic.

The idea had always been to consolidate the environmental problems and resolve them in a way that wouldn't absolutely ruin the country's standing with the rest of the world. That certainly hadn't changed.

"Have we completely disregarded the use of force here?" one of the men in a lab coat asked the others gathered around a conference table. All available data on the Zoo was laid out in a number of charts hung on the walls.

"Yeah, let's charge into a place that has resisted all attempts at attack and invasion. Oh, and which adapts and evolves so anything larger than small salvage teams is immediately swarmed by thousands of mutated creatures," another responded sarcastically and shook his head. "I'm sure that won't backfire in a spectacular way. Come on, man. We've already tried the brute-force tactics. It's time for a little subtlety."

"We could always drop a couple of nukes on the place," someone else suggested as he removed his glasses to rub his sore eyes. "We could level it and turn it into a desert again and have us all home before dinnertime."

"Yes, because we all know that to nuke the place is the epitome of subtle, especially when it's on foreign soil," the second man said and now looked annoyed. "Of course, that will have no repercussions, either environmental or diplomatic." He snorted disdain and ignored the hostile stares of some of his colleagues.

"It sounds like all you're doing here is using sarcasm to shoot down other people's ideas instead of coming up with any of your own," the first man said, his tone angry.

"Can you really call those ideas?" the challenger asked with a snort. "I've been around here the longest because I haven't come up with any new and cool ideas and have only nitpicked and destroyed everyone else's ideas. It's about job security, man. That and being able to say I told you so as much as possible."

"You're an asshole," the first man said with a groan.

"Realistically, there aren't many options we haven't tried already," a fourth man interjected, one in a suit instead of a lab coat, which indicated that he was the one in charge. "Which is why we need a think-tank to come up with something new and exciting to present to the new budgetary hearing in the Senate next week."

"What about the plans for the mech suits?" another scientist asked. "Will those be ready at any time in the foreseeable future?"

"The technology is all there and is already being tested in the Zoo environment, albeit at a lower capacity," someone else replied. "We're essentially waiting on the big bucks to flow in."

"Why do you ask, Brian?" the leader asked.

"Well…" the younger man began and gave Dr. Sarcasm a hard look before he continued. "The Mechs look like they're the only things we have available that might be able to handle the ever-changing environment of the Zoo with any degree of reliability. If we send them in larger numbers, it could be exactly what is needed to curb the jungle's growth."

"The only problem is, they aren't exactly available yet," Sarcasm said with a chuckle. "Although that is the closest thing to a good idea that I've heard all day. And it's only been…five hours." He took a moment to check his watch to be sure of the timeline.

"The only terrain we can trust is anything not taken over by the Zoo," the leader said and shook his head. "And the priority should be to keep that area clear and untainted by the goop. We need to find a way to detect its spread across the ground."

Sarcasm rolled his eyes and leaned back as another barrage of so-called creative ideas surged. He must have done something terrible in his last life to have been cursed to deal with this many idiots on a daily basis.

Gregor rubbed his eyes and returned his attention to the newest shipment of supplies that had arrived from the home front. Well, no, he doubted that they had been flown in all the way from Russia. India was the most likely origin of all this food, although that sounded ironic in his head. He wasn't sure how the people managed the deal in light of the problems the country had faced over the past couple of years, but damned if he would complain about it. He had been with one of the first companies to arrive to start the base, and memories of half-rations in the early days were enough to still his beating heart.

He moved away from the crates the teams unloaded from the massive plane, worried they might call him in to help if he looked too idle, when his gaze identified the base commander Commandant Solaratov making his rounds. To Gregor's surprise, another man he didn't recognize and who sported a horde of medals on his chest berated the man.

It merited a closer look if nothing else, he mused, and sidled forward casually.

"While our technology research into vehicles outstrips the American competition, our other research sadly lags behind," the new man stated. He seemed to have some difficulty with moving at the same pace as his fitter companion.

"If the Kremlin wishes us to focus more on research, they must send us more researchers," the commandant said. He seemed calm despite the reprimands delivered by the man whom Gregor could now see was, in fact, his superior. "Scientists, specialists—someone who could actually make heads or tails of what we encounter out there.

We have beasts with venomous fangs, trees that use vines to trap and eat our troops… We simply don't have the time to test weapons as well as deliver a competitive amount of intel to Moscow. If they would send us proper researchers—"

"That will certainly not happen," the superior said with a chuckle. "Too many children of high-ranking officials work for the government-funded labs for them to be spared in this decade."

"Could we not bring in third-party contractors?" the commandant asked. "It's what the Americans do with great success. So much so that all the other nations now want a piece of the action."

"There are talks underway, but you know how the government is back home." The man sounded calmer than he had been before. "They are bidding on the projects, so that could mean anytime this year—or maybe not at all. We have to wait and see."

"And knowing all this…" Solaratov said. He stopped and turned to face the other man. "How do you expect us to bring in research that is worth anything?"

"I only relay the orders that sent me here, Commandant Solaratov."

Gregor couldn't help a smile of his own. The base commander had dealt with bureaucracy in Russia for decades longer than anyone else and knew how to work men like this one effectively. He had all the right excuses and all the right lines and knew exactly when to deliver them to make people defensive around him.

It was a good trick to learn, and Gregor himself had put it into practice as much as possible. Which was why he was there, still out of the Zoo even though it had been almost a week since his last run and he had long since recovered from his ordeal. Most of the others were already scheduled into the rotation with the other teams.

All except Solaratov's son, of course. He had been sent to Moscow for further treatment.

"I brought a couple of new Spetsnatz-trained teams with me to make sure you have the people necessary to handle your new responsibilities." The new man seemed to suddenly remember that he was the superior in this conversation, not the other way around. "Men who have been trained in jungle warfare in the worst conditions around the globe and should be ready to deal with wild animals."

"If you think all they will face is wild animals, I am afraid you are the one who has not done his research." Solaratov chuckled. "We have videos that have been shared with us by our American friends as well as their reports on what they currently face inside. These are more than enough to convince you that standard training, no matter how advanced, can in no way prepare any man for what he will encounter in there."

The commandant nodded toward the jungle. The eavesdropper narrowed his eyes. Solaratov's fears of the place were well-founded, and yet Gregor had never seen the man enter himself. He must have spent a great deal of time studying the reports they were able to acquire.

That or the man had enough sense to know he wasn't cut out for missions into a place like that.

"Their reports have clearly been altered and their videos exaggerated." The other man gave a dismissive wave of his hand. "The Americans have grown very skilled at spreading fake news and would obviously rather profit from our lack of presence in the jungle instead of having our help. The new teams will be entered into the rotation immediately, and I want all reports about what they encounter inside to be sent to my office first. I will then share what I have found with you if I deem it something you need to know."

Solaratov now clearly fumed at being talked down to like that—like he hadn't read the reports from his own teams and had a fairly decent idea of what they would face in there.

But, again, he was the consummate bureaucrat. He knew when fights could be won and when it was time to step away. This was the latter. The new man needed to prove his superiority to his troops, no matter how many were killed in the process, and would only then consider listening to any ideas that had the potential to save lives.

Careers were more important, always, Gregor thought with disgust.

Solaratov saluted quickly as his new superior marched away but his stern look changed to one of scorn and disgust while he watched the man's movements across the tarmac.

"Send in these idiots with more muscles than sense and think they'll survive one trip into that fucking jungle," he muttered. The lieutenant wondered if the man had seen him but quickly realized that the commandant was simply talking to himself.

Gregor pulled away from the conversation and headed to the plane and from there, to the mess hall. He wasn't crazy enough to volunteer for any missions inside until it was absolutely necessary, but that didn't mean he couldn't warn the friends he'd made there—who numbered more than a few—that the new boss on base would increase the number of rotations.

Maybe the information would come in time for them to fake some kind of injury or sickness to get themselves out of the few first trips that would have the most casualties— and maybe for long enough that the new man would gain some sense and change his rigid stance.

Not everyone would make it, but if he could save a few lives, he would consider it worth it.

CHAPTER FIFTEEN

A JLTV pulled up near the tarmac as Sal and Kennedy clambered out of the loading bay of the Hercules. He could tell it was one of theirs. First, it wasn't standard military issue and was therefore slightly more expensive and second, because he could see more than a few modifications made to the bodywork.

He confirmed what he already knew when his gaze settled on a blonde with short hair and a pair of aviator sunglasses who eased it forward to where they now stood.

"Hey there, strangers," Gutierrez said with a smirk. She lowered the sunglasses dramatically. "Do you ladies need a lift?"

"Only if I drive," Kennedy said with a broad grin.

Amanda shook her head. "If you think I'll let you drive my baby when I've barely finished repairs on her from the tear-up you caused, you're crazier than I am, Sergeant."

"Shotgun," Sal called and sprinted quickly around the vehicle to scramble into the copilot seat. He grinned when

Kennedy scowled and flipped him off as she took her place in the back.

"I hate riding bitch," she said and shook her head as their driver accelerated away from the massive plane. "Hey, wait, how come this is your baby? As I recall, you weren't around while we bought these or the compound. As far as I'm concerned, this is my baby."

Gutierrez looked at Sal, who shrugged.

"Don't mind her," he said. "She didn't get much sleep on the whole flight over here."

The woman chuckled. "Heh. Very nice work there, stud. I wouldn't have thought you could get it up while that high in the air. Pressure and all that."

"It's nothing like that," he retorted, a little uncomfortable. "We simply had a ton of reading material."

"And like that, you lost my interest," Amanda said with a grin. She glanced into the rearview mirror at Kennedy. "By the by, you made this one my baby after you drunk-drove her and trashed the shocks and the transmission and ruined not one but all six of the wheels. I put in too much work and trouble to get her back in working order—I'll bill you guys for the parts later—which, for all intents and purposes, makes her my baby. The rule on my baby is that you don't drive until you take lessons that involve teaching you not to drink and drive."

"Ugh. Fine, Mom," Kennedy muttered, leaned back in her seat, and closed her eyes to nap during the hour-long ride to the compound.

"So, how have you settled into your new surroundings?" Sal asked after they'd traveled for a couple of minutes in silence.

"Not too bad, actually," Amanda said with a bright smile. "I have a room all to myself. I got your message and moved all Dr. Monroe's stuff into storage. Do you really think she won't come back?"

"She inherited a damn fortune," Madigan said and didn't bother to open her eyes. "Do you really think someone who made that much money will come back to poke at animals that are more than likely to poke back?"

Sal's face fell but he said nothing. Amanda noticed, though, and raised an eyebrow.

"Yeah, that's a good point," she conceded. "Anyway, the former owners left us all kinds of materials to work with. I appreciate you leaving all of it in the garage for me. I've organized everything to my specs, worked everything out, and now, you have a fully functional workshop at your disposal."

"That's worth every penny," he said with a smile. "It sounds great. Quick question, though. How mobile do you think that workshop could be in a pinch?"

Amanda narrowed her eyes. "Are you joking? There are literally tons of stuff to move. If you want me to look into getting a truck to put it all into, I could, but that wouldn't really help with mobility. It would be more a way to get it from here to one of the other bases."

"That's not what I mean," he replied and shook his head. "I'm more interested in...well, what would you need to carry so you could make repairs to suits out in the field?"

"Oh." She frowned as she considered this. "Well, that's more complicated, obviously. I've tinkered with Kennedy's suit over the past couple of days, got it back into working order, and made some improvements too. But I'd have to look at the inventory to see what I'd need to bring into the Zoo for repairs. I'll get back to you on that ASAP."

"Thanks."

"Anytime, boss."

"You don't have to call me boss. You know that, right?" he asked.

Amanda shrugged. "If you really mind it, I can stop, but it's easier than calling you Jacobs, and I don't think we're close enough for me to call you Sal yet. And I most definitely won't call you Salinger. That's way too much mispronunciation simply waiting to happen."

"Fair enough. Boss it is until you feel comfortable enough to call me Sal."

She nodded and silence prevailed during the rest of the drive to the compound. None of them were great at small talk. Well, he was, but he wasn't really in the mood to carry the conversation by himself. Madigan snored softly in the back and Gutierrez seemed more than happy to fiddle with various buttons and gizmos on her new baby. He leaned back in his seat. He hadn't had much sleep on the long flight either and yet he had something of a wired sensation in his body that kept the weariness at bay. He would feel it soon, he knew, but that obviously wouldn't happen until later.

They entered the compound and the garage, which was an opportunity for her to show off what she'd done with it in their absence.

"By the way, boss," she said as they walked into the residential part of the compound. "A guy approached me who wanted a job or something. A Corporal Brandon. Ever heard of him?"

"Yeah, he's the guy I drank under the table, right?" Sal asked Kennedy, who yawned and stretched after her nap.

"Yeah," she replied, still on the tail-end of the yawn. "The guy who I then beat up after he tried to steal my food while you were getting checked at the hospital. Fucking jet lag. Why can't it be nighttime already?"

"I think we're stocked with some melatonin," he said with a smile and patted her on the shoulder. "Take one and sleep until tomorrow."

She shook her head. "That's fine. I'll last for a while after that nap."

He nodded and turned to Amanda, who had averted her eyes at the scene of oddly intimate affection.

"Anyway," the armorer-mechanic continued, "he asked about work, and I told him I'd pass the word along— although, if you want my opinion, hard pass. The guy is a serious asshole who worked very hard to cover it, which didn't make it any better. I could still smell the bullshit the guy tried to sell, no matter how much he spray-painted it gold."

Sal laughed. "I'll steal that description, and I hope you don't mind. And yeah, from what I saw of him, he's a real piece of work—and not in a good way."

"I agree that he's an asshole." Kennedy raised her hand as she moved to the kitchen to make coffee.

"It would seem we have a consensus," he said with a soft chuckle. "Motion passes. The good Corporal Brandon will have to find employment elsewhere."

"Do you want coffee, Sal?" Madigan asked as the aroma drifted to fill the common room.

"I'll pass," he said. "I think I'll take a melatonin myself

and be dead to the world until tomorrow. Unless you need me for something?" He aimed the question at Amanda.

"Not really." She made a face and shrugged. "Nothing that can't wait until tomorrow."

"Cool," he replied with a grin. "I'll see you delightful ladies later."

Once he had gone, Kennedy brought an extra mug of hot coffee over and handed it to Amanda.

"Will he be okay?" the other woman asked and took a small sip.

"Yeah, but he's a little heartbroken." Madigan fixed her attention on her mug. "Our last talk with Courtney before we left didn't exactly go great. Everyone was civil, of course, but she practically insisted that we head back while she stayed behind and worked out whatever family affairs she still needs to resolve. Sal tried to cover it, but I know him well enough to know what hurts and what doesn't. And that hurt."

"I'm sorry to hear that," Amanda said as the two of them moved to the couches.

"Well, it's not the first time he's lost people," Kennedy said and shook her head. "Given our line of work, it probably won't be the last. At least Courtney walked away from here alive. Not many people can say the same."

"True. A little morbid but true."

"So…" Madigan suddenly needed to change the subject. "I heard on the ride here that you tinkered with my suit. I spent hours getting it to work the way I want it to, and if you fucked that up in any way, I'll tear into your baby and make you fix it yourself."

Her companion laughed loudly. "Yeah, you don't want

to do that. I may only be a mechanic and an armorer but I know how to feud, Madigan, and believe you me, there haven't been many where I've walked away the loser."

"What a coincidence." She tilted her head. "My experience has been the same."

"Well, hopefully, it won't be necessary," Amanda said with a chuckle. "I didn't mess with any of the settings. Whatever the two of you ran into in the Zoo did a number on the outside protective layer, so I had to weld it all together. I had a sudden spurt of inspiration and decided to cut off a piece of that leg you guys brought back to use as welding material. It's very easy to use and once cold, it's incredibly strong too.

"I tinkered with the power armor as well—added weight to the gyros in the midsection to help you keep your balance better and allow you to move faster. I also spent maybe five hours cleaning gunk and dirt from the joints, so I took the time to install flaps over the ankles and knees to keep the gunk to a minimum. You might want to give that a look for yourself, though. If those get clogged and you can't move in the middle of a fight... Well, that's not an enviable position to be in."

"Hear, hear," Kennedy responded with a chuckle as they both raised their mugs to clink them together softly. "You know, that's the biggest problem I have with the full power armor. It works best and moves the easiest over tough terrain, but in a place like that, moving easily is a second thought, you know? When you fight something that can tear through the armor faster than a welder with a grudge, you may not want all the extra armor to weigh you down. What if the electronics fail? What happens if a bug squirts acid on the controls and suddenly, all you have is a big suit that weighs a ton and doesn't help you move it anymore? We ran into a Russian in there who had that very problem, and it made me think."

Amanda smirked and took another sip of her coffee. "You know, I think I like you, Madigan. I may not feud with you after all."

CHAPTER SIXTEEN

G regor studied the group of men assembled in front of him. These weren't new recruits, of course. Special forces troops like the Spetsnaz didn't get where they were without dropping a truly spectacular number of bodies in a wide range of very exotic locations. These were hard men in a profession where most hard men died young.

And they were all in their thirties.

It didn't mean they were fully qualified for the Zoo, of course, but it meant they had a higher chance to survive their first trip and all subsequent trips too. Once you had a feel of what it was like, it was easier to predict and follow the moods of the jungle, which made survival so much easier.

Thankfully, he'd had very experienced Americans to help him when his luck turned sour. That said, he still wasn't sure he was ready to go back into the Zoo. Which was why he was there now, running the tape on what the new guys could expect in the jungle.

He'd anticipated that they would be cold and stand-offish. Most men in special forces were, after all. Even so, they listened very closely and quietly and some even took notes, while a couple more recorded the lecture for later use. They were professionals above all, and this was their job. They could joke as much as they wanted in their off-hours, but when it was time to work, they were willing to do what was required without any fuss.

It was oddly unsettling. Gregor had made his living by rising in the ranks of soldiers who refused to take anything seriously, which made the men before him the oddest of oddities.

"New images have been taken of these locusts, of course," he advised them and played the video taken by his team when they'd been swarmed. "They started out as basically little more than cannon fodder. Usually, they would rush any teams they encountered in huge swarms and try to overcome through sheer numbers or as a distraction to allow the deadlier animals to attack from the flanks or sides—and sometimes, from the trees above.

"However, in later trips, these creatures have been seen with tails like scorpions. The venom in these stingers can literally kill grown men in a few seconds if it can punch through armor and inject enough. Or it can travel through the bloodstream and kill slowly and painfully if death is not instant."

"Is there video where these creatures use military tactics as you mentioned?" one of the men asked and looked firmly at him. There wasn't a hint of mockery in his voice but there was some disbelief.

"Fortunately, yes, and they've been included in your

study packs," Gregor replied. "However, I've been instructed by our new commandant that these images were provided to us by our American friends on the other side of the Zoo and should therefore be studied with caution."

The man nodded and turned to his notes. He used a notebook and a pencil, Gregor realized. Did they honestly make these guys live in the Dark Ages?

"That concludes this presentation," he said with a small sigh and dropped into his seat as he watched the troops prepare to leave. "More information has been provided to you for study. Be safe out there, and there's a bottle of surprisingly good vodka waiting for you when you get back—on me."

The men stood quickly, and a couple came to shake his hand as they headed toward the doors.

They were good men, he thought with a small smile. Too bad most of them wouldn't find their way out of there. If they went together, maybe, but they would go with a mixture of mercs and man-children, which lowered their chances of survival significantly. He was sure their presence would improve the others' chances by a massive margin, though.

Gregor scowled at the desk in front of him, his head angled in thought. He didn't want to go into the jungle but seeing the young men who would put their lives on the line to keep the rest of those assholes alive made him feel a little guilty.

Besides, he'd been in before. He knew what he would face and in all fairness, what were the chances that he would run into another swarm like he had the last time anyway?

Finally, he shrugged and pulled the phone from his pocket. If he died, he would come back to haunt the absolute shit out of these people.

He'd have to send Madigan the message about when the hacker would reach the drop-off point when he left. There was no point in doing it when someone might track him.

Gregor shifted in the armor and grimaced at the memories of when he'd been stuck in the damn thing that was too heavy to move without power. He'd been set up with one of the standard suits and allocated to a team that was heavily populated with the new special forces boys, all eager to get into the Zoo and do some damage. They still chuckled and discussed all the unbelievable stories they'd heard about it.

In fairness, a few of the stories were far-fetched and yet not quite as unrealistic as they seemed to think. Gregor himself chuckled nervously when they talked about videos of a massive, four-eyed creature that spat venom and could crush suits of armor under the weight of only one of its six legs.

"There is a saying out here—" he said as they began their march through the thick jungle. "Well, it's not really a saying but more of a common superstition. Try not to think of your own personal nightmares. They have a habit of coming to life here."

One of the men raised an eyebrow while the rest shrugged. They didn't feel comfortable enough around him to crack jokes but it was clear they weren't convinced.

"These plants are odd," one of them said and poked at the bark with his rifle. "But so far, there's nothing out of the ordinary. We were on a mission in the Amazon of Venezuela about three...four years ago? The monsters there were damn fucked up. And I'm not even talking about the animals."

The rest of the special forces men chuckled, but those who didn't have any part in whatever had happened laughed nervously. There was talk about black operations run all over the world but there was very little proof, which was the point. Hearing about them actually happening was worrying, if only because people were killed all around the globe for knowing less.

"Look out!" one of the men called as something big and black bounded from the trees above them. Gregor had his gun up, but the sound of gunfire already filled the jungle. A low roar from the massive panther was difficult to hear after the shots but it whined pitifully for a few long seconds before it lowered its head.

"Well," one of the men said and moved closer, "that was interesting, but they sure do go down easy, don't they?"

He shrugged in response. "In all fairness, for most of them, it becomes a matter of bulk. These smaller groups tend to leave us alone unless we get close to their young or something like that."

"These creatures have babies?" the man asked as he poked cautiously at the panther's shoulder.

"I wouldn't do that," Gregor warned. "They tend to travel in packs. Did none of you read the information I gave you?"

"Not all of it," the man said with a shrug and straightened from his study of the body of the creature they'd killed. "Then again, it doesn't look like we needed them. As you can see, there is no second crea—"

His boast was cut short as the second animal pounced from the shadows, almost as if it had waited for him to deny its existence. This one was considerably larger than the first. Gregor knew that meant it was male…or was it female? If the truth be told, he had only skimmed those information packs himself, so he wasn't entirely sure which was which. Or even, come to think of it, if they had that kind of gender distinction.

Weapons were raised instinctively, but there was some hesitation from him and the mercs as the massive panther was tangled with the special forces man. It bit and thrashed in an effort to get past his armor while he screamed for someone to do something.

The other Spetsnaz fighters were quicker on the draw, however, and aimed their shots high while their comrade was pinned beneath the enormous creature. Slugs blasted into the panther's shoulder to draw blood and throw it off balance and away from the man. As one, they lowered their aim and released a smoking volley into the animal's chest and head. This one fell without a sound and only a heavy thud indicated that it was dead.

"Fuck!" the man who had been attacked roared and pushed to his feet. He scowled at the obvious damage to his suit, especially around the right leg where the creature had clawed in its attempt to reach him.

"Are you all right, Vasili?" one of the Spetsnaz men asked and hurried toward him, while the others stepped forward to make sure the creatures were really dead and no others lurked nearby. Gregor and the two mercs joined them, although with less of the military precision the special forces men displayed.

"All good, Sergeant." Vasili hissed and tried to hide the slight limp that had developed from the fight. Gregor wasn't sure if that was only because of the damage done to his power suit or if the creature or the struggle had damaged the leg within. He supposed the man was lucky the panther's venomous fangs hadn't pierced his suit. Otherwise, he would have to deal with a much larger problem than an iffy power leg.

The sergeant looked at the team and it seemed clear that he had taken command of the situation. Gregor didn't mind. Let him deal with the problems that arose from the need for the six remaining combatants in his squad to take care of the one whose suit had malfunctioned.

"It seems you might have a point about these fucking animals," the man muttered to him as one of the others crouched to try to make emergency repairs to Vasili's legs. "We'll be more careful from here on out."

"This was nothing," he responded with a soft chuckle and checked his weapon. "You should see what happens when we pluck those fucking Pita plants."

"Pita plants?" The man looked intrigued.

"Yes...the plants with the blue flowers?" Gregor asked and gesticulated with his hands. With the armor he wore, there wasn't adequate translation between what he tried to show with his hands and what was displayed so he gave up. "The ones that all the companies back home are pissing about? The one that's funding all this?"

"Oh, right," the sergeant said with a nod. Gregor had a

feeling he didn't have a single clue of what he was talking about but didn't want to seem ignorant. They would learn eventually, he thought with an internal shrug. Hopefully, they all survived to laugh about this later or he would feel guilty about it. He intended to survive, even if all the rest died, but he didn't want to feel bad about if they didn't make it.

He knew it was a little selfish, but he was in there in the first place to save all their lives if he could. It was the least that they could do to allow him some survival ground rules. The first and foremost of these was that he wouldn't stick his neck out to save anyone, especially not one of them. They might think he held no grudge over being left behind that one time, but he did. Everyone was still on the hook for that particular brand of bullshit, whether they'd been there or not.

"We need to keep moving!" the sergeant called, and the others regrouped and began to head out. They ended up leaving Vasili with someone to help him with the repairs to his suit since they didn't want to have to carry him if his armor might give out at any time. It was clear the man didn't care for this arrangement, but he also obviously knew it was the right choice. He would be able to catch up with them if they managed to fix his suit. If not, they would find him on the way back.

Gregor assumed that one of the reasons included the small matter that the rest of the men had begun to take what he'd told them about this fucking place more to heart and were now far more wary. Their heads remained on what was essentially a constant swivel and each man always checked their corners to ensure there were no blind spots on their peripherals. He was actually rather impressed by how quickly they had adapted to their surroundings.

It was almost like they knew how to work in combat situations while in a jungle, he thought to himself with a grin.

As they delved deeper and ran through a small group of the scorpion-tailed locusts, he could see the tensions rise within the group. The Spetsnaz professionals remained collected, although the casual conversations had quickly dried up. It was the mercs Gregor was concerned about. Well, himself too. Mostly himself, but he had a feeling they could rely on these new guys not to leave them behind when things went sour. Not if, when.

They finally caught sight of one of the tell-tale clearings that indicated that they approached one of the collections of Pita plants. He had been around when there were clearings all over the place, so you had to go from one to the other in the hope that you would find one that had these expensive flowers. But as the jungle expanded faster, it grew thicker too, which meant that the clearings now only occurred when there was a Pita plant.

That still seemed odd to him. Of course, there were a hundred thousand different things that were odd around there, but this was one that really stuck in his mind. It was like the jungle wanted the plants to have full access to sunlight, which he didn't need to be a biologist to know was extremely weird, especially since everything else seemed to grow perfectly fine without it.

As they moved into the clearing, he focused his eyes on their surroundings and tried to make sure that nothing headed their way. He caught sight of a few whispers of movement immediately outside the sensor range.

The teams began to collect the flowers, and he continued to watch the movements which now drew closer and moved within the sensor range. Most of the creatures were small or medium-sized, which indicated that they were the hyenas or locusts with a couple of panthers interspersed, but one shadow remained obscured toward the back.

He remembered the videos passed on by the Americans that revealed the massive, dinosaur-like creatures that made all the other animals go crazy when they were killed, exactly like they would if someone plucked a full plant. One of the whitepapers had described a couple of sacs at the base of their skulls that contained a huge concentration of the same goop as was in the flowers, which meant there was considerably more money to be made beyond the clearing. All they had to do was survive and get it out of the jungle.

The other three mercs glanced around. They had clearly noticed the opportunity too, although he wasn't surprised when they all seemed to decide not to mention the massive beast's monetary value to their new Spetsnaz friends. It seemed they all intended to get out of there alive.

It soon became obvious that the special forces men were nervous about the number of creatures that had assembled immediately outside their line of sight in the darkness under the cover of the trees.

"We should probably leave now," the sergeant said when they had finally picked the bushes clean of their expensive

flowers. The animals were uncharacteristically friendly—
or less hostile, anyway—but none of the men really wanted
to test them.

They pushed into the jungle once again and the animals
seemed to part directly ahead of them as if to show them a
way out as they trudged toward the vehicles. It had only
been one day, but as things stood, none of the men
involved wanted to linger when so many animals waited
for an excuse to start a fight.

"This feels odd," the sergeant said softly to Gregor
when he stepped beside him. "Why do they watch us? It's
like they are here to protect those fucking plants."

"I've given up on trying to understand what drives
these fuckers," he replied and adjusted his hold on his
weapon. The creatures remained out of sight, but he could
hear them as they shuffled through the underbrush. The
motion sensors identified hundreds of them now, and the
large one still lurked beyond real visibility. "Sometimes,
they leave us alone. Or they seem curious about us and
actually approach one by one for a closer look. At other
times, though—"

"They swarm and run into gunfire and in general, act
like rabid motherfuckers," one of the other mercs interjected. Gregor could tell that everyone on the team was on
edge. The ones who had wandered the jungle before knew
it well enough to not pick a fight that should rather be
avoided, but it was a testimony to the training of the first-
timers that they were willing to wait things out instead of
engaging in an immediate preemptive strike.

"If there's anyone who knows what they're doing out
here," he continued, "it would be the two who brought me

out alive the last time. Now those were crazy mother-fuckers—freelancers on the American side of the Zoo who walked around like they owned the place. They've been around here the longest, I think, and they have one of the best scientists on their side too."

The sergeant looked oddly at him like he hadn't expected to hear anything good about the American side from someone like him.

"What?" he responded to the unasked question. "I was told to trash the Americans by our new commandant. Since he's not here, I'll speak my mind. Most of them are rat bastards, although no more so than the assholes who left me behind to die. Those freelancers seemed like they wanted to make sure there were good relations on both sides of this fucking jungle."

The sergeant smirked. "I'll keep that in mind. If we ever need Zoo Whisperer motherfuckers to help us communicate with the jungle, we know who to call. At least we have the technology."

"What technology?" Gregor asked. The sergeant didn't grace him with an answer but instead, moved forward quickly to take point on the team.

When they reached the place where they'd left Vasili and the other member of their team to fix the man's suit, it was clear that something was wrong. It had only been a few hours, yet the special forces soldier was nowhere to be seen. A body lay in the vicinity and they could assume it was the merc they'd left with him, but it wasn't a sure thing. The acrid smell of acid on flesh still lingered and the evidence of what had happened was difficult to refute.

Something had spat a large glob of acid that had melted

through most of the man's helmet and the head within, which made it difficult to identify him apart from his armor.

The Spetsnaz men obviously had some kind of rule about leaving their comrades behind as they picked the body up quickly, hefted the heavy combat armor between two men, and set off through the jungle without another word.

"Shouldn't we look for Vasili?" Gregor asked the sergeant quietly.

"He would know to head to the vehicles if he runs into trouble out here," the man responded in a low tone. "We can only hope he made it—"

"Sergeant!" one of the other Spetsnaz men called. A couple of them were gathered around a second body and Gregor didn't need to move any closer to know it was Vasili. They weren't that deep in the Zoo, so it wasn't likely that they had come across any of the other teams that had been sent in and had made their way deeper into the jungle. Hopefully.

"*Cyka Blyat*," the sergeant muttered.

What was interesting to see was the way he had been killed. Gregor had assumed he had fallen victim to the same acid flinger that had taken down the other merc. Instead, six extremely narrow punctures had somehow penetrated completely through the chest piece, supposedly the hardest part of the armor. The punctures didn't look like they were enough to kill a grown man in armor that was supposed to provide emergency first aid, which meant there was most likely venom involved. The punctures didn't look like fangs, though, not unless the beast was truly massive and had multiple rows of them.

That was out of character for this fucking jungle, he mused as he stepped in to help carry the second body to the vehicles.

"At least we still have the technology," he snarked as he struggled under the heavy weight of Vasili's armor.

The sun had almost set by the time they slipped out from under the heavy cover of the trees. It washed vivid orange and red over a purplish-pink sky. It was truly a wondrous sight, he acknowledged.

As the bodies and the Pita haul were loaded into the vehicles, the sergeant moved to where Gregor stood to one side.

"About those freelancers you mentioned," the man said and looked into the forest with an angry expression. "Do they join trips out of the Russian base or only American?"

"I've heard they're looking to expand," he replied and tried to sound casual. "Why do you ask?"

"I think we should contact them," his companion said with a nod. "Bring them over for our next run. We could do with a couple more veterans in our crew."

"I'll pass you their information," Gregor said with a small smile.

CHAPTER SEVENTEEN

Airports were usually busy places, and around this time of year, that effect was enormously increased. It was why she had chosen to travel at this time. Well, that wasn't quite true. Her house and those of all her friends were being watched, with what remained of her family brought in for questioning and watched as well.

You didn't get to fuck the FSB over without consequences. She still maintained that she had been in the right in doing so, yet she might have profited if she'd had an escape plan in place for when she was caught.

Which—surprise, surprise—she had.

It had been an impetuous act with a great deal more impulsiveness that kept her doing it over the span of months until finally, she realized someone was tracking her movements. At the same time, her employers quietly ran checks on her to determine how difficult it would be to find a replacement. It didn't take a significant mental leap to realize this would not end well.

It hadn't been difficult to buy an airplane ticket under a

fake passport with cryptocurrency. She'd done that to make spending money for years now. The hard part was to make it to the airport and from there, across the damn world to someplace that would let her live out the rest of her life in peace. Or with less threat of death, anyway.

She hadn't bothered to bring any luggage. A backpack contained one of her laptops and whatever clothes she'd been able to get her hands on the last time she'd been home. For a brief moment, she wondered how suspicious it would look for someone with a ticket to Casablanca international airport.

"Ticket and passport, please," said the bored-looking woman who managed the customs line. She presented both with a small smile, careful not to look shifty or uncomfortable.

Well, who was she kidding? Everyone felt uncomfortable at the port authority, right?

"Reason for leaving St. Petersburg?" the woman asked as she typed the name and passport number into the computer in front of her, which could easily have been from the seventies.

"I'm visiting my brother who works in the embassy there," she said smoothly. The ID had been stolen from someone with connections in the foreign ministry, but the woman was currently on an illegal spending spree in Monaco. The ID would be safe for as long as she needed it.

"Please put your baggage through the machine." The woman indicated the x-ray machine to her left. "Remove all electronics to be scanned separately."

She did as she was told, removed her laptop, and placed it beside her belt, keys, and phone in a small bin that went through ahead of her backpack. The woman's bored expression shifted in a moment. Traveling that far with only one piece of luggage was suspicious, no matter who your brother was. She checked the ID again, this time against the federal database on a no-fly list, but when nothing came up, she leaned back in her seat and assumed the expression of a bored airport official once more.

The passenger smiled, collected her belongings on the other side, and slid her laptop quickly into the backpack before she jogged toward her gate.

While she did have family in that area, it wasn't her brother and she really hoped that the flight wouldn't be late. She had no money and no other connections and now headed off to a different continent with only the slightest assurance that she would be able to make a living in one of the quickest growing markets in the world.

The harsh reality was that she didn't look forward to being so close to what ZooTube told her was one of the most dangerous places to live at the moment, but at the same time, it was a new adventure. And she was nothing if not an adrenaline junkie.

Sal blinked a few times in an effort to force his pupils to function as they should. With the shades drawn, he was unable to focus on anything. The light that shone between the cracks told him it was daytime, although he wasn't sure what time. If the truth be told, he wasn't even sure what date. He'd taken melatonin to help with the jetlag, but it had the small side effect that he woke like he'd come back from the dead. His brain was fuzzy, and he wasn't sure if anything in the world made sense anymore.

It didn't matter, he reminded himself with a yawn that seemed determined to dislocate his jaw. He pushed himself out of bed.

"I need to clean this place," he muttered. He located his phone, which told him the alarm he'd set the day before had gone off fifteen times and was thirty seconds away from another attempt. He growled, shook his head, and turned it off before he slipped the device into the pocket of the pants he'd slept in. It was nice to know his sleep had been deep enough that the obnoxiously loud alarm in his phone hadn't woken him—although not for lack of trying, evidently.

As he stumbled out of his apartment, he realized he could smell breakfast. He paused to sniff the air—a mixture of the instant waffle batter that had too much vanilla and the dry-frozen bacon that almost smelled like the real thing but not quite.

He shuffled down the steps and rubbed his eyes to force his pupils to contract as he moved to the shared kitchen area. He could have complained that the living situation was much like the one where he'd shared an apartment with five other dudes while working on his masters. But in all honesty, with the amount of space they had, it was nice to have one place where they were all bound to congregate eventually.

Only one member of their team stood in the kitchen when he reached it. Their new arrival listened to eighties rock on her phone while she moved around the space.

"You look like you've made yourself quite at home," Sal said and fought back the urge for another yawn.

"Well, I know this is our shared living quarters," Gutierrez said with a grin. "I thought I might welcome you two with breakfast. It's the same quality as what you'd find stocked in the apartments at the base but still, it's the thought that counts, right?"

"Absolutely." Sal wandered to the counter and picked up one of the pieces of bacon that were already cooked. He bit into it and chuckled. It tasted almost like bacon too. There was something else in there—probably some kind of preservative—but he still couldn't make out what it tasted like. Almost like maple, but not quite. It was interesting, and after having had it a few times, he'd acquired a taste for it. While it didn't mean he'd give up real bacon, this would do in a pinch.

"So, how was the flight?" Amanda asked as he heaped his plate with more bacon, a couple of waffles, and some jelly packs and butter.

"Loud, crowded, and full of uncomfortable silences," he said with a grin. "Your average plane flight, I suppose—or I assume so, at least. I didn't do much traveling before I came here, and that was on one of those huge fucking Hercules planes. When it comes down to it, that sums up my average flight experience."

"Wow," she said as she filled a couple of mugs of coffee from the machine. "You're much better at small talk than I thought you'd be."

"I hate awkward silences more than I hate small talk," he admitted around a mouthful of butter-and-jelly-smeared waffle. "So I learned to make sure that if some item of small talk was offered, I could carry it until the conversation was interesting. It took some doing—a whole lot of practice and awkward silences caused by my failed attempts—but I'm happy with the results."

"You talk a lot, don't you?" She grinned, placed his mug down on the table, and sat opposite him.

"When someone has as much to say as I do, that does tend to happen." He grinned in return.

"And so modest too," she said with a chuckle. He shrugged, his mouth too full to respond politely, when Madigan stepped inside. She looked worse than he did, with bleary eyes and an almost permanent scowl on her face. Her hair was rather neat, though, which told Sal that she'd kept her drinking in-house the night before.

"I smell coffee," she croaked.

"On the counter." Amanda pointed at the pot. "Bacon and waffles too, if you want them."

"Bacon and waffles?" Madigan asked and raised an eyebrow. "That's an awkward combination if I've ever heard one."

"Oh, look whose glass is half-empty," the other woman responded with a laugh. "In all seriousness, though, they were all that was left. We need to get supplies tomorrow, so we'll restock then."

Sal smiled. It was nice to hear Gutierrez talk like she was a part of the team. She was, but the fact that she saw herself as that meant she had fit in better than he'd thought.

Kennedy piled a plate with bacon but avoided the waffles before she joined them with a mug of piping hot black coffee. He knew she took it without any sugar.

She'd once mumbled something about suffering through the bitterness of it without any help being a part of the waking up experience. He wasn't sure where the logic was in that, but everyone had their own personal morning rituals. Who was he to tell her not to do something?

"So," he said once half her mug was empty—which was usually about the time when she was in the mood to answer without any bite or sarcasm. "Should we address the elephant in the room?"

"The fact that Amanda moved all the tools in the suit repair shop?" Madigan muttered, still a little hoarse. Maybe more than half a cup was needed today.

"It's my job to fix the suits now, so the shop has to be set up how I need it," Amanda said with a shrug.

"Not that." Sal chuckled. "Well, maybe that too, later, but for now, we seem to be down one full-time specialist."

"Isn't that your job?" Gutierrez asked with a slightly confused expression.

"He's been a hybrid gunner-slash-specialist for the past couple of months," Kennedy said with a shrug. "It works better since he has some skill with weapons while still able to be a specialist. It would be better to have someone on that full time, though."

"I don't think I can pull the specialist role off in the Zoo," the other woman stated with a shrug. "I could probably only be a gunner."

"Good call," he said. "But at the same time, we might want to find ourselves another specialist until Courtney gets back."

"If she gets back," Madigan corrected. Sal didn't want to

openly admit that she wouldn't, so he didn't dignify that comment with an answer.

"The ones in the base are locked tight," Amanda said. "They didn't like how you guys stole their best away, so they rewrote the contracts to keep the geeks happy after Courtney left them."

"It makes sense," he said. "Still, some must prefer to go freelance rather than be stuck with forced runs into the Zoo."

"Not really," Kennedy said. "They're light on specialists as it is, given the kind of death rates they have in there."

"Huh." He grunted. "No wonder they grabbed my ass all the way from California."

"As fun as that would be," Amanda said, "I think we might have better luck if we poach the talent in the new UN base. The folks they brought in are still green, metaphorically speaking. They wouldn't mind the extra cash that comes from working for themselves while still being a part of a team that knows a thing or two about how to get in and out of that fucking jungle alive."

He nodded. "That makes sense, yeah."

Madigan looked thoughtful. "We could probably arrange a visit there later today. I have contacts who helped to build the base."

"Any word on our plans from the Russian side?" Sal asked.

"I gave Gregor the green light to bring our new friend over," she said with a nod around a mouthful of almost-bacon. "He'll let us know when he's ready for retrieval."

Gutierrez narrowed her eyes. "What are you two talking about?"

"A prospective Heavy Metal member should arrive in a couple of days," he said. "I'm not sure when, though."

"Would this guy be someone to take the specialist position?" she asked.

"No, his job will be more focused on security around here," Sal explained and waved vaguely to indicate the whole compound. "A Russian IT specialist who will help to keep our firewalls in place as well as with some other tasks we need done."

"Awesome," she responded although she wasn't sure how she felt about someone she didn't know keeping an eye on her belongings while she was in the Zoo. In fairness, the others had trusted her to manage the compound while they were gone, but she knew herself. She didn't know some Russian hacker dude with a neckbeard. Probably.

"I'll get cracking and arrange visitor badges for us," Madigan said and shoved her mug and plate aside before she walked off.

"Who will do the dishes?" Sal asked.

"Hey, I made the breakfast," Amanda said with a laugh. "I think you can afford to get your hands dirty there, Salinger. Or clean and sudsy, rather." She pushed her plate and mug to his side of the table, stood, and stretched. "Have fun!"

"Goddammit." He collected all the dishes, carried them to the sink, and grinned. On the upside, she seemed to have moved beyond her need to call him boss. Maybe a few dishes weren't so bad after all.

CHAPTER EIGHTEEN

As it turned out, much of the French base had been copied from the design of the US base. The Americans had made more progress with the wall, even though they no longer provided the only staging area from which missions into the Zoo could be carried out. There were four bases now, with plans already laid for a couple more.

If you build it, they will come, said that insanely sappy movie from the late eighties. The building part, of course, meant the Zoo—and the amount of money that came out of it. The people running the American base had, for a long time, been the only ones to profit from it, but no longer.

All kinds of logistical complications would arise from this. Sal knew it with a kind of vague but absolute certainty.

It seemed the French sector had been built more as a landing point for the militaries and lab workers of all the represented countries, which had been slow to arrive of late. The French were already established alongside the Israelis, and the Indians had brought in a token fighting force in advance of their more scientific support of the project.

A large number of empty and unclaimed housing buildings and unused warehouses were earmarked for future arrivals. Work on the wall seemed to indicate that the nations who oversaw that sector, like the Americans, would ultimately house the official, administrative, and research divisions alongside the military in the mammoth wall when it was complete. Although the details regarding the company names that would host the labs and weapons departments were still to be decided, effort had been made to erect temporary structures that would enable the base to function until the long-term vision was achieved.

Bureaucracy was terrifying, Sal mused as they drove their vehicle through the fully built yet empty base that nuzzled up against the inner section of the wall.

There was a bright side to that, though. The fact that everyone was late to this particular party meant those who were there were desperate for work. They were anxious to enter the Zoo as quickly as possible, which meant many freelancers were already stationed in the area. Amanda was right, as it turned out. They had their choice of specialists and gunners. Now, all they needed were a couple of runs into the Zoo to make sure the people they considered for the job were suitably qualified for it.

"I think we may have jumped the gun by coming here," Kennedy commented as they found a quiet corner in the local bar to compare notes. "We should have brought our suits and weapons if we planned to make runs into the Zoo."

Sal nodded. "The bartender filled me in on a grab and

dash mission which heads out tomorrow. It seems exactly what the doctor ordered if we want to test new recruits."

"Did he ask you for your ID first?" Madigan asked with a grin.

"Yeah," he replied. "I don't know if I should feel flattered or offended."

"You might want to grow some facial hair," Gutierrez said with a low chuckle. "You know, age that babyface a little."

"Yeah, yeah, whatever," he grumbled and shook his head. "Anyway, the bartender said the mission will head out tomorrow, so if we want to be a part of it, we might want to grab our stuff and have it ready to go tonight."

"And who will drive all the fucking way to the compound for it?" Amanda demanded, her chin raised in a challenge.

"Not it," Sal said quickly.

"Not it," Kennedy said in quick succession.

"That'll teach you to make fun of my babyface." He grinned cheekily. "Y'all drive safe now, ya hear?"

"You two can go and fuck yourselves," the woman said with a scowl on her face as she pushed out of her seat. "Not literally, of course. I feel it needs to be said since you're both nasty like that. But since I am the only one of the three of us who hasn't had a drink while here, it was probably the best choice anyway."

She glowered at her companions, who merely grinned in response. "Don't forget to message me the details of where to meet," she added and pointed at Sal. "If you think I'll drive all over the place looking for you, Salinger, you're wrong."

He nodded and leaned back in his seat, grinning broadly.

"Why does she keep calling you Salinger?" Kennedy asked once the woman had gone.

"I think that's her way of middle-naming me," he said and took a sip from his drink.

"Middle-naming?" she asked in evident confusion.

"You know, when someone is so mad at you that using your first name only is not enough," he explained, "so they use your middle name too?"

"Oh, right. I remember my mom doing that. Chills of terror every fucking time."

He grinned. "Yeah, I know the feeling. Wait—does that mean you actually have a middle name?"

"Of course." She looked strangely at him. "Who the hell doesn't have a middle name?"

"I don't know," he said with a shrug. "How about that one guy, what's his name...oh, right, Salinger Jacobs?"

Madigan laughed. "Oh, yeah. But Salinger counts as two names, doesn't it?"

"Fair enough," he conceded. "And I have to be honest, I do have a middle one. But how come I've never heard this middle name of yours? Did you ever plan to tell me about it?"

"Let me think about that," she said sarcastically and tapped her chin for a moment. "Um, that's a no, but thanks."

"Ugh, fine," he muttered with pretended irritation. "Keep your secrets. Now, we should probably get back to our search for specialists who are looking for a job. And we can also look for a place to stay for the night so we should maybe split up."

Kennedy nodded. "I should probably stay here since I'm the one with the connections."

"And since it's the place that sells alcohol for about half the price they have it at our base?" Sal asked.

"One of the perks of having connections, I'm afraid," she said with a sweet smile. "Have fun finding us a place to spend the night. Make sure it has sturdy beds, hmm?"

He chuckled. "You'd better hope I do."

The Heavy Metal duo were not the first to arrive at the assigned area next to the wall from which the teams would head out. A large number of people had already assembled and begun the preparations required to ready the entire operation for the mission.

One of them was Gutierrez, who unloaded the heavy suits from their JLTV. She looked up with a scowl and patted the crates as Sal and Kennedy arrived.

"This shit needs to be more portable," she complained as they approached.

"Hey, if work were easy, it wouldn't be work, right?" Sal replied. He tried to dodge a smack she aimed at the back of his head with only partial success.

"Smartass," she snarked before she glanced at Kennedy. "So, did you two lovebirds have a nice beauty sleep?"

"It wasn't terrible," Madigan said with a chuckle. "Before that, though, we managed to get possible names from the bartender. He works part-time as a billboard for all the folks who want their names out there for hire. We narrowed it down to three. Unfortunately, only one of them will head into the Zoo with us, so I talked to the operation leader and he's assigned to our team. The downside is that they could spare only one for a new team, so if he ends up a bust, we'll be stuck with him until the operation ends in about…what, two days from now?"

"Give or take," Sal confirmed. "It's a quick run to get people used to the operation as well as maybe get some money flowing through here. I imagine we can help with that. But yeah, in and out, two days tops."

Kennedy thought for a moment about making some kind of stamina joke about Sal lasting for two days tops. She doubted he could or would be able to no matter how much of the blue stuff he took, but it was still a good laugh. For her. Maybe less so for him and definitely even less so for Gutierrez.

She quickly decided against it. That would play fast and loose with their professionalism rule, and she would only make those jokes if there was guaranteed enjoyment for all parties involved.

"Okay, ladies," Amanda interjected and looked around pointedly. "It seems like folks here are almost ready to lock and load. Suit up!"

"Is that a reference to something?" Sal asked as he hefted the pieces to his suit out of the crates and put them on, starting with the boots. Always start with the boots, he'd learned after a few ill-fated attempts.

"Shut up and get moving," Madigan responded.

It wasn't long before the three of them were ready for action. Gutierrez knew about the mechanics of the suits better than anyone else, which meant that despite the fact that this was the first time she used the suit she donned, she was the first one to finish. Kennedy came a close second and Sal lagged behind as his hybrid suit had far more moving parts to put together and prep for a trip into the jungle.

"So, where's our new prospective member?" he asked when he had finally settled everything to his satisfaction.

Kennedy checked the list that had been passed out to the various teams to which the three dozen or so people involved in the mission were allocated. Most of the groups contained six or seven members each, which made theirs the smallest at only four.

It was probably better that way, Sal mused. This was a test run for a potential new member of their team, which meant they didn't need to keep an eye on more than one newbie in the Zoo. It increased the chances that they would make it out alive.

A man approached, dressed in an older model of a specialist's suit.

"*Je suis le Dr. Adrien Couture. Êtes-vous...Heavy Metal?*" he asked, his expression hopeful.

"That's us, yes," Sal replied and took point on this one. "I'm Salinger Jacobs, and these are my partners, Madigan Kennedy and Amanda Gutierrez. I take it you received our message last night?"

"*Oui,*" the man replied with a polite smile. "I was told you looked for someone to work with your team full-time, yes?" He spoke with an accent, but his command of English was almost impeccable.

"That's right," he said with a nod. "We need someone

who can operate as a full-time specialist. The person who handled that role before had to leave to attend to personal matters, so we'll work with you to see if you're a good fit for our team. Kennedy and Gutierrez will be our gunners. I will help them, but I'll help you too. I'm something of a hybrid that way."

"*Pardon*," Couture said, raising his hand. "No offense, but if you needed help as a specialist, why would I need yours? Perhaps it is best if you help your friends to keep me alive while I work as I do best. Alone."

"Hah, good point," Sal replied and forced a smile. He'd heard that Frenchmen could be arrogant, and kudos to Dr. Couture for living up to the stereotypes. Either way, it was still too early to make snap decisions, so he decided to put the casual insult to his abilities aside until he had a realistic view of what the man was capable of.

The sirens wailed, the signal for everyone to move to their JLTVs. Sal assumed this was the kind of thing that resulted when comms systems could still not be automatically activated by the base's database. Everything was so low-tech around there. The American base still operated the management side largely by paper, but that was for the pencil-pushers in the US. Everything else—which meant anything that anyone paid attention to, including such important things as work contracts and payment slips— was all done electronically.

Sal smirked, grasped his gun with his power arm, established the connection between that and his HUD, and activated the combat software. He would never get used to this, he thought. The cold pit in his stomach always came when he prepared to go into a place where he would put his life on the line. It was exciting and terrifying.

And it had started to grow on him, he realized with a smile.

As it turned out, maybe he should have listened to his first gut impression of Dr. Couture. Sal grimaced as he slapped another magazine manually into his rifle. The autoload feature was problematic after they'd had to drag the dumbass from a nest of the acid-spitting reptiles.

Gutierrez had done her best to fix the damage done and in all fairness, the mother hadn't been around and the acid spat by the tiny creatures wasn't half as destructive as that of one of the full-grown assholes. Yet there was still damage and he'd given up on the mechanism after it dropped the magazine it was supposed to bring to his rifle for the third time. They would have to make repairs when they returned.

The most infuriating part about it was that the man liked to flaunt his doctorate over them and insisted that they call him Dr. Couture—instead of say, Dumbass, which was more appropriate—and had the attitude that he was the one who did them the favor. Not only that, but he seemed to think being hired to work with Heavy Metal was already a foregone conclusion.

Sal realized then that he'd failed to mention that they were the founding members of the start-up and would therefore be the ones who decided whether he would be hired or not. Maybe the idiot thought there was someone higher-up who would make the decision based solely on whatever the man's qualifications were.

Either way, he counted down the minutes before they got rid of him forever. Given that this was already day two of the short operation and they were on their way to where they'd been dropped off, there was a definite sense of relief. This was doubled by the fact that Couture had stopped talking for a moment to check on something with his HUD.

There had been talk between the three of them over a private comm about the option to prank the man by inserting faulty software into his next update, but Sal had overridden the idea. They might not like the dude, but that didn't mean he'd earned a death sentence out there in the Zoo. Realistically, that was what a malfunction to his suit could mean. Since they were supposed to be the veterans who knew better than to get people killed, Kennedy and Gutierrez finally agreed, albeit reluctantly.

It didn't save him from their constant grouching about the man for the whole of the next day, but he stood by his decision—barely.

"We must stop," Couture said with a grunt.

"We're behind schedule thanks to our last stop," Sal pointed out and tapped the scars the acid had left on his armor. "We need to keep moving or we'll be left behind. Believe me when I tell you that you don't want to walk all the way to the base. If you think moving through the jungle is difficult, wait until you have to get through the dunes out there."

"Even so, we must inspect these...these plants here," the specialist protested and dropped to one knee to study a couple of the smaller bushes—or pretended to, rather, as he obviously needed a break.

Sal took a deep breath. It was hard not to remember his first time out there when he had run for his life in a suit very similar to the one the man wore while carrying the packs and weapons of those who had fallen earlier. Sure, it hadn't been pleasant, and if he'd had the option, he would have preferred to take it easy too. Maybe he was too demanding. They weren't even that pressed for time. He simply lacked patience and wanted this to end. While it was the man's fault since he was the reason why he wanted it to end quickly, if the idiot broke or sprained something, it would mean they would have to spend much more time stuck out there with him.

Overall, it had been a decent run through the jungle. The team had found three Pita locations and stripped them bare, which would net them an impressive payday. They would take money out of Couture's pay if the suits needed new parts due to acid damage, but the specialist would walk away with a good payout and, hopefully, no hard feelings.

The past thirty-six or so hours with the man told Sal he would take it as a personal insult if they didn't think he was the absolute best teammate ever, but at this point, he was beyond caring. He would make sure Couture never worked with anyone they liked because he would never subject a friend to this kind of torture.

He looked up when Kennedy pinged him on his comms. Something moved outside his line of vision. The motion sensors picked it up, though—in the trees and approaching from the direction from which they had come. Following them, he thought and gritted his teeth. He didn't like that. His mind didn't want to think about something out there capable of tracking them.

It looked like he would have to, unfortunately.

"We need to keep moving," he said forcefully, leveled his weapon, and aimed it at the faint movement.

Couture looked up from his rest with a scowl. "You have pushed us far too hard these past few hours. Do you think what I did was wrong? As I recall, there has only been one young creature brought back from the Zoo, and I tried to acquire the second. None of these reptiles have been studied up close before. All we have is blurry videos of them attacking. I tried to advance science, and what did you do? You pulled me out like I am some child and injured my back in the process. Now, you must let me rest."

"Look, we're moving out," Sal told him bluntly. "If you don't follow, we'll leave you behind."

"You cannot!" the specialist snapped angrily. "You are gunners, my protectors in this horrible place. It is your only job as useless weapons of violence to keep me alive long enough to change the world, and if you don't comprehend this—"

The man's pontificating was cut short when Sal looked up sharply with a hissed intake of breath. A couple of vines snaked from the darkness of the trees above them and aimed toward what he assumed they had identified as the source of all the noise—the two men and their altercation.

He reached forward to grab the specialist, but the man backed away, apparently thinking he meant to drag him out of there by force. Couture pushed Sal back and drew in a breath as if to give him a much louder piece of his mind. Before he could begin, however, two tentacle-like vines wound around his neck and waist to drag him into the jungle they'd come from. Sal reacted quickly and Gutierrez did the same. Both surged forward to take hold of him and, hopefully, to save him.

Whatever the tentacles were attached to was strong enough to drag them for a few meters before Sal's grip was knocked loose when he impacted with the ground. Gutierrez was harder to dislodge, and she was hauled a little farther before she smacked painfully into a tree.

"Fuck!" he roared and scrambled to his feet. Kennedy moved quickly and fired into the darkness to try to hit whatever was out there, but the effort was futile. They heard one thin scream from Couture before he disappeared into the Zoo.

"What the hell was that?" Gutierrez asked and pushed herself from the ground.

"I've seen tentacle-vines like that," Sal said as he hurried to her. "Are you okay?"

"I banged my shoulder a little, is all." She shook his concerned hand off. "It sucks that we have to keep an eye out for the plants now as well as the animals."

He looked into the Zoo and ground his teeth. Part of him felt bad since he had wished the jungle would swallow the asshole more than once, but it sucked that it had happened under his watch.

"Should we go in and find him?" Kennedy asked as she reloaded her weapon.

Sal checked his motion sensors for any sign of the tentacles or even any motion at all. For a second, they shifted on the very edge of his vision but disappeared quickly like one person was all they'd come for.

He was tempted but only for a brief moment. No matter how much he detested the man, this was not the kind of death he would wish on even his worst enemy. If they could rescue Couture from this, it would put him in his place and help him to be more than simply an asshole with a doctorate.

Finally, he turned away and rolled his shoulder, which had been bruised and wrenched in the effort to help the specialist.

"There's no way to save him from that," he reasoned aloud. "And there's no assurance that it won't come back for the rest of us. We need to keep moving."

Both women looked a little relieved. For a moment, he had a warm feeling. They would have gone with him into the Zoo to save the bastard, even though at least a part of them wanted to leave him out there to die. It was something a guy could take to heart.

"Let's hope the next one we test isn't that much of an asshole," Kennedy muttered as the vehicles came into sight. Most of the other teams had already assembled and now waited for the rest to return before the trip back to the base.

"Less of an asshole," Sal said and winced as he pulled the suit-clad body over his shoulder.

"Oh, definitely," Kennedy snarked and managed to hold her rifle at the ready as she helped Gutierrez. Most of the left side of Amanda's suit had been shredded and she tried to repair it as Kennedy half-carried, half-dragged her out while she also provided cover. Sal had helped with that as well, although he had carried the body of the specialist they had brought with them on this second trip into the Zoo from the French Base.

"It would be nice if these guys managed to be even a little competent," the armorer added belligerently. She had been the one closest to the man when he'd stumbled face-first into a pit of angry locusts. In all fairness, it was an interesting discovery to find that the locusts actually built nests.

Too bad it came at the price of the man's life. It was doubly frustrating because he was a Canadian and very eager to learn and a real pleasure to work with, unlike Couture. Unfortunately, that eagerness had been coupled with complete cluelessness as the man seemed to think this was a place of wonder and beauty. In all fairness, it was precisely that, but it was also a death trap if you didn't treat it like an adult and watch your goddamn step.

"At least they can't argue that we left a man to die out here this time," Kennedy hissed and swept her rifle to gun down a couple of locusts that jumped out of the under-brush. They hadn't swarmed, which seemed interesting to Sal since they usually did when they acted like this. They approached piecemeal like some creatures could smell the blood and tried to see if they could get a quick and easy bite to eat before they backed away when they realized the wounded had friends with guns.

"Well, that was a very short argument," Gutierrez responded and managed to limp through a couple of steps when her power armor began to work again. As frustrating as these jobs had been, at least the woman had more than proved her ability to fix the suits on the fly and under pressure.

Sal tightened his hold on the body as he scanned their surroundings. The jungle had broken barely a few meters back and gave them a full view of the desert in front of them.

He glanced at the two women as Amanda dropped to the ground, breathing hard. There had been more than mechanical damage when she'd dragged the man out of the nest, but with some help from the best mechanic around, the suit was able to keep her more or less on her feet despite a broken leg.

"Are you all right?" he asked and his concern showed in his tone.

She nodded, but the way her hands clenched and unclenched in time with her jaw told him otherwise. He didn't need to be a mind reader to tell that she was in an enormous amount of pain and barely held it together. He retrieved his first aid kit and drew a syringe full of morphine. After a few attempts, he injected it into the port of her suit. A few seconds passed before she breathed more or less normally again.

"Thanks," she said and nodded curtly.

"Don't thank me." Sal patted the side of her helmet. "I wasn't the one who dragged your ass out while shooting a whole horde of ugly motherfuckers."

She smirked and looked at Kennedy. "Thanks to you too. I guess I owe you one now."

"You know it, girl." Madigan helped her to her feet

again. "And if you think I won't collect, you're dead fucking wrong."

Sal grinned. He liked the fact that they were still able to joke about this shit. Gutierrez hadn't had as much experience in the Zoo as they had before she'd joined them, but damned if she wasn't virtually a veteran now. She'd shown heart and grit to keep up with them and had saved their lives and worked well to cover and help them out when she could.

She would need time in the French base's hospital, though.

He picked the body up and hauled it to where they'd brought one of their vehicles this time.

"Another job, another dead scientist," Kennedy snarked as they settled into their seats at a table in the corner of the bar. This one was more traditional, at least to Kennedy and Sal's sensibilities. It looked more like a pub, with an Irish bartender-slash-owner who had been a bartender before he joined the military, and it absolutely showed. The man had some panache and showed off his skills in drink-making at every opportunity.

Sadly, in their case, he'd simply poured them a couple of pints and there was little potential to show off.

It didn't matter. They only needed a drink after they'd booked Gutierrez in for a night of observation at the hospital.

"Did you catch the commander's attitude, though?" Sal asked and took a sip of his dark beer.

"Yeah," she replied. There was nothing worse in the world than knowing your life didn't mean that much to the people in charge of risking it.

The man had seen them return with another body, and while he'd asked pointed questions the last time about why they weren't able to recover the body and even implied that they hadn't done their all to save Dr. Couture's life, this time, there was no such annoyance. He merely seemed happy that they'd brought back another heavy haul of Pita flowers. When they asked him about why he didn't seem more upset about losing research personnel, the annoying little man had merely shrugged.

"They know better than us," he said in a thick French accent. "We warn them, and they ignore us. If they are the kind of idiots who want to go in without knowing if they have what it takes to come back, who are we to deny them? They are adults, yes?"

Sal had to grudgingly admit that their physical ages might make someone mistake them for adults, yes.

"I hope your payment was to your satisfaction?" he'd asked next.

It was. Over the past couple of days of intermittent trips into the Zoo, they had made more money than on most of their other longer and more arduous trips that usually ended up going deeper and being more dangerous. They were paid in euros around there, of course, but the conversion was still good. They would come away from their time working with the French base considerably richer for their efforts.

Would it be worth it, though? He wasn't entirely sure. The death toll of their shorter and supposedly less dangerous trips was now up to two. What was more, he wasn't sure he really cared for the blasé attitude the locals had about the loss of life.

He rubbed his temples and tried to forget about all that for one night.

"Hey, you two are the Heavy Metal people, yes?" someone said with a heavy German accent.

He looked toward a couple of men who stood near the bar and stared at them. They didn't look hostile but he really couldn't tell. Their whole culture was completely foreign to him.

"Yeah," Sal said, not in the mood to play games at the moment. "Yeah, we are. How can we help you?"

"You bring in much more money than the rest of the teams," the man said with a chuckle. "Almost more than the rest of them combined. You know how to run operations into the Zoo. When next you take a trip, let us know if you need gunners, yes?"

He nodded and narrowed his eyes as he turned his gaze to Kennedy.

"What's up with these people?" he asked with a chuckle.

She shrugged easily. "There are mostly mercs here at this point. Even the specialists. They're all here to make money. Since they risk their lives anyway, it might as well be with someone who knows what the fuck they're doing."

That made an annoying amount of sense, he realized.

"You're not actually considering their offer, right?" he asked.

"Hell no," she muttered under her breath. "If we march into the Zoo with a group of gunners, you know I'll only go in there with people I trust, not some random German dudes."

"I can respect that," he said with a nod.

Kennedy pulled her phone out of her pocket and indicated that a message had been received.

"They've tagged us for another run tomorrow," she explained. "Should I turn them down? I don't think Gutierrez will be good to go so soon unless you decide to give her a lick of Madie."

Sal grinned. "I'll hold off on that for the moment. But we can do it with only the two of us. A one-day trip since we have one more specialist to test. Let's see if the third time isn't actually the charm in this case."

"That hasn't been my experience," she retorted.

"Yeah, well...if all else fails, we'll make one last load of cash before we leave this hellhole."

"I'll drink to that," she said with a chuckle and raised her glass to clink softly with his.

CHAPTER NINETEEN

She looked around warily. Casablanca, of course, was a city bathed in all kinds of film history, but unfortunately, the city was nothing like the movie that had made it famous. In fairness to the film, it did show that it was ridiculously hot and crowded, even back then, but most of it had been done inside a café-slash-casino while some very charming not-African people had innumerable conversations about a war that happened on another continent.

When she landed, she came to the not so shocking realization that there was far less appeal than one might have expected. The scenery was fantastic, but it was difficult to truly enjoy all the natural and man-made wonders it had to offer when you constantly looked over your shoulder for someone with a gun and a black head bag.

She stepped into one of the local dive bars and looked around to make sure she hadn't been followed. Satisfied, she made her way to a table with two chairs and took the seat that gave her a decent view of the door. There wasn't much point in hiding in there. If one of the people who hunted her made their way inside, she would rather know about it immediately and be on her way out before they saw her instead of waiting for them to find her while she tried to remain hidden.

It made sense in her mind, even if she wasn't entirely sure if there were any stats that would define whether she had made a good decision or a mistake. She shrugged and followed the instinct that told her to stay where she was.

He said he could come here. He was a little late, was all.

As the waiter moved away after taking her order, she looked around again and scanned the clientele.

Wait.

She startled and pushed herself out of her seat in a way that she hoped was subtle. There hadn't been that many expectations, of course. It wasn't that she had no skills when it came to this kind of thing, but a cold feeling still settled in her stomach when she saw a couple of men stand when she did.

The two were much better at this than she was. They didn't even look at her and merely moved calmly to the bar to pay their checks before they sidled closer and cut off her exit. There had to be another way out, though. The kitchen door was behind her. They couldn't make a scene while she was in a public place, so if she moved now, it might put some distance between them and her.

All thoughts of escape disappeared, however, when something cold and hard pressed into the small of her back.

"You won't be staying to eat," a man's voice said in English but with a familiar accent. She inhaled sharply and clenched her hands to keep them from shaking as the man guided her away from the table and marched her toward the exit. The other two men followed closely behind them.

She wondered if the rest of the patrons were aware of what had happened or simply blissfully ignorant. Either they were not observant enough to see the gun against her back or if they did see, with this kind of thing as common as it was around there, they simply didn't want to get involved.

Neither would surprise her, she realized as she stepped out of the café and looked hopefully around for someone who might interfere with this kidnapping. The street was entirely deserted. The two men who had followed them out broke away and walked down the street as the man behind her opened the trunk of a sedan and shoved her inside.

She really hoped this was all worth it.

Sal shifted his shoulder and scowled at what his HUD was showing him. In retrospect, it might have been a stupid decision to take the first job they could get their hands on. Maybe they should have taken the time to ensure that Gutierrez was all right and barring that, take more time to ensure that their suits were in working order.

He patted the reloading mechanism which was still problematic after it had been attacked by a group of acid-spewing reptiles. Of course, he should count his lucky stars that they hadn't been fully grown, which was why he only had trouble reloading and not with missing a whole arm.

Power arms were so expensive to fix, he thought with a shake of his head.

"Are you having trouble there, Jacobs?" Kennedy asked and glanced at him with concern.

"Only some software issues while trying to get to the specialist side of my suit," he responded and tapped his mask, more out of instinct than because he thought it would actually work.

"Do you think we jumped the gun coming out here?" she asked.

He looked up from the plant he tried to take samples of. "Do you say that because we should have probably waited for Gutierrez to recover and make sure our suits were back to full functionality, or because it made our prospective specialist bail because he thought our little team was cursed?"

"You don't see many superstitious scientists," she observed and shifted her rifle. "But you're right. Well, I'm right, and you made a good observation. We certainly jumped it on this one. Maybe if we'd waited the whole operation out, we might have been able to get the guy to come in with us while working with functioning equipment."

"Are you having trouble?" Sal asked when she scowled and fiddled with her weapon.

"Yeah, I have a fucking nick in my rifle that makes it jam all the time. How about you? Do you have your suit fixed yet?"

Sal nodded. There were a couple of glitches but nothing he couldn't sort out later. Besides, he wasn't sure how he was supposed to feel about having to double as a specialist and gunner for this run. It was supposed to be a smash and grab operation with lower numbers to make sure the teams moved quickly to collect hard drives from the suits of those who had died on previous missions. A couple of Belgian companies were willing to bet there was enough on those hard drives to warrant the amount of money they had sunk into getting them back.

They had already found a couple of dead teams. As usual, no animal bodies were found around them, although the sight of half-empty magazines and the heavy tears in the armor suits told them the story of a hard fight which had ended poorly. No carcasses simply meant the Zoo continued to do its thing and collect the bodies of the dead animals.

He ground his teeth in frustration and pushed forward into the jungle. While he didn't want to say it, he missed Courtney more than he wanted to admit. Despite that, he didn't want to irritate Kennedy by bringing the woman up. The two of them had been friends but she didn't seem like the kind of person who obsessed over having her friends around her all the time. She had more of a love the person you were with kind of philosophy. Not that there was anything wrong with that.

Then again, he hadn't actually had the opportunity to talk to her about it, so he might have been completely off base. Maybe she missed Courtney too and only wanted to seem tough about it. That wouldn't be out of character for her either, he supposed.

But this was neither the time nor the place to have a conversation about their feelings. They were in the middle of one of the most dangerous jungles in the world—if not the most dangerous—and had bigger problems to deal with.

The nostalgia was probably something along the lines of being in there alone, only the two of them, and having to watch each other's backs while they tried to get a job done. It wasn't an impossible job, Sal mused and tapped the reloading mechanism again to make sure it still worked. Merely annoyingly difficult.

The hours passed while they made the rounds through the jungle and tracked the suits. It was tedious work as the GPS locators emitted a signal with limited range so they had to work on estimates of the location before they picked up actual confirmation. When they found each one, they stripped the suits of the hard drives and worked their way slowly back to where the vehicles waited. It was supposed to be only a day's work, max. The company involved didn't want to have to pay for more than that.

"Do you think we'll find a body belonging to that asshole Couture?" Sal asked and adjusted his rifle to bring it closer as he carried the pack with the hard drives on his free shoulder.

"I doubt it," Kennedy answered but glanced reflexively at the trees. "Whatever that vine shit was that snagged him probably took his suit apart to get the juicy human inside. I doubt there'd be a hard drive left to recover."

He nodded. The details they'd been given about the GPS locators didn't provide the names of the men who had worn them when they went down, only the model number. As this was meant to be a brute-force kind of operation, they would only look for the markers that had more than one suit in close locations, since that improved the chances of getting something worthwhile from them. It also reduced the chances that they'd run into a body belonging to the once great Dr. Couture.

Of course, the company that paid for all this had taken an enormous gamble that there would be something of use on the drives. They paid per item, whether they held something useful or not.

As they made their way out at the end of the day, the signal interference from the trees around them gradually lifted. They reached the edge of the ever-advancing tree line and Sal glanced at Kennedy with a grin.

"What?" she asked bluntly.

"Your butt's vibrating," he said helpfully.

"That's an odd way to put it," she returned with a smile. "But thanks. Your ass is pretty vibrant too."

"That— No, well…yes, it is, but that's not what I meant." He laughed. "There's something vibrating is what I mean."

"Oh." She grunted and her head moved to indicate that she used her phone through a wireless connection to her HUD.

"Our Russian friends have gotten back to us," she said after a pause. "They've let us know there will be a trip into the Zoo tomorrow and they want us to be a part of it. They're willing to pay top dollar for it too, but we have to head to their base to get in on the action."

As they stepped out of the Zoo, it was hard not to smile at the view that greeted them. Sunset was still a couple of hours away and they looked out over a sea of sand from the pleasant shade of the heavy tree cover behind them. The massive girth of the wall, sections of which were still under construction, loomed large on the horizon. It looked truly impressive, Sal had to admit. Considerable work, creativity, and money were poured into a project that no one was sure would work, and yet they insisted it was the way to go.

He had to admire a gamble like that.

"I'm sure we don't have the option to turn them down," he said. "But we might have to take a job with the Russians minus two members of our team and head in with iffy suits."

"Which one of us will give Gutierrez the news?" she asked.

"I guess we could always go into the hospital and tell her together," he said with a chuckle. "I have no idea how she'll feel when we break the news that we have another job on the other side of the Zoo we need to do. How do we even tell her? Sorry to abandon you here in this half-finished base to recover from that broken leg that may or may not be our fault."

She chuckled. "She's cool. I think she'll take it in stride."

"I hope you're right."

Sal's grip on his gun tightened as he looked out into the jungle behind them and ground his teeth. Ever since he'd seen those fucking tentacles in the trees, it had been hard to get the image out of his head. The awful truth that they'd tracked the team through the jungle like they had ears and a mind of their own was the stuff of nightmares.

Well, he supposed there were people with all kinds of weird fetishes and fantasies, and he certainly wasn't one to judge. His time spent on the Internet had taught him that.

Kennedy nudged his shoulder. "I'd pay a penny for your

thoughts, but I don't want you to go through the trouble of having to reimburse me."

He grinned. "I'm thinking about the amount of crazy we have to deal with on a daily basis. I've actually kind of forgotten what it's like to live a normal life with a normal job and nothing alien trying to kill me."

"Do you miss it?" she asked as they strolled toward where the vehicles had been left.

"Not really," Sal replied and eased his painful shoulder, the price of tinkering with his less than reliable suit. "All the getting shot at, bitten, and everything else is probably something I could do without, but at the same time, living on the edge and fighting for our lives—it's hard to imagine a life where that isn't something I would wake up every morning to dread. It's like the feeling that you can literally bash anyone for complaining about their jobs, you know?"

"Well, given that I've been in the military for most of my adult life, I'm not really sure what a normal life is supposed to be like," she answered honestly and picked up the pace as the vehicle came into view. "My time in the Marines was spent either getting shot at or doing mind-numbingly boring work. Out here, there's less mind-numbing, but that means more action. On the plus side, it also means better pay, and that's something I can definitely live with. My drinking problem is starting to get expensive."

Sal laughed as they pulled themselves into the vehicle and started it. Kennedy turned it and eased down the road toward the French base.

"Do you miss her?" he asked into the extended silence. "Courtney, I mean."

She sighed and gripped the steering wheel tightly enough that her knuckles went white.

"Yeah," she answered finally after a long pause. "Of course I do. She's my friend and I like having her around. That said, I'm also happy for her. Despite everything I said about never wanting to give this kind of life up, at the same time, I wouldn't wish it on anyone. I'm glad she got out and could head back home and play gazillionaire."

He chuckled. "Yeah, I guess I can agree with that."

CHAPTER TWENTY

"Igor Khorokhorin," the brig guard said and had to lean in close to make sure he read that correctly. He looked at the man in front of him. There was a lean look about him and slightly feminine features but not overly so. A couple of bruises under his eye indicated that his capture had been more difficult than anticipated.

This Igor character should count himself lucky that he was alive at all. Most of the time, if the people who were sent there made trouble for the people who brought them in, they were simply shot and driven out to be disposed of somewhere near the Zoo. No bodies would be found and no one would question what happened in there.

It was a chilling situation, but it was the world they lived in now. Survival was the idea, one way or the other, and those poor, unfortunate souls who didn't learn that lesson fast enough would never be found again.

Sure, he'd heard they stuck GPS locators in suits these days, but that was only for the people who went in with suits.

He looked at the man who still stood in front of him. There was something about him that simply didn't fit. He looked like what they said the scientists would look like—those who people constantly complained they needed—but in the end, if they were willing to break the law, who cared if they were necessary or not?

The guard examined the paperwork for the prisoner again and narrowed his eyes when he saw the section marked off for reason of arrest was left blank. He looked up from his desk and called the arresting officer.

"There's nothing here about he was taken into custody," the guard pointed out belligerently. "You should know we can't legally hold anyone here without reason for more than twenty-four hours."

"I know," the man said in a calm, collected voice. "We only need the prisoner kept here until later tonight. We hold him for questioning, then he's sent into the Zoo to run recon for another team."

The guard turned to the man, who looked at the ground and tried to avoid his gaze.

"Fucking assholes," the official muttered and signed off on the paperwork. Sending someone into the Zoo was as efficient an execution method as any, but that didn't mean he approved of it. Still, who would listen to the opinion of a man whose bad knee made him ineligible to use the power suits they needed to head in there?

"Here today," he said and spoke softly so only the prisoner could hear, "dead ten feet into the Zoo." He shook his head in sympathy, but there was no response from the man in front of him. "Who the fuck did you piss off, anyway?"

Once again, he received no response. Not that it would

have made any difference, the guard realized since there was no way to save him from the reality that he would be sent off to be some animal's meal. But it didn't mean that a show of sympathy couldn't help.

The guard shrugged after the moment of silence stretched on into almost half a minute. He leaned back in his seat before he pressed an ink-covered stamp to the arrest papers.

"You can take him to holding," he ordered and turned away as the prisoner was hauled up by the man who had brought him in and marched to the cells down the hall.

It was a pity that they didn't offer last meals to the poor fuckers sent out there to die.

"So the last guy simply quit on you, huh?" Gutierrez asked as she toyed with the Jell-O left in her bowl with a scowl. Sal couldn't tell if it was because she didn't like the sour apple flavor or if it was because she would be stuck in the damned hospital for another couple of days.

"Well, yeah," he said. "He'd heard that the last two guys to head in there with us hadn't walked out, so he thought we were cursed or something. No mention that our team was the one with the least casualties. Of course, all they see is that the veterans walk out while the rookies are all dead, so yeah, they think we're cursed or something."

"Look at you, using sports lingo," Kennedy said with a grin. "Trying to be all cool and shit. We might make a man out of you yet, Jacobs."

He grinned at the woman who had now joined him in

Amanda's room. The fact that the base was so empty meant there was more than enough space for each individual patient to have their own room.

"Did you tell her yet?" Kennedy asked as she moved to the chair beside the bed and plopped on it with a groan.

"I was waiting for you to get here," he said uncertainly.

"Tell me what?" the patient demanded.

"We received word that our hacker will be available in the Zoo for a limited time," Sal said, speaking in a low rumble of a voice. He didn't think anyone would listen in on what they had to say but that didn't mean he shouldn't be careful. "We'll have to work it undercover, but the only way to get there is to actually join one of the Russian teams heading into the Zoo."

Gutierrez raised an eyebrow. "Exactly how narrow is this window of ours?" She looked like she already knew she wouldn't like the answer.

"They start their run tomorrow," Kennedy said and followed his example by keeping her voice down. "We need to head there tonight to be ready for it. We might actually have to sleep in the vehicle, now that I think about it."

The other woman scowled at her leg still encased in a cast. "Doc says I won't be Zoo-ready for another couple of weeks. It wasn't a full break, but there were some cracks that showed up on my x-rays along with a sprain on my hip, knee, and ankle."

Sal nodded. "I'm really sorry about this, Amanda."

She smirked. "That's nice of you to say, Sal, and I appreciate it. But you guys have a business to run. As long as I get my fully paid sick leave while I lay here on my ass, there won't be any hard feelings. But only as long as this new guy you bring back is worth leaving me here on my own."

"We'll make sure he's worth the trouble," he assured her and patted her shoulder gently. "Just…get better, Gutierrez. You are a part of the team now, and I need my engineer in top form out there, after all."

"I'm not an engineer," Amanda retorted with a chuckle. "I simply fix shit. Now get out of here, both of you. You're cramping my style."

"Of course, we are, Spring Apple," Kennedy said with a smirk and indicated the woman's uneaten Jell-O. "We'll drop you a message when we head back to the compound. Depending on when that happens, we might swing by and pick you up."

The duo made their way out of the hospital and shared what felt like a very comfortable silence before they reached the parking lot and climbed into their JLTV, already loaded with their suits and supplies and ready to start on their trip to the Russian base. The sun had barely begun to set, and from there, they had a good few hours of driving, depending on how fast they went.

Given that Kennedy would take the wheel for this one, he assumed they would try for a record run.

"She's a cool cucumber, that Gutierrez," Madigan said as she started the engine.

Sal waited for the initial rumble of the powerful motor to settle into the normalized sound before they pulled out of the parking lot.

"Very cool," he agreed. "She's good with mechanics and a gun when needed. We're lucky to have her on our team. You know, I think she likes you."

His companion looked at him with a very unamused expression. "Are you kidding me? Can't two women be friends without a guy starting to wonder if they'll make his lesbian fantasies come true?"

"Come on, you know what I'm talking about," he said and shook his head in protest. "I don't mean it like that. You two seem like you're almost close friends already, and that's a good sign for Heavy Metal for the days to come. That said, you are more her type, and let's be honest, if she were to develop a crush, you are the obvious choice."

"Don't think I don't see through the compliments into your inner sleazeball," she warned, but when she looked at him, he could see a glimmer of amusement in her eyes. "That doesn't mean you should stop trying with the compliments, though. Practice makes perfect and all that."

Sal grinned, tugged the lever on the right side of his seat, and let it lower into a more comfortable recline. "Wake me up when it's my turn to take the wheel."

"Sweet dreams," she said with a grin and pressed her foot harder on the gas, looking for a reaction from him. There was none as he covered his eyes with his forearm and quickly dozed off.

CHAPTER TWENTY-ONE

He looked at the clock and willed it to move faster. Right now, he needed a cigarette but he'd made the promise to himself that he wouldn't have another one until his shift was over. The decision had mainly to do with a desire to get home to his wife and surprise her with how he'd quit a decades-old habit, but he'd slowly lost the will to do it. The old hag probably cheated on him with the single guy across the hall anyway, so why should she get to enjoy what he had to work for?

The guard was distracted from his train of thought when someone entered the brig building. His visitor was easily recognizable, even though he didn't know much about the man aside from name and rank, and even those were somehow shrouded in mystery. Military police were difficult men to really get a bead on, which meant that as the man moved to his desk, the guard straightened from his habitual slouch and matched the visitor's glare.

"I'm here to release a prisoner you have," the newcomer

said and clearly hadn't recognized the guard from six hours before.

"Igor Khorokhorin, yes?" he asked and withdrew a handful of forms from the second drawer of his desk. "I will need you to fill all these out and hand them to the release guard outside."

The man nodded, clearly aware of the red tape surrounding even something as simple as a prisoner transfer. He went through the forms quickly like he'd practiced for them as the guard pushed out of his seat and walked slowly to the holding cells. Reluctantly, he tugged to retrieve a couple of keys that were roped to his belt.

Igor looked up from staring at the floor as he'd done for the past few hours, clearly terrified as the door to his cell was unlocked. The guard had no real desire to go in there and drag him out and was thankful that the prisoner came out of his cell without having to be coaxed.

He took hold of the young man's arm and half dragged him to where the Military Police Lieutenant Andrej Mikael Khadev finished the paperwork required for the release. There was no delay before he pushed the completed documents across the desk and stood decisively.

"I can't do this," Igor said softly, a hint of a tremble in his high-pitched voice. "I can't."

Khadev looked angrily at him, ground his teeth, and was about to snap off a string of insults when the guard stepped in.

"Look, maybe it's not so bad," he said in a soft, reassuring voice pitched low but loud enough to be heard by the frightened inmate. "Maybe you will be lucky and get to walk out of there too. Find a way to get as close to the other side of the jungle as you can and make contact with the Americans. Maybe they get you out of there without too much trouble. It's not like it's the end of the world, right?"

His words didn't seem to have any effect on Igor, who still looked absolutely terrified. At any other time and in any other place, he would have told the man there was no need to fear. He would reassure him that the only reason he felt apprehensive about what he faced was because it was something unknown, something that would never live up to the horrifying expectations.

But this was the Zoo and it had all kinds of ways of bringing nightmares to life. The guard hadn't been in there himself but the footage that had been brought back by those who had was enough to make a man doubt his own sanity.

Khadev shook his head and chuckled as he grasped Igor by the arm and dragged him out of the building. The only words the guard had heard the prisoner utter in his six hours in the place still rang in his ears as one of the other guards hurried up to his desk.

"Damn it, why did you do that?" his colleague asked and sipped from a mug of coffee. "There's no need to get anyone's hopes up about that particular kind of death sentence."

He shook his head and leaned back in his seat with his gaze glued to the door the two had left through. "It's rough. That man is on his way into a place to be 'released,' not knowing that he would be better off simply being shot in the back of the head. The least I can do is give him a little hope as he heads off to the gallows."

He stared at the door for a few more seconds before he glanced at the clock. Another thirty minutes to go. Fuck, he needed a cigarette.

Her eyes jerked open as the alarm on her phone went off. It was supposed to be the soft and soothing tones from Beethoven's Fifth, and yet she realized that her heart pounded and a cold sweat formed on her brow despite the fact that the environmental controls maintained her room at a pleasant and balmy temperature.

How long would it be before she no longer dreamed about the Zoo? Would it ever really leave her? She knew she didn't miss the damn place, even though the only pleasant part of the dreams involved having Sal and Madigan around her again. In a time when friendships had always been less important than pushing the boundaries of science, she had managed to forge a couple that made her miss being in their compound.

Yes, it was the compound she really missed. The jungle could go and fuck itself with all kinds of cacti.

Courtney dragged herself from the comfort of her queen-sized bed and pushed the down comforter aside before she moved across the carpeted floor to the bathroom. There were certain comforts she'd learned to live without, she realized as she turned the shower on and slipped under the steaming stream, but the longer she stayed there, the more she adjusted to having them in her life again. Like decent coffee and not having to get up at a time that only the military thought was civilized and go to work.

And she'd missed the bacon. Real bacon that tasted like it hadn't spent the past three months in a freezer.

Almost an hour after she'd woken up, she checked her watch and pulled on the pantsuit she'd set out the day before. Nothing really felt quite as powerful as wearing a suit of armor, but there wasn't much that could protect her from the poison she'd face in downtown LA.

She looked around at the various decorations and the furniture that had been chosen. Her dad had never really had the best eye for décor, but that was why people hired decorators. And from the looks of things, the man could certainly have afforded it.

Not that Courtney actually thought she would stay there for much longer. It was cheaper to be there in her childhood home than stay in a hotel. Yes, she had inherited it along with the rest of the man's possessions, but she didn't think she wanted to disturb what had to be at least one lifetime's worth of memories. She preferred to sell it, let someone else form memories around it, and find something she could feel more comfortable in.

She wasn't sure why she felt guilty about planning her life without Sal and Madigan involved. They were her friends, of course, but they had to understand that she had a life now, and until she sorted out everything that her father had left her, she wouldn't be able to go back to them.

They had to understand that, right?

Courtney put on a pair of pearl earrings and slipped into her comfortable yet stylish shoes. Satisfied with her appearance, she drew her phone from her purse and sent a message to the town car company, which promptly responded that her transportation would arrive in a few short minutes.

It annoyed her that her driver's license had expired while she'd been in the Zoo, and without any time to get it renewed, they couldn't have the heiress to the Monroe fortune riding around in the city's public transportation system. Besides, she doubted that they even had buses this far into the suburbs.

Sure enough, a few minutes later, a limousine drew up in front of the house and the driver waited patiently as she came down the steps and locked the door before she walked to the car. She didn't wait for him to get out and open the door for her, being perfectly capable of doing it for herself, thank you very much.

With a murmured greeting, she slipped into one of the passenger seats and stared out the window as the various houses and trees flashed by. Distracted by her earlier thoughts that still nagged at her, she noticed very little of the journey until they pulled to a stop in front of a massive building downtown.

Courtney blinked a few times and wondered how long she'd been lost in thought since it had to take at least an hour to get into the city at this hour, usually more.

She shook her head and nodded as this time, the driver was given ample opportunity to come around and open the door for her. With a bright smile, she gave the man a generous tip and a word of thanks before she went into the building.

It was an investment company, one that had handled most of her father's investments into research grants and the like and allowed him to make money from his scientific advancements without having to step into a lab for almost a full decade before his death.

An aide waited for her at the front desk, smiled broadly when she came into view, and quickly waved the security men who approached with metal detector wands away.

"You don't need to worry about that, Dr. Monroe," the young man said in a pleasant voice as he guided her to the elevators at the back of the lobby. "The people around here are paranoid enough to make J Edgar Hoover drool. Anyway, I made sure they knew you were one of the owners of this place, but they still need to be reminded that some people don't need to deal with the red tape involved in getting into this building."

Courtney smiled pleasantly as they walked. The young man continued to talk, although she filtered out most of what he said. A part of her knew these people were paid to be pleasant and to make conversation, but she didn't feel in the mood to deal with that right now.

She wasn't in the best frame of mind and honestly hadn't been since she found out that her father had died, with a few very rare exceptions. Those grew rarer by the minute. Having to deal with all the business of his estate had grown tedious to the point where she almost longed for the non-existent comforts of the Zoo.

At least the animals in there had the good manners to not sidle up to her, smile, and try to stab her in the back. They might want to kill her ass dead, but they were upfront about it.

Her companion led her into a conference room filled

with two dozen office chairs she would have killed to have in her apartment at the compound.

"It doesn't seem like your party has arrived yet," the aide said, his smile intact. "Might I get you something to drink or eat while you wait? We have a delightful sandwich bar on the second floor. Perhaps some juice? Water? Coffee?"

She put her hand on the boy's shoulder in an effort to stop him talking as pleasantly as possible. Now that she thought about it, this kid couldn't be that much younger than Sal. In fact, it looked like he might be a couple of years older. That was a truly odd thought. Here she was, thinking of the aide as a kid and yet thought of Sal as one of her peers.

"Only water, thanks," she said and maintained her smile as she moved to take a seat at one of the chairs at the end of the table. She made herself comfortable and pulled a laptop from her bag, set it up on the table, and connected it to the building's Wi-Fi before she pulled up the document she'd worked on since before she'd returned.

The title still made her smile, but she moved past it quickly. She'd worked on this description of her experiences at the Zoo for her father, and now that he was gone, she did it in his honor. It was something that might help people remember him and everything he'd done.

The reasons for wanting to come out from under her father's shadow were still present but less important now. There was no point in outscoring a dead man, after all. She could still put out as much work as she needed to be remembered under her own name.

This was something for him, and it was something she would finish in his memory.

She looked up from her work as the young aide peeked his head into the conference room once more.

"I'm so sorry, Dr. Monroe," he said in the same pleasant voice he probably practiced in front of a mirror. "I've received word that your party's been caught up in traffic and should be a while. Can I get you anything in the meantime? Have I mentioned that we have an amazing sandwich bar—"

"On the second floor, yes," Courtney said with a chuckle. "Yes, you did. I don't think I'm ready for a sandwich now, Mr…"

"Gregory Pedersen," he said with a smile. "But you can call me Greg."

"Well, Greg, I think I might take you up on that coffee."

"Coming right up, Dr. Monroe," he said with a snap of the fingers. He was back in less than two minutes.

Damned if the coffee there wasn't better than what she had at home, she thought and inhaled the rich, bitter aroma of the brew before she ventured a sip. She liked to add a little cream and sugar to it, but when it was this good, what was the point?

She had barely drunk half of it when Greg stepped into the room, closely followed this time by three people. One was a woman dressed in as severe a pantsuit as Courtney wore herself, with her dyed blond hair tied up in a rigid bun and a pair of delicate glasses perched halfway down the bridge of her nose.

The other two looked like they would be perfectly at home in the Zoo. Powerful shoulders needed no padding to fill out their suits and the heavy hands and bulky coats were more than capable of hiding concealed weapons.

She stood with a broad smile and offered her hand to the woman, who wore the same fake smile Courtney had put on herself this morning.

"Miss Courtney Monroe?" the woman asked with a mild Boston accent. "I'm Andressa Covington. I was friends with your father and I've managed his estate during his tragic absence. I'm so sorry for your loss."

"Thank you," she said with a smile. "It's Dr. Courtney Monroe, by the way."

"Of course, sweetie," Covington said with a condescending tone. "These are James and Giles. They're my accountants and have helped me with the management."

Courtney nodded and took each of the men's hands in turn. If they were accountants, she was a venom-fanged panther she mused before she took her seat again.

"Now, I know you've been read into your father's will, which means you've been told about the kind of investments he was involved in," the woman said quickly as she sat a couple of chairs away from Courtney. The two so-called accountants remained on their feet behind her. "I won't bother you with the details—it's all so very complicated, you understand—but in the end, I want you to know that your father's estate, and yours in turn, is very well taken care of. So well, in fact, that I'm not even sure why we're here. I'm sure the portfolio you were given was more than sufficient."

"I was given a portfolio," she said, withdrew it from her bag, and placed it on the table. "And I came here because I was alerted to a couple of discrepancies in the accounting —" Courtney paused to give the two men a pointed look.

"More specifically, in the very generous expense accounts you've assigned yourself."

"Please take no offense when I tell you that you have no idea what you're talking about," Covington said but her polite façade began to disappear very quickly. "I've worked accounts like your father's and many others for over ten years. I have a degree from Harvard if you'd like to check my credentials."

"I have no doubts as to your capabilities, Miss Covington. I'm afraid that's the problem, though, since it took my lawyers the better part of a week to sift through all the various charities and businesses you funneled my father's money into the moment he died," she explained and took care to keep her own façade firmly in place. "Would you like some coffee?"

The other woman opened her mouth but, clearly stumped by the out-of-nowhere offer, snapped it shut again. She fidgeted with her watch for a few seconds and looked at the two lugs behind her before she nodded.

"I'd love some coffee. Half caf, mocha latte with soy—" She paused when she realized that Courtney had stood, pushed her own half-drunk and very cold cup across the table, and placed it in front of her before she resumed her seat. Without a word, she slid her laptop and the portfolio into her bag.

"Look, I'm sure you're a very busy woman, so I'll cut right to the chase," Monroe said, her voice soft and civil. "I don't work for you and I never will. And until your company is willing to send someone to work with me who has a modicum of manners and doesn't try to steal everything my father worked so hard to achieve in his life, I'm afraid I'll have to take my business elsewhere."

She picked her bag up and started toward the door. Covington snapped her fingers and one of the lugs turned, marched over to her, and placed a hand on her shoulder to stop her.

"Now, Miss Monroe," the woman said as she pushed from her seat and turned to face Courtney. "I'm terribly sorry that you are unable to be civil in such an important meeting. Believe me, I understand the pain you are going through at the moment, but I'm afraid that's no reason to be ru—"

Courtney couldn't help herself. There were more than a few issues that she had to work through as she tried to get back on track with living where the biggest threat to one's life was high fructose syrup. She tried to keep things under control, but at that moment, as the man's hand tightened on her shoulder and he tried to drag her to the conference table, something in her snapped. As far as metaphorical straws that broke camels' backs went, this one was heavy—which, she felt, explained her reaction.

She reached over her shoulder, grasped the man's fore and middle fingers, and twisted them as she turned. The motion enabled her to use her body weight to add increasing pressure to his joints until she heard the tell-tale crackle and pop as fingers pulled out of their sockets. The thug screamed in pain and dropped to his knees as she continued to twist. She took advantage of his exposed position and hammered a jab at his nose. A satisfying crack didn't quite convince her, so she hammered it again, this time with her elbow.

Kennedy would be disappointed. She had failed to keep up with her training regimen.

With his nose and fingers broken, the man was a pitiful pile of soft whimpers and cries as she reached into his jacket and found what she'd suspected was in there. She pulled the handgun clear, made sure to flick the safety off with her thumb, and released the man's broken hand to drag the slider back and chamber a round before she aimed at man number two. He already had his hand tucked inside his jacket to draw his weapon.

"Let's not be hasty here," Covington said, her voice suddenly soft and pleasant again and her bright green eyes as wide as saucers as she stared at the gun in Courtney's hand. "There's no need to resort to violence."

"There certainly isn't," Monroe said coldly. "Is that why you brought in a couple of armed 'accountants' who were here to hold me down if I disagreed with the idea of you stealing from my father's estate? Because there was no need for violence?"

"You have no idea what kind of person you're dealing with here, Miss Monroe," the woman all but snarled.

"It's Dr. Monroe," Courtney snapped and shoved the wounded man to his knees. She kept the gun trained on the second one, who had removed his hand from his coat and now raised both of them in response to her closing the distance between them. "You've done this for a while now, right, Miss Covington? You know your job well enough to research your clients—well, let's call them victims because that's more accurate. You've done your job. You researched me before coming here. The little blurb that said that I'd spent the better part of the last two years in one of the most dangerous places on earth—a place where you wouldn't last ten fucking minutes? That didn't ring any alarm bells?"

"I have friends in places you wouldn't believe," Covington retorted as if she'd somehow forgotten who held a gun with a round in the chamber. "I have power you couldn't even dream of."

"I, on the other hand, have friends in very dangerous places," she retorted and gritted her teeth as she pointed the gun at the woman, who gulped very audibly. "And unless you are willing to find death knocking on your front door selling girl scout cookies, I suggest you never, ever threaten me again." She moved a step closer so that the barrel of the handgun hovered less than an inch away from the woman's forehead. "I've been there and done that more times than I can count. Can you really say you've done the same?"

A moment of tense silence followed in which Courtney seriously considered pulling the trigger. The woman was terrified now, yes, but there was little hope that this would show her the error of her ways. No, she would continue to rob other people blind until she was caught and sent to a minimum-security prison for a couple of years. Inevitably, she'd be released and allowed to live the rest of her days in the luxury of the money she'd acquired from others. Pulling the trigger would be the best kind of justice.

You're not in the Zoo anymore, Courtney, she reminded herself, closed her eyes for a second, and backed away. *Do you really want to go to jail for this bitch?*

Finally, she stepped aside and released the magazine

from the gun. With slow, deliberate competence, she drew the slider back to eject the single round in the chamber.

She dropped it in a gesture of utter disdain and moved out of the conference room toward the elevator, where Greg stepped forward to intercept her.

"Dr. Monroe, I'm so sorry to see you leave so quickly," he said and almost stumbled over himself to find the right words to say. "I trust you enjoyed your visit?"

"I had the time of my life, Greg," Courtney said with the first genuine smile that had touched her lips all morning. "Although you might want to let the maintenance department know there's been a small spill in the conference room and they might want to get right on it and clean it up. No hurry or anything, and if there's a bill, please don't hesitate to send it to me."

"Of course," he stuttered, not sure why there was such a change in her demeanor. The elevator doors opened, and she stepped inside. She continued to smile as the doors dinged shut again.

"Oh, you poor, innocent summer child," Courtney said. If punching a man and breaking his fingers wasn't enough to get her blood pumping, nothing else would.

CHAPTER TWENTY-TWO

I gor looked around the base. A host of people moved about despite the late—or maybe in this case, early—hour. The man who provided escort didn't seem concerned by the number. Igor assumed this was regular activity around there. It was a military installation, after all, and they adhered to all kinds of silly protocols like getting up early.

The escort hadn't made an ass of himself. He wasn't especially friendly either, but then they weren't really expected to be. There had to be some kind of overlap into asshole, it could be assumed, but he showed no signs of it. He remained the ultimate professional, even though he effectively led a man to his death.

The guard pushed Igor into one of the six-wheeled all-terrain vehicles and made sure to lock her in the back seat before he moved to the front. The vehicle rumbled to life and they pulled away from the base. The small round windows gave her a limited view as it slipped slowly into the distance to be replaced by the massive and apparently still growing expanse of the Zoo that moved steadily closer.

She gulped. The ZooTube videos had to be fakes, but there was a small chance that the reason there was this much armor between her and it was because there was something out there that wanted her for a snack. As much as she slipped into the mantra that it couldn't be as bad as it seemed, the nagging feeling remained as the ATV slipped in under the heavy tree cover. Maybe, just maybe, this one time it was so much worse.

She felt a buzz inside her sealed suit and pulled out a comm device with trembling fingers. She glanced at her captor before she attached it to her ear.

"We're in deep enough that we don't have to continue the charade," her guard stated through the commlink. "You can come up to the front if you'd like."

"Thanks," she replied and looked quickly away from the Zoo that was barely one pane of twenty-centimeter bullet-proof glass away. "But I think I'll stay here."

"Understood," he replied. "You can take the chains off, though, Anja."

That was something she was willing to do, and she tugged at the manacles around her wrists and ankles until they came free. They had to stand up under quick inspection, even if they'd not encountered any difficulties, so they couldn't simply be left unlocked.

Anja took a deep breath and scowled at the smells that seemed like they had been trapped in this confined vehicle forever. Like it had rolled out of the factory in Vladivostok already smelling like sweat and engine grease.

She gripped her seatbelt tightly and realized that the

only lights illuminating the cabin were those from the dashboard and the HUD on the vehicle's windshield, which she assumed was also thick and bulletproof. The ride was rather bumpy but not as bad she imagined it might be, all things considered, and she was only slightly sore and aching by the time they came to a halt.

The driver put the vehicle in park. He unbuckled himself and climbed through the porthole that connected the driver's section and the passenger section. It was meant to be sealed off, she realized, and would have been if she were an actual prisoner.

"You shouldn't have to wait too long," he explained as he dragged a pack from under the seats. "But in case the people who are supposed to pick you up are delayed for some reason, this holds food and other necessities. They should last you for a couple of days—longer if you pace yourself. I'll seal the place off, and this part of the vehicle is built to withstand an RPG hit, so you should be safe. That said…" He retrieved a heavy pistol from the pack and put it in her hands. "Here's the safety. You need to click it off and pull this back to chamber a round. It has eight rounds, and if things get bad… I hate to say it, but you might want to save the last round for yourself. It's up to you."

Anja nodded and her eyes widened as she stared at the pistol like it would bite her. She'd never held a weapon before, and if all had gone well, she would have preferred to keep that record intact. Even so, she was willing to part with morals if it meant she could get out of this situation alive. It was hypocritical, she knew that, but at least she would be alive to feel guilty about it later.

"Thank you, Andrej," she said softly, wound her arms around his neck, and hugged him. "For all of this."

"We're family," he said with a smile. "It was the least I could do."

"Could you tell Grandmother that I'm alive and all right?" she asked and struggled to hold back the tears.

"I will," he replied and his voice was oddly raspy with suppressed emotion. "It's up to you to not make a liar of me, hmm?"

"I'll do my best." He nodded, not in the mood to talk anymore.

With a final wave, he pushed through the porthole and sealed it. A heavy clunk sounded as the front disengaged from the back and an iron rod dropped to keep the remaining section of the ATV propped up. The part with the engine roared off into the darkness. She thought for a moment that it was night but knew it was daytime. The darkness of the jungle was what made it seem like night.

That same darkness soaked into her very soul, with only a flashlight for company. She wasn't even sure it was safe to use out there.

"*Cyka blyat*," Anja muttered softly and leaned back in her seat. She never thought she'd miss the dull growl of a diesel engine, but right now, it beat the hell out of the deafening silence that slowly surrounded her.

Courtney raised her head from the papers she'd been studying. She wasn't even sure what time it was or what day it was. It was hard to tell in the basement.

This wasn't really out of character for her. She tended to get intensely involved when she studied something she was interested in, to the point where sleep and food became a secondary consideration. It was what had earned her top grades in all her schools, but there were also problems that came with it.

Problems that had mostly dissipated during her time with Heavy Metal. It was good to know she was in a regression stage of her life.

She still wasn't sure why she had decided to look through her dad's notes. The book she'd written for him was almost finished and she would now maybe publish it with a little blurb dedicating it to him.

There hadn't been enough pills in the world to deal with the guilt she felt, although Dr. Pierce, the psychiatrist her parents had sent her to when they were considering a divorce, would have told her that what she was doing was classic survivor's guilt. Outliving your parents was something kids would have to face eventually, but finding out that a man she'd initially had been terrified of and spent most of her life trying to impress felt outshined by her? It was so much to take in.

So what was she doing down there? She'd rationalized it as the need to compare notes and make sure that nothing she'd written conflicted with anything he'd published. Although she'd found a couple of discrepancies, they could be easily explained by how quickly the Zoo evolved past the knowledge of the people who didn't engage with it on a daily basis. What he had noted was a couple of months out of date, but that was to be expected these days.

Her head whipped around when she heard the doorbell

ring. Not for the first time either, she realized. She'd had a power nap over the papers and wondered if there was any coffee left in the house when the doorbell rang the first time. A little bemused, she looked around and tried to think of who might be calling at...well, eight at night. She hadn't exactly isolated herself from everyone, but at the same time, what friends she'd once had were currently busy elsewhere in the world. That meant there shouldn't be anyone trying to get her out of the den after business hours.

She moved to the kitchen, where there was a screen connected to a camera on the front door. A car with a pizza restaurant's logo on the side idled out front and a young-ish kid stood on the porch, grumbling something the microphone didn't pick up.

He looked around and clutched the thermal bag more firmly as the camera above the door finally swiveled to focus on him.

"Sorry, I didn't order a pizza," a woman's voice said over the speaker.

"Hey, I have a large, extra pepperoni with cheese crust," he said and checked his phone. "And this is the address. Are you seriously going to leave me hanging here?"

"Look, maybe it's for the people across the street," said the voice. "They said they were having a party there."

"On a Monday night?" He sounded incredulous.

"It's Monday?" the voice asked and sounded both shocked and disappointed. "Anyway, it doesn't matter. I didn't order anything. There must be some error with your online ordering service or something. Sorry."

"What? Are you kidding me?" he asked, but there was no response. He shook his head. Normally, he would have put something into her food as payback like he often did for bitch customers. But given that she obviously wouldn't eat anything, it wouldn't work and he would simply have to eat it himself instead.

Well, at least this trip wasn't a total loss, he thought as he trudged to the annoying little electric car the pizza place insisted he drive. With the extra money he made on this trip, he could afford to have the pizza for himself. He pulled out onto the road and made his way slowly about a block down to a black van with the logo of an exterminator company on it.

As he pulled in close, the window of the driver's side rolled down to reveal a man with a beard and bright green coveralls.

"So?" he asked. He could see another man in identical coveralls in the driver's seat. They both looked incredibly uncomfortable in the attire which did little to hide the kind of bulk that meant they probably weren't exterminators. He didn't really care, though. There wasn't much he wasn't willing to do for the amount of money they paid him.

"Yeah, she's home," the delivery boy told them. "Not in the best of moods, but she's there."

The man didn't say anything but instead, handed the kid a roll of bills, which he took quickly and eagerly. He didn't even bother to count it.

"Hey, do you guys want this pizza?" he asked, feeling a little guilty that he would have it all to himself.

The two men glared at him and seemed annoyed by the question.

"Got it!" he called, rolled his own window up, and pulled away. Who would have thought it? The two creepy stalker guys weren't in the best mood either.

Courtney hung the speaker up as the pizza boy left. He'd clearly been very unhappy that he hadn't been paid either for the pizza or what he'd probably hoped would be a very hefty tip. She felt a little bad for him, but the mild regret was rapidly overtaken by a very real sense of dread as she moved away from the screen and headed to her father's study.

News had recently come to her that other parties were very interested in what she would do with her father's estate, and a slight sense of paranoia had crept in with it. While she assumed it would entail innumerable discussions with lawyers to get it all out there, a part of her suspected there would be attempts at foul play.

She was sure someone would tell her she was paranoid and to knock it off. Maybe they'd be right, too. But if her time in the Zoo had taught her anything, it was that if things seemed to go a little too well, it was time to check the branches. There wasn't always something lurking there, but the number of times there had been made her always trust this feeling in her gut.

The same feeling that now demanded her full concentration.

Her heart thudded a little faster as she moved into the

den and examined the various shelves and pieces of furniture. She knew her dad had installed various panic rooms and the paperwork had indicated that one had been in his study. Now was as good a time as any to check it and make sure it was all up to code or whatever.

She finally found a loose lamp hanging from the wall and twisted it gently to the side. A click sounded from the other side of the room behind her dad's desk where she'd worked for most of the…well, weekend, she supposed.

Her instinct spurred her toward the hidden door that had revealed itself, but she stopped short when she saw a keypad and a hand scanner. She didn't know the password and her dad probably wouldn't have been able to get her biometrical handprint anyway. It didn't really matter, fortunately, since the heavy safe door was already open. It had probably been left that way in case he wanted to get in when time was of the essence.

She stepped inside and looked around. The space had been equipped with the necessities. Apparently, her father had expected to spend considerable time in there since all kinds of dried and canned goods were stacked on the shelves. A small bed was built into the back of the room and a fully stocked wet bar stood in the corner near a bathroom. Courtney remembered reading that it had been installed with its own independent water and power supply.

All thoughts that her father was a prepper quickly disappeared when she reached a desk with three screens, all awash with live feeds to various cameras around the house.

Huh. It looks like ol' Pops was more than a little paranoid

247

too. Well, were you actually paranoid when there really was someone out to get you?

Which, as it turned out, there was. The cameras that overlooked the back door revealed a couple of men in full tactical gear. One tried to unlock it and one worked on the alarm system, while another two snuck in through the flower beds and attempted to jimmy one of the windows open on the side of the house.

She would be cleaning the mud from their tracks out of the carpet for days, she realized. The sprinklers had only now switched off.

Courtney wasn't sure what she was supposed to look for if she wanted to identify a professional, but they were certainly equipped like she imagined they would be. Sub machine-guns hung from their shoulders, and sidearms and Kevlar vests told her that whoever had sent them was exceptionally well equipped for this kind of situation.

Panic was an immediate response, but she pushed it aside, shook her head, and snatched up the landline phone beside the screens. She knew for a fact that the hideaway was a signal dead zone intentionally created by the lining of the walls around her. Her cellphone would be useless down there.

This was probably the simplest call she would ever have to make. She punched the three digits in quickly and waited for it to ring through.

"Nine-one-one, what's your emergency?" A soft woman's voice answered.

"Hi," Courtney replied and tried to keep her tone calm and civil. "My house has been invaded by four men. All heavily armed, all dressed in black. I can see them from my panic room. I think you can tell my address from my call, so if you could send police, I'd really appreciate it."

There was a pause on the line, which Courtney hoped was because the woman checked for her address on her side.

"You said you're in a panic room, is that correct, ma'am?" the woman said after a few seconds' pause.

"That's right," she replied.

"Please lock yourself in there, and if you can, stay on the line for as long as possible," the controller instructed. "We have a couple of vehicles in the area, and they should get there in a few minutes."

Courtney nodded, placed the handset on the desk, and moved to the door of the panic room. She pulled it shut and locked it, then moved around the room and looked into one of the cabinets on the right. The contents brought a grin to her face. A couple of suits of light armor lay inside, as well as some of the usual self-defense apparatus that could be found in a place with strict gun laws like California—pepper spray, a baton, and even a baseball bat.

It didn't look like the armor would fit her, though. It had been made for her father, and while they were similar in almost every respect, he had lacked what she had in her bust area.

"That's some sexual discrimination right there," she muttered.

"Ma'am, are you still there?" she heard the operator ask from her phone. She moved to the still open line and picked it up.

"I'm here, but I'll hang up now," Courtney said, not sure where the eerie calm that entered her voice had come from. "Please let the officers know they can come directly into the house when they get here."

She hung up before she received a response and hurried to the cabinet. What the hell had her father been preparing for with this? It went beyond the common garden variety paranoia. Were these the same people he had prepared for, and if so, did that mean there was the possibility that his death hadn't been from natural causes?

Not now, Courtney. She drew in a ragged breath and rolled her neck to ease the tension before she readied herself. There was no way she would stay in there and wait for either the police or the gunmen to find her. She was better than that now.

CHAPTER TWENTY-THREE

Anja peered out the small window and tried to make something out—anything would do at this point. She wasn't sure of the time and was too scared to look at the watch on her wrist. Whether she was afraid it would tell her that days or hours had passed, she wasn't sure, but one thing was certain. She wasn't sure how long she would last in there.

Normally, she would have been more comfortable in closed, tight spaces than vast, open ones. She wasn't sure if it was possible to develop claustrophobia or if it was something you were born with. In her present circumstances, she could swear she could feel it grow in her little by little with every second that passed while she remained enclosed in this metal coffin on wheels.

The first couple of hours had gone by in constant worry about her cousin. She had tortured herself with speculation about what kind of trouble he would be in for losing a prisoner and half a vehicle in the Zoo. Then she'd remembered that his supposed purpose was to leave her there to die, their own twisted manner of execution. And, since the jungle was reputedly full of monsters that were able to tear shit up, the missing piece of the ATV would probably be easily blamed on one of them. She doubted he would need to come up with a better excuse or even that he would need to put on too much of a show.

Her eyes opened—which made her realize that she'd closed them in the first place—when the vehicle jolted with some kind of impact. She hated to remind herself that it was only the back of the vehicle because it increased the sense of vulnerability.

On to more important questions. Had she fallen asleep? Was that even possible?

What had made the vehicle move?

She shifted closer to the window and tried desperately to see something other than her breath fogging the glass. There wasn't anything out there. For a moment, there wasn't even any movement—until there was.

Not movement, not really. It was weird that it took this long for her eyes to adjust to the darkness, but as she looked into the Zoo, tiny little pin-pricks of light drew her attention. Blue light gleamed impossibly in the darkness. It was hard to make out exactly what it was. Maybe she simply had a problem with her contacts, or maybe she had finally gone crazy. There really wasn't anything that shone the light, not that she could see, and it was so tiny that she couldn't make out what it was at all.

Anja froze when something moved and a shape blocked out the small lights. It drew closer and nudged the vehicle again. A low growl prickled the hairs on the back of her neck and more lights appeared. In a second, a line of blue lights moved and sidled around the back of the ATV she was trapped in.

It was beautiful, she realized. Like she was out in space and the stars had drifted close to her.

Suddenly, two lights came up to the window, bright enough that there was a reflection on the glass. They vanished and appeared again, one after the other.

It took her longer than she wanted to admit to realize that they were eyes. Only when a row of teeth gleamed with that same beautiful blue glow did she realize that they were part of something that was very big and quite probably very, very hungry.

"Oh, fuck." She gasped and stood instinctively as the teeth lashed toward her. They hammered hard into the ATV and she stumbled back into the seat from the force of the blow. The whole vehicle rocked. With another roar, the monster attacked again and the ATV shook and shuddered. This time, it didn't stabilize but tilted over and groaned loudly before it fell on its side.

Massive claws scratched at the outside and her skin crawled as she curled up and covered her mouth to suppress her scream. She didn't want to cry, but hot tears already tracked down her cheeks and she whimpered. Chills raced down her spine as the eyes returned to the window and flicked from right to left.

"Shit...shit...shit...shit," she whimpered into her hand between deep, ragged breaths as if the air had suddenly been sucked out of the cabin and she couldn't get enough into her lungs.

Where were the people who were supposed to pick her up?

"What's taking you so long with that fucking lock?" Al snarled when he returned after successfully deactivating the alarm. "I've had time to cut the alarms and the landlines and you're still tinkering with the back fucking door. What the hell is wrong with you?"

"This is a delicate process, you moron," Kelson protested and remained focused on his work.

"It's the back door to some rich woman's house," his partner said with a chuckle.

"Wrong," Kelson said and smiled when he heard his picks find the right tumbler. He twisted and pried the door open. "This was the house of a very paranoid security freak."

"How do you know?"

"No one installs a three-thousand-dollar pin lock on their back door unless they are really terrified of who might use it without a key." He pulled the door open slowly. "That is unless they're really paranoid."

"Are you really paranoid if there's actually someone out to get you?" Al asked. He hefted his gun and grinned behind his mask. "Someone being us, in this case."

"Shut up," Kelson admonished him as they slipped into the house. "We're supposed to be in and out without making a mess. The cops need to think it was an accident."

"Do you seriously believe we need four people for that?"

"I assume the client doesn't want anything to be left to chance," he responded, his tone curt. He'd helped to run a job in this house a couple of months before which sent an old man to his death a little faster than nature wanted. Everything had gone according to plan that time and he'd only had a security specialist with him. He wasn't sure why the client had switched it up to four this time. The target was younger and had some combat experience, though, and would thus probably be more difficult to put down.

Still. Four seemed like overkill at this point.

He froze when the power was suddenly cut to the rest of the building. His nerves taut, he looked around and blinked quickly to force his eyes to adjust to the blackness that had blanketed them.

"Good evening, gentlemen," a young woman's voice said from the loudspeakers on the walls.

Al looked at him as the second team moved forward hurriedly to coordinate with them.

"There are four of you," the voice said softly like she whispered into the microphone, "and one of me. We can play hide and seek but only if you hide. I'm not my father, you sons of bitches."

"Oh...not good," Kelson stated and adjusted his grip on his weapon. It was one thing to clamp down on an old man's mouth and nose until he died. But it was another thing entirely to make a kill on someone who knew they were coming and seemed determined to put up a fight.

"We have four minutes until the cops get here," she continued and even seemed a little excited. "Let's see how long we can play."

"Well, there's something seriously wrong with this bitch's head," Al muttered. One look revealed that he was as uncomfortable with this as his partner was.

"It doesn't matter," Kelson whispered. "We're on a

timetable. We need to find and kill her before the cops get here. Let's go hunting."

If she thought they would simply run and hide because a crazy rich lady wanted to play mind games, she would be sorely disappointed. He made a quick gesture to the other two and directed them to stick together and take the second floor while he and Al would cover the first. They nodded and made a beeline for the stairs.

Courtney had spent literal days poring over all the records of the money her dad had put into converting the house—secret stairways, hidden passages, and more panic rooms, one for each floor. The one in the basement seemed to be the master room, but her dad apparently didn't want to risk having to go all the way down should something like this happen.

That and he wanted to leave a way open for himself to go down there should the situation call for it.

All of which worked out rather well for her. She wouldn't hide in a room while there were men in her father's house. No way in hell would she give them that satisfaction. She had made her mind up not to be the prey anymore. For once, she was the huntress.

She found the staircase that brought her to the second floor without having to openly follow the two men who had gone up there. As she climbed the stairs quietly, she wondered if the cops would give her enough time to play with the home invaders. If they wanted to complain about what she was doing, she would make sure they had a nice long conversation with her lawyer about personal property.

When she reached the second floor, the walls were thin enough that she could hear the men's footsteps as they moved through the living room which had been styled as some kind of oriental peace garden or something. She pushed the secret door open and took a breath as it moved without a sound. The coast was clear, so she stepped out, closed it again, and kept to the shadows behind the two men who tramped across the polished oak floor.

Courtney gripped her baton firmly in her hands as she snuck in behind them. Her bare feet moved silently, unlike the racket their combat boots made on the timber.

The first man screamed when she hammered the baton across his knee. A soft crunch confirmed there were broken bones and torn soft tissue as he dropped and gave her the perfect opening to slam the baton across his jaw. She leapt over him and closed quickly on the second goon.

He had only half-turned to try to find his comrade in the darkness when she took hold of the barrel of his gun and brought the baton down hard on his wrist. Another crunch was followed by a satisfying scream and he stumbled and almost fell over his partner. She reversed her strike quickly to drive the steel pole firmly against the man's temple. The scream cut off abruptly and he dropped without a sound.

Courtney disarmed the two unconscious men hastily, kept one of the guns for herself, and tucked the rest behind the door of the secret staircase. She moved to the intercom system and keyed the microphone.

"Two down, two more to go, with two minutes and

twenty seconds left," she whispered, unable to keep a grin from her lips. "And now I have a pistol. Ho, ho, ho."

He should have been excited by this. They were supposed to respond to every call like it was a life or death situation.

Still, they got prank calls from this neighborhood all the time, so even though they weaved through the heavy traffic in LA on a Monday night with sirens blaring and lights flashing, it was all Officer Williams could do not to yawn.

"Come on," Officer Keno admonished but without aggression. "You could at least act a little more interested."

Williams looked at the younger man. Six months out of the academy meant the guy had already begun to struggle with his sense of identity in the force. He still believed he could make a difference, but he had been knocked down a few times by the red tape involved and the hordes of rich pricks and their complaints. Every now and then, he had second thoughts about his choice of career.

"Yeah, about that," Williams said as he steered the patrol car onto the sidewalk to get around a red light. "This isn't the first time we've been called to this address. The other two times were merely an old man off his meds. Sure, the guy died, but lung cancer does that. And now, his daughter moves in and two weeks later, we get another home invasion call to the same house? It's hard not to think that this is merely another wild goose chase."

"Have you always been so cynical?" Keno asked with genuine curiosity.

"Hell no," he exclaimed and grunted as the squad car lurched onto the road and picked up speed. "You have to work hard to be as cynical as I am. And if you plug away and keep your nose to the grindstone, maybe one day, you'll get here too."

"You should write inspirational speeches," his partner said with a sarcastic chuckle.

"It can't be a worse paying job than the one I have now," he said airily. His eyes turned to the road. He would make his best attempt to reach that fucking house as quickly as possible. That was what he was paid to do but damned if he would take it seriously. The DA wouldn't ever press charges on something like this, but it was nice to know he could wave that story around to make sure she never clogged the emergency lines like that again.

"Like father, like daughter," he grumbled under his breath.

CHAPTER TWENTY-FOUR

Courtney slipped into the hidden staircase, careful to be as quiet as possible. While she was definitely a predator there, she wasn't the only one around. She held her pistol firmly and tucked the baton into her belt before she ventured down the stairwell. The second team would be on the first floor, but she wasn't sure exactly where. It was a difficult choice to make. Logic told her to use the surveillance system, but she wouldn't have time to locate them on the cameras and deal with them before the cops arrived. She would need to take some chances.

They had come into her father's house with the sole intention to eliminate her. Before she'd gone into the Zoo, she would probably have followed the emergency operator's advice, locked the panic room, and remained there until the cops arrived. Sal and Madigan had helped to transform her into something better, but out in the world without them, she wasn't sure if better didn't actually mean much more dangerous. Humans weren't Zoo creatures, after all.

She moved quickly and silently to the entrance that would lead her into the first floor. A trickle of sweat traced down her spine and she dragged in a deep breath as she opened the door. Like the one upstairs, it made no sound and swung open smoothly. She stepped out and constantly checked her flanks while she moved swiftly over the stone floor, soundless with her bare feet.

The tramp of boots on the floor caught her attention and she turned, tense but ready, and flattened against the wall to peer into the shadows.

Two men moved toward the stairs, the shape of their readied weapons barely visible in the near darkness. They were professionals, she mused, but not the best. They should have anticipated that since they hunted someone who was familiar with the territory, she would know the layout better than they did.

There was the possibility that her decision to come out and fight had knocked them off balance, which would make this more complicated than what they had signed up for. She didn't think that was very likely, although the possibility made her smile.

They eased up the stairs and whispered urgently. She couldn't make out what they said but waited a few seconds before she hurried in pursuit.

Kelson looked furtively around once they reached the second-floor landing. He scanned the area to make sure no one lurked in any crevices or blind spots as Al moved forward. It wasn't the smoothest of coordinated room sweeps, especially with no lights to aid them, but it wasn't bad given that it was the first time they had worked together.

"Holy shit," his partner said and moved forward a couple of steps after his initial hesitation. Kelson froze and squinted to see what had disturbed the man, his senses on high alert. Unfortunately, it didn't take him long before he made out two bulky, motionless figures on the ground. He didn't need to check to know they were his boys. Well, on this job at least.

He cast another careful glance around the shadows before he approached the two men and dropped to one knee to check if they were still alive. The first was, although for the life of him, he couldn't remember the man's name. He looked at Al, who checked their second accomplice. His partner glanced at him and shook his head.

"Holy fuck, she wasn't joking," the man exclaimed in a low tone as they stood and shifted their weapons into a ready position once more. "They're missing their weapons too."

"That's not the worst of it," Kelson said. He inclined his head toward the window, through which headlights and red and blue flashes could be seen. "Let's grab them and get out. We can regroup and—"

His words were cut off when the flashing lights gave him a view of a silhouette that moved in from behind them. He thought he'd imagined it out the corner of his eye for a second, but as he turned, it stepped directly into his path.

"Too late," the figure snapped in a feminine voice. The

arm raised and a swift flash and loud bang followed quickly. Something struck Kelson in the stomach and the sudden pain forced the breath out of him. He stumbled back before his foot caught on a rug and he catapulted hard onto his back.

His ears rang but he heard the second shot a split second before a body hit the deck. Al, he assumed, since the figure still stood motionless before them and there hadn't been any of the tell-tale buzz of the sub-machine gun. The shadow moved to where Al had fallen and with a calm, deliberate movement, pulled the trigger again. Kelson flinched when she fired another two shots. She had made sure that the other two were dead before she turned her attention to him.

He tried to lift his gun, but it had somehow become too heavy and slipped from his fingers every time. His brain registered that his body armor had done nothing to stop the single round to his stomach. He wondered briefly what the hell kind of cut-rate Kevlar they'd fitted him with before he remembered that their weapons—which was what she carried, he assumed—had been fitted with armor-piercing rounds. They were designed to shred Kevlar with ease.

"Shit," Kelson said and gave up on his attempt to aim his weapon. Instead, he focused on the need to apply pressure to his wound. There wasn't much else he could do except try to save his life.

The figure crouched beside him. People shouted outside—the police presumably tried to get in while they called for backup after hearing the gunshots.

"That's the thing about the Zoo," she said and patted his

chest lightly. Even that barely-there touch still made him groan in pain. "It changes a person. It conditions you to be ready to fight whatever and whenever. That means you are either my teammate or part of the Zoo."

Kelson looked into her eyes. This close, they were illuminated only by the flashing lights outside, but he saw enough to urge caution. He might still have tried to make her see the error of her ways but the effort to speak alone would be too painful to contemplate and he decided against it. Persuasion wouldn't do much at this point, anyway, he consoled himself. She was as nutty as the shit someone took after eating fruitcake.

"And my teammates are in the Sahara," she stated coldly as she pressed the gun to his forehead and pulled the trigger.

Courtney pushed to her feet and rubbed the side of her head. One tended to forget how loud gunfire was when it was always heard through the suit filters. She hadn't had that luxury this time around and her ears would probably continue to ring for a while.

Footsteps thudded on the front porch—most likely the cops, she reasoned. They wouldn't know that the other door had already been opened. She rolled her eyes and wondered if she should go downstairs to the front door, then decided against it.

"That should give these fuckers a new attitude," she said gleefully.

"Repeat—shots fired, shots fired," Williams called over the radio. His own .38 was drawn but he maintained his distance from the house. Keno, to his credit, tried to gain entry, but given the kind of security the old man had put in before he died, the kid was likely to break a few bones before could actually break through the door.

"Squad three-four-seven-six, responding to a ten-sixty-two reporting shots fired," Williams shouted into the radio again. There had been some seven or eight shots—or maybe more—since they'd pulled up in front of the house, but it had been quiet since then. That generally didn't bode well for the people inside. If there was still someone alive in there, they would have tried to get out and access police help. The perps should try to escape too.

No sound meant everyone was probably dead or down. He didn't intend to risk it, though, not without backup. The reality was that he wasn't paid enough to risk his life in these situations.

Keno didn't seem to think so, but he had now taken a break from his failed attempts to kick the door open. He panted and scowled at his partner as he threw his hands in the air in a what-are-you-waiting-for gesture.

Williams opened his mouth to make a snarky comment about what the kid was trying to do but he was cut off when an engine roared into life nearby. It was loud and rumbled closer, and blinding headlights swept the officer and the vehicle as what looked like a van barreled down the street. He circled quickly behind the squad car and held both his gun and the radio as he focused on the vehicle.

It screeched to a halt across the driveway of the house and a man scrambled from the passenger side, a pistol in hand. Williams ducked behind his car and dropped the radio but readied his gun as he took cover. He wasn't sure what the fuck was going on—or even if he wanted to know —but as of right now, someone seemed about to shoot police officers. If that didn't spur the rest of the force to hurtle down there with all kinds of hellfire, he didn't know what would.

The stranger glanced at the patrol car but despite the officer's original misgivings, didn't seem at all interested in either of them. Williams still crouched behind the car and Keno had dived behind some bushes, but both were reasonably easy targets. Instead, the intruder focused on the house as he shouted into a radio for someone— presumably someone inside—to answer.

The entire situation seemed like something from a bad movie. Williams wanted to act but couldn't be certain that the man was, in fact, on the wrong side. He could challenge him, of course, but his natural instinct for survival persuaded him to reconsider. Reinforcements were no doubt on the way, and he had a better chance to get out of this in one piece if he simply waited for the bizarre scenario to unfold.

An answer to the man's repeated shouts finally came, but it was clearly not the one he had hoped for. One of the second-floor windows flung open and the shadowed man immediately directed a few shots at the woman who was now framed in the aperture. She yelled something indistinguishable and returned fire. The stranger hesitated, obviously surprised that she was still alive, and wasted valuable seconds he could have used to escape. He fell with a grunt of pain and blood soaked into the manicured lawn.

More shooting erupted, this time from the van as the driver tried to return fire. The woman ducked below the window ledge but only for a second. Her shadowed outline was barely visible against the far edge of the window frame where she sought cover behind the wall while she extended her hand out the aperture and resumed firing. The van skidded into motion and raced away.

"Fuck!" The woman leaned out the window to shout at the police officers. "There went my intel, you useless bitches. I don't suppose either of you got the guy's plate?"

Williams stared at her. If she had made the call to nine-one-one, she wasn't what he'd expected at all.

"Wait. Is that dumbass still alive?" she asked and indicated the man who lay face down on the lawn. The policeman glanced at the body and when he looked at the window once more, she had gone.

"What...the actual shit?" Keno exclaimed as he straightened from behind the bushes, covered in dirt and mud.

CHAPTER TWENTY-FIVE

Anja gritted her teeth. She wasn't sure how long it had been since she'd been left there. It could have been a day or it could have been more, but with no apparent change in the unending fucking darkness out there, it could also have been years. The creature with the glowing dots on its skin and the vicious row of teeth had left a while before, but she still couldn't shake the feeling that she was far from alone.

The APV was on its side, but its structure ensured that it retained its shape no matter which side was up. Still, that really wasn't her chief worry. It was more than a little uncomfortable since all the seats were designed to be used with the vehicle on its wheels, but she was more than happy to remain on her back and look at the window. Some light filtered through the dense, shadowed canopy she could see, but it was little more than tiny pinpricks that provide almost no illumination. If she didn't know better, she would have thought she was looking at the stars.

The ground under her shuddered for a second and

drew her attention back to the moment. She scrambled around, hesitant to use the flashlight unless she absolutely had no choice. There was no way to know how long the batteries would last, and she preferred to believe she still had something in reserve if things truly went bad. The light itself wouldn't save her, but it might help her to save herself—or, at least, make her feel better.

She finally located the pistol Andrej had given her and held it tightly as she aimed it toward the window. Logic told her that any attempt to shoot anything from in there would, at best, break the environmental seal that currently protected her from whatever was out there. At worst, the bullet would strike the armored shell and ricochet. In that case, it was more than probable that it would skewer her a few times before it ended up buried in one of the seats.

That, plus the fact that the gun's safety was still on. Even with her limited knowledge of firearms, she knew that was a dumbass move. She shook her head.

"Stupid, idiot girl," she admonished herself and thought about it for a few seconds before she flicked the safety off. After a moment, she clicked it on again and placed the weapon down beside her, then lay back. She didn't want the damn thing to go off accidentally, but she wanted it close. So far, none of the beasties that had snooped around the overturned ATV had been able to find a way in but she couldn't assume it was strong enough to hold up against everything in the Zoo. She didn't want to be one of those people whose assumptions finally killed them.

Claws scrabbled shrilly for purchase on the sides and she jerked to a seated position again. She'd spent most of the first couple of hours in this armored bubble trying not to sob too loudly but now, she felt like she was all cried out. She'd survived a death sentence from the mother-fucking FSB at home and, while that was a completely different challenge from what she faced now, she would make it out of this. She would survive—thrive even. She wouldn't make a liar of her cousin.

She took a deep breath and held the gun tightly with both hands. Caution kept her finger off the trigger but she nevertheless clicked the safety as she drew a deep breath.

"Get a grip on yourself, Anja," she whispered, nodded, and steeled herself when she saw a hint of movement over the window. "You've got this."

Sal snarled his discontent and shook his head to wake himself as he pulled his armor on. He'd spent more time in the Zoo these days than out, and he now felt more than a little fatigued by even the thought of going in there again. Still, it was something he had to do. He'd signed up for this mission for more reasons than only the money they would receive, but he couldn't help another grumble of annoyance as he looked at the wide expanse of green out there.

"Well, you look like shit," Kennedy commented from behind him. She was already halfway into her suit and now tested the pieces of leg armor she'd had trouble with before.

"And you look...damn good," he responded and raised an eyebrow.

She grinned in response. "Why, thank you. I do try to moisturize."

"No…well, yeah, that too, but how come you don't look like you've spent half the night driving through the desert?" he asked. He dragged his power armor on and connected it to his helmet. The power functions came online with a satisfying blip.

"Well, there's this magical potion that was unlocked by the ancients," she explained sagely. "It's made when you burn a bean, grind it, and boil it in hot water." She paused for a moment and searched his unamused expression. "Coffee. I got some coffee."

"I don't suppose you got enough to share?" Sal asked and managed a hopeful grin.

"I needed all of it," Kennedy replied unapologetically. "Besides, what would you prefer—having your own and feeling slightly less miserable with me in a bad mood, or having none with me in a better mood?"

"Don't even talk to me right now," he muttered as he shifted the various parts of his body to ease the armor into a more comfortable fit and slipped his helmet under his arm.

"Seriously?" she asked and stepped beside him as he headed out to where a small van waited, ready to roll out.

He smirked. "I don't think you'd be able to stand me in a bad mood. No offense, of course, but I think anyone would have trouble with that. And without coffee to help, I might realistically be in a bad mood all friggin' day long."

"Heaven spare me from your wrath—ow!" She jumped as he punched her in the shoulder with his power arm hard enough that she stumbled a couple of steps to the side.

"You watch it, missy," he said and pointed a finger at her. "I may put you over my knee."

"And I may let you," she retorted with a wink. The conversation ceased when they moved into earshot of the Russian group that appeared to be all ready to leave and only waited for the two of them.

"Jacobs! Kennedy!" someone called from the back of the convoy. They turned as a familiar figure strode toward them with a broad grin. "Where is Dr. Monroe?"

"She needed to take some personal time, unfortunately," Sal said. He gripped the Russian's hand. "Nice to see you alive and well, Gregor."

Kennedy shook his hand and managed to fend off his attempt at a hug. It would have been awkward with that much armor between them.

One of the men in full power armor approached them. They could see little of him except the clean-cut blond hair and muscle-heavy features. It was hard to say how much height was added by the armor itself, but he appeared to be a solid foot taller than Sal.

Even so, he had a professional look to him as he shook their hands, first Sal's and then Kennedy's.

"I am Master Sergeant Volkov." He introduced himself in good English with a heavy accent.

"I'm Salinger Jacobs and this is my partner Madigan Kennedy. Thanks for thinking of us for this mission."

"Of course," Volkov said with a stern nod. "I was told that there would be three members from your company?"

"Our specialist had some family issues that called her back to the US," Sal explained. "I'll take over in that capacity myself. I hope that's not an issue."

"Of course not," the master sergeant said with a small, professional smile. "You come highly recommended by those who tell me the two of you are some of the most experienced in what the Zoo has to offer. We are glad to have you on our side. Regarding scientists—or as you say, specialists—we have two with us, so maybe you won't be needed in that respect, not for the most part. We have been called in for a job regarding one of our other teams. Most were killed but one managed to bring out footage of a beast we have not seen before."

Sal looked at a file that had been transmitted to his HUD. He opened it and watched a couple of videos of a fight between men in the rustic Russian power armor and something long and winding. The carapace shield that covered it told Sal that the body itself would most definitely be smaller than the outward size. Large jaws lunged in attack and broke through armor, but more importantly, Sal thought, the hundreds of legs all seemed to be tipped with venom like a centipede's.

Interestingly enough, though, it seemed that these men had stumbled on what looked like a nest filled with insectoid eggs, perfectly spherical and mostly white, and all larger than an ostrich's egg.

"Well, that'll haunt my nightmares for a while," Kennedy muttered. "Thanks for that."

"You are welcome," Volkov said, although whether he returned her sarcasm or not was difficult to tell. "It will be our duty to find that nest and, if possible, recover the eggs and maybe some parts from the mama nightmare for study."

"Have you guys named it yet?" Sal asked. "Something like that needs a cool villain name. Something like a... killerpillar?"

Volkov smirked. "Nyet, this was done by John Ringo and David Weber. We love their books. We call these ones *ubiytsa gusenits.*"

"Yeah, I won't even try to pronounce that," Sal said and shook his head firmly. "But anyway, how do you plan to track the nest?"

"Many dead men were left in the area, as you can see from the video," the Russian responded. "We know there is a possibility that the *ubiytsa* has moved since the attack two days ago, but it is a place to begin our search."

"So, we track the nightmare factory down," Sal said.

"Is this a problem?"

"Not really," Kennedy said. "It's not like it's the first time we've gone in there to hunt something big and nasty. We simply like to complain about it. Is everyone ready to go?"

Volkov nodded and hefted his weapon. "We waited only for you two before heading out."

"Fantastic," she said cheerfully. "Let's get the hell out of here and into some hell ourselves."

They boarded the APVs and the entire team checked their weapons and equipment in preparation for the trip into the Zoo. Sal was a fan of not having to walk all the way into the jungle. The Russians had developed their APVs for travel inside, which meant what would normally have taken a day or two could be traversed in a couple of hours. It was a pity they hadn't had Gutierrez in on this one. She would have been able to isolate what made these vehicles so much sturdier than those they had at the US base that usually fell apart after a couple of klicks into the damn jungle.

They drove through the rough terrain for a couple of

hours and their surroundings grew steadily darker the deeper they went. When they finally halted, Gregor and Volkov exchanged a concerned and muted conversation in Russian. The GPS signal was picked up as soon as they were in range and they followed it to the designated location. Oddly enough, there were no bodies, no nests, and no killerpillars.

Sal had decided to stick with the name. It was cooler than whatever the Russians had come up with.

The team scrambled out of the APVs and unloaded their equipment. A couple of men remained behind to watch the vehicles while the rest moved deeper into the Zoo. There were more than enough of them to keep any oncoming horde of critters off their backs until they did something stupid like trying to pull a plant or kill one of the huge bipeds.

Sal shook his head, adjusted his rifle for better grip, and joined the group. The two scientists led the way but they peered around and tried to identify tracks that would indicate a direction for their search. As it turned out, a centipede the size of an anaconda that carried a nest full of eggs wasn't that difficult to track, even through there. With their night vision on, there was a very clear path to follow. It seemed like the creature had dragged its nest away and the visible swath it had left in its wake led them in a firm southeasterly direction.

The group moved quickly. Many of them had the look of people who were new to the Zoo. In fairness, if you hadn't been around for the past year or so to get used to the dramatic changes that had taken place, it would be difficult to acclimate to the darkness, the number of dangerous creatures, and…oh yes, the plants out there that attacked people and dragged them away to be eaten in some horrifyingly slow death.

Sal wasn't sure there was a mentally stable person alive who would feel comfortable about acclimating to that—at least not if they planned to remain mentally stable.

Did that mean he was something less?

Probably.

He raised his hand quickly and glanced around. Kennedy and a couple of the others immediately stopped but the bulk of them continued to follow the tracks.

"What?" she asked. She'd already learned to trust her partner's gut in these things.

"My motion sensors picked up on something," he said. That much was true, but the fact was that he'd noticed his senses had adjusted far more to the darkness around them. He would have to find out later whether it was one of the effects of the blue stuff he took or if it was simply him now used to not being an apex predator around there.

For now, he was sure something was following them. If his experience counted for anything, it was something that wanted them eaten, dead, or hurt. In the Zoo, things either ran away from you or stalked you. There didn't seem to be any room for coexistence with the humans who came inside.

Sal raised his rifle, his eyes narrowed as he looked for what moved in the darkness. He couldn't help a smile when four eyes turned toward him, reflecting what little light was in the Zoo, and stared at him from up in the branches. He tagged the familiar creature with his HUD to alert Kennedy and the others to its location.

It seemed to sense this and bounded down from the trees with enough force to make the ground shake. It was smaller than the one they'd encountered before. That wasn't saying much, though, and in this light, it was still large enough to be terrifying. It stood almost as tall as a horse at the shoulder and slithered like a lizard, with massive jaws more than willing to tear into armor and a lightning-quick tail that could rip a man's head clean off.

Good times.

Sal opened fire first and tracked the creature with the combat protocols in his suit. It moved quickly, which made the soft target of the eyes almost impossible to catch. Even so, as it ducked and rolled, the bullets didn't ricochet but seemed to be absorbed into its skin.

Its body stiffened and he flung himself quickly to the side. He brought Kennedy down with him as the tail whipped and deflected across one of the Russians. The power of the strike hurled him aside with a chunk of his chest armor missing. Sal didn't have time to check if he was wounded but scrambled up hastily and maintained a steady stream of fire until his rifle clicked empty.

"Fucking...useless...suit," he complained and reloaded manually while the creature circled the group. Orders were shouted in Russian, and while he couldn't understand them at all, it was easy to deduce that Volkov had told his men to form a perimeter against the attacking beast.

"Yeah," Sal snarked as he dragged the slider on his rifle back to chamber a round. "This time, you have to deal with a whole shitload of us, you ugly motherfucker. Do you think you can handle that? I didn't think so!"

"Do you still harbor some resentment from the last time we ran into one of these critters?" Kennedy asked.

"It's probably not fair to hold a grudge against an entire species for what one of them did to me," he conceded, "but yeah, kind of. I hate these guys. With a burning passion."

"Come on, Jacobs. When it was only the two of us, I think we were lucky to get out of that situation alive."

"Of course you'd say that," he grumbled. "You got to shoot that one in its face."

"You really do get grumpy without your morning coffee, don't you?" She grinned. The gunfire continued, but as Sal looked around, he couldn't see where the creature had vanished to. The motion sensors went crazy but nothing moved out there.

"Yeah, the coffee is what's making me grumpy," he said and glanced at Volkov, who had called out an order, presumably to cease firing.

"What the hell was that?" the man asked once they were on the move again.

"We don't have a scientific name for it," Sal said. "But since I was the first person to write up a whitepaper on it, do you think it would be overly egotistical to name it after myself?"

"What, like Salingerious Rex?" Kennedy asked and chuckled. "I think the monster would hunt you simply for trying to paste your name onto it."

The Russian shook his head. Gregor had warned him that the two liked to bicker and fight about nothing in particular. Honestly, if it was something they did to keep their morale up out there, he was all for it, but when it interfered with his ability to have a conversation with them, it would be a problem.

Sal shook his head and turned to Volkov. "The basics. In terms of behavior, that critter's damn unique. I won't go into the details, but any attempt to anticipate what it does next would be nearly impossible."

"Right." Volkov clearly did not like that news. "What would you say about...I don't know, how do we fight it? What do we do to kill it?"

"The last time we had an encounter with one of those beasties, virtually nothing we did could bring it down," Kennedy said with a shrug. "That tail is perfectly capable of cutting into armor, though, and the claws too. It left this one in the hospital for a few days and almost killed him until I put a couple of bullets through the eye."

"So, the eye is...what you call soft target, yes?" Volkov asked.

"Right," she agreed. "And I don't think I need to tell you how difficult it is to get that shot in, although it's something to aim for."

Volkov nodded, apparently not too keen to be involved in their particular brand of banter as he turned and headed to his men and communicated the news of what they were supposed to do if the creature returned.

"What kind of name did you have in mind for it?" Kennedy asked as they pushed forward through the jungle again.

"What, you mean Salingerious Rex doesn't do it for you?" Sal asked and grinned. "Come on, it's not a dinosaur. It's not even in the same species."

"Ugh, fine," she groaned. "What were you thinking about, then?"

"I thought…Varanus Jacobis," he said with a small grin.

"Huh…that's actually not too bad," she replied. "Where does it come from?"

"Well, it shares a number of physical characteristics with a Komodo dragon, and so it seemed fitting to put it in with the same family, right?" Sal asked.

"Look at who you're talking to, buddy." She chuckled. "Anyway, I think that's a good name. I don't suppose you have anything else out here with your name on it?"

"That would be the first," he confirmed with a nod.

"Still, it's a good choice. Besides, given that it's a creature you got to study while it actively tried to kill you, I'm reasonably sure no one else will try to get their names in first."

He nodded but paused when the rest of the team stopped suddenly. The conversation would have to wait, he realized as they moved closer to the scientists still in the lead. It wasn't difficult to make out what they were saying, even though they chattered in Russian. Context was everything, and the context of their obvious confusion was that the tracks had essentially disappeared.

"These scientists don't know much about the Zoo," Volkov explained. "And they are not sure how a creature of that size carrying something that heavy could have simply disappeared."

"Well, the fact would be that the…uh, whatever the hell it is you guys call it would have looked for a new location to set up camp, right?" Sal asked and studied their surroundings.

The Russian nodded and the scientists fell silent and leaned in closer to listen. Sal had the feeling they were too arrogant to ask for help themselves but wouldn't be above taking advice that was freely given.

"The fact that everything has gone and the tracks disappeared would indicate that our hundred-legged buddy found a place to nest again," Kennedy said. "Somewhere it would feel safe. Arthropods tend to prefer nests in the ground, right?"

"Right," Sal said. "But when they feel endangered, they aren't against setting up camp in the trees. And since this is the Zoo, you should note that many of the creatures use the trees for cover. So, if what we're after isn't anywhere on the ground, our best course of action is to probably look up."

Sal could hear the moment of terrified silence from the group as everyone froze. There were more than enough monsters out there, but there seemed to be something about having to look for their predators above them that genetically terrified humans. Before he could say anything further, he heard something move in the high reaches of the jungle. Instantly alert, he hefted his rifle and aimed it upward.

The motion detectors identified something large slithering through the branches, but by all appearances, it hadn't noticed them yet.

"I don't suppose we could...um, ignore that?" Kennedy asked.

"Most certainly, no," Gregor replied. "And it doesn't look like it will ignore us either, so—"

The odd riffling sound as needle-like legs dug into the wood of the tree trunks around them yanked their attention to the reality of their predicament. It was likely that every member of the team now realized that the creature above them had all but destroyed another group of men in suits of armor like theirs. The soft click of mandibles warned them that the break they had taken was not appreciated by a creature that guarded her young against the invaders who wanted to take them away.

Sal could appreciate that. Protecting their young was one of the most vital roles of any mother out in the wild, and he had all kinds of respect for that.

At the same time, there wasn't much he wasn't willing to do at the moment to ensure that those mandibles and venom-soaked legs didn't get anywhere near him. He raised his weapon as Kennedy obviously came to the same conclusion as he had at almost the same time. She aimed her weapon in tandem with him.

He pulled the trigger first, though, and kept his rifle set to three-round bursts. The first three struck the creature dead center on one of the carapaces and dislodged it slightly from its hold on the tree with a loud, high-pitched whine that hurt his ears even through the sound filter. He could feel it in his bones in a way that made him want to turn away and run as fast as possible.

His partner's aim was far more accurate, and she delivered a couple of rounds in a semi-automatic setting on her rifle to the head of the beast. Another blood-curdling screech issued into the split second of silence before the Russians followed suit. They opened fire as one at the creature as the scientists, inexplicably unarmed, cowered behind the gunners.

Not that it would have mattered, Sal mused while he reloaded as quickly as his hands could move. The mutant was large enough to be tangled around all the trees above them. If it fell, it would probably crush them all... *Oh, that's a good point.*

"Keep formation!" he called and motioned with his free hand as the power arm continued a steady barrage of fire at the creature that now circled down toward them. "Back up! Back up!"

Kennedy fell in behind him and adjusted her shooting pattern to cover for him as he reloaded. A cloud of locusts and hyenas now also approached, but they seemed to have the good sense to know they were no match for the massive centipede and backed rapidly away into the darkness.

The Russians followed the Heavy Metal duo without hesitation. They were new to the Zoo, that much was apparent, but other than the scientists who had to be dragged into formation, they all looked like they had some experience in combat situations. The men moved quickly and precisely and followed orders without question. In addition, they maintained ongoing pressure on the creature with a constant stream of accurate fire.

Unfortunately, none of the bullets seemed to be able to pierce its armor. Like they had with the lizard they'd encountered earlier, the bullets seemed to sink a few inches into the carapaces and go no further. Worse, they served only to enrage it further.

It reached the ground. The body was almost as thick

across as Sal's torso and what looked like hundreds of spindly legs worked feverishly and in coordination to propel the beast—about six or seven meters long—forward. It was hard to tell exactly how long it was, though, since it coiled around trees to take cover against the bullets. It became extremely difficult to continue to fire at it while still moving backward step by step to avoid it.

It was only a few meters away when Sal decided to take matters into his own hands. He was accustomed to that personal idiosyncrasy by now. While he wasn't usually in a leadership position when it came to the gunfights—that was Kennedy's job—he liked to think he brought some creative thinking to their little mix. It was his turn to initiate something innovative.

He motioned sharply for them to split up. Kennedy took half the gunners and one of the scientists to the right and Sal led his group in the opposite direction. Gregor was a part of his team, while Volkov joined Kennedy as they circled. The left was closer to the centipede-like monster, which was what Sal had in mind while he fired without ceasing until his mag was empty. He was now close enough that he didn't need his suit's sensors to see the mandibles snapping at his throat.

"This is a bad idea!" he screamed to amp himself up as he dropped his rifle, drew his sidearm, and charged forward past the vicious jaws. He caught one of the legs as it moved forward to impale him and squeezed the trigger on the pistol a few times. He couldn't make any eyes out, unfortunately, and the carapace extended over the head too, which meant the slugs did little damage. The creature powered forward, knocked him onto his back at least a meter away, and hurtled forward again for the killing strike.

Out of pure instinct, Sal twisted his body and shoved his power arm forward to hammer the reinforced fist into the creature's armor. The carapace cracked and the centipede emitted another fearsome scream. Undeterred, he scrambled to his feet as the beast fell back a few steps, fisted his power arm, and punched his adversary again. Its armor broke this time and the resultant hole exposed a massive section of soft flesh which Sal quickly took advantage of. He aimed the pistol still gripped in his hand to shoot through the hole until the sidearm clicked empty.

Quickly, he yanked a spare magazine from his belt and slapped it in, but it wasn't needed. Not for the centipede monster, anyway. The mandibles had gone still although the rest of the body seemed to have a hard time accepting its end as it thrashed in violent death throes.

Sal looked at the blue blood that coated his power arm and made a face.

"That will never wash out." He hissed in disgust and shook his arm with little result.

"Come on, do you really want to get rid of the blood of your vanquished foe that quickly?" Kennedy asked as she slapped his shoulder playfully.

"Yes," he said firmly. "I can tell this stuff smells horrible and that's not something I want to greet me when I get out of my armor."

She nodded. "Agreed. That was quick thinking out there. It seems it's armor was made to take bullets better than a punch to the face, right?"

"Yeah." He grunted and still tried to dislodge the blue

gunk from his power arm. "That's what I was doing when it charged me with venomous mandibles and legs. Thinking."

She grinned but he blocked her attempt at a response with a sharp wave when one of the scientists moved toward the now completely still dead body.

"Give it a second, Doc," he said with a knowing smile.

"What are you talking about?" the man said with an intriguing mixture of Russian and British accents. "We must take samples as quickly as possible."

"The man said to give it a sec," Kennedy interjected. "I suggest you do as he says."

Sal's hesitation was rewarded with the sound of straining and cracking wood. The way the creature had climbed had weakened the trees and they were no longer able to support what looked like a massive weight elevated high in the canopy. The group backed away hurriedly as the noisy evidence of distressed timber increased. Broken branches crashed haphazardly into others and added to the damage as they fell.

Before anyone could react, the structure now visible in the treetops succumbed to the pull of gravity, along with a large portion of the vegetation. A solid burst of sunlight streamed in its wake as everything landed with a thunderous whump that came close to a roar. The creature had definitely set its nest up in the trees above, and all the shooting and the needle-sharp legs had weakened the already strained vegetation.

"See what I mean?" Sal said and grinned smugly at the scientist, who rolled his eyes and shrugged disdainfully. He didn't mind the silent rebuff as he'd managed to pull off the impossible. The nest was down and unprotected by the very dead mother. He couldn't see if any of the eggs had survived the fall, but he imagined that even if they hadn't, it wouldn't be enough to stop them from gathering specimens.

"You know," he said as the scientists brushed him aside as if to make sure he didn't steal any of their samples. "I know there's a movie or TV series that highlights the dangers of bringing the young of some super powered evil insect monsters back to civilization, but I can't think of any right now. Should my geek card be revoked?"

Kennedy grinned at him. "First of all, that was an arthropod, not an insect and...I think *Arachnid* had a plot like that? Maybe *Arachnid Two*?"

Sal nodded. "Maybe, but I never paid attention when I watched those movies."

"Yeah, they were basically drinking game movies for me too," Kennedy agreed. "But watch a movie for drinks enough times and you seem to understand the plot by the fourth or fifth time."

He gestured to Kennedy that Gregor was walking over to them.

"Well, orders have come in for us," he said when he came into earshot. "We are to collect the specimens and leave immediately. The commandant doesn't want us to risk any of what we collect now by moving deeper into the jungle."

She looked at the man and scowled. "Wait a minute, Gregor. That wasn't part of our deal. We agreed to be paid half the standard salary you guys get because we would have time to hunt for more of the Pita plants. That was the deal."

"It has changed," the Russian replied with an apologetic shrug. "You will receive the full payment, of course, plus more for helping us get the specimens back."

Kennedy smirked. "Hell no. We agreed to this deal for a reason. We make more money with the plants than with the salaries anyway. That's why we schlepped all the way over here to help you guys with this."

Volkov came forward to see what the problem was and caught the last of what Kennedy had said.

"Is there a problem?" he asked.

"Yes," she exclaimed. "We made a deal and now you guys are trying to back out of it."

"We have our orders," he muttered. "And we can't disobey. We cannot accompany you simply for your own personal profit."

"Well, we accompanied you guys for your profit," she retorted.

"And we appreciate that," the master sergeant said in an effort to defuse the situation. "You two have lived up to your reputations, which is rare in places like this. However, we cannot stray from our orders. Once the scientists have collected their samples, we will head to the base."

"And we won't join you," Kennedy advised him coldly. "Although I do expect to be paid in full for our efforts anyway."

"I will make sure it happens," Volkov said and moved away before she could respond.

"There is nothing we can do," Gregor said, his expression still apologetic. "I'm sorry."

"That's fine." She shook her head. "It's not your fault, I know. Although I expect you'll be right there to fight for them to pay us the full amount promised."

"Of course."

"And you will pick up our tab the next time we drink at the Russian bar," she added with an affirmative nod.

"I never agreed to that," the Russian protested.

"You will." Kennedy patted him on the shoulder before she moved away from him. Sal had returned to bother the scientists.

"I would appreciate it if you guys could forward your whitepapers on this beastie," he said. "I have enough to write something basic, but if you could get me results from your lab testing on the carapace especially, I'd really appreciate it."

"Jacobs!" she called. "We're moving out."

He nodded. "Oops, got to go." He'd collected a few specimens while the scientists had been busy. The Russians probably wouldn't appreciate him digging into their first major discovery in the Zoo, but he was out there for himself. The way he saw it, the only people who would be hurt by his actions were those who had bravely sent other people into the Zoo while they sat around in comfy chairs and complained that the people sent out to die didn't do it fast enough.

In all honesty, he was perfectly all right with fucking those guys over.

Sal grabbed his rifle from where he'd dropped it and dusted it off before he connected it to the power arm that was still coated in bug goo.

"Do you think they bought it?" he asked once they were moving at a good speed away from the Russians.

"Well, Gregor did sell us as greedy mercenaries whose sole objective in this mission was to make a quick buck," Kennedy replied. "I don't think they'll have too much trouble buying it."

"Gee," he said with a grin, "thanks."

CHAPTER TWENTY-SIX

She blinked and fought to keep her head from nodding forward. It had to have been at least a day by now, and she hadn't had a wink of sleep since she'd been picked up in the bar in Casablanca. That had been three or four days ago, by her estimation, and it began to tell on her. The adrenaline still pumped through her body, but it had dwindled somewhat and she'd caught herself nodding off half a dozen times.

It wasn't that she didn't want to sleep. That was almost all she could think about, to the point where she now even negotiated with herself. A significant part of her seemed determined to convince the rest that a couple of winks couldn't be that bad.

The one thing that kept her awake was the fact that she still held a gun in her hand. It had the safety off and now lay on her lap.

She breathed deeply and stared at the dim light that seeped in through the windows to give herself something to focus on. Over time, she'd realized that no other animals had poked around her little sanctuary for the past couple of hours, which really didn't help to keep her awake.

For a long time, she'd constantly reminded herself of the dangers that faced her should something get in as an inarguable reason why she had to remain awake and alert. Without that terrifying truth to sustain it, her will wavered under the oppressive need to rest.

"Is this the comm line?" a man's voice asked and jerked her from another almost-nap. She glanced around and aimed her weapon vaguely at the still empty cabin of the APV while she tried to find the source. It took a moment for her to realize that the cabin itself had its own comm line and someone tried to speak through it.

"Yes, that's the one," a woman's voice said in quick succession. She sounded annoyed.

"Okay," the man replied. "Well, I don't know if you're listening, but if you are, Anja Petrovitch, this is Salinger Jacobs and Madigan Kennedy. We were sent to pick you up and ask that you don't shoot at your potential employers. That tends to make a black mark on your resume."

Anja scrambled to the comm device and tried the various buttons, but nothing seemed to work. Then again, she should consider herself lucky that the receiver worked, all things considered.

"We're at the APV and we'll open the seal now," the man said. Her gaze snapped instinctively to the part that had been connected to the motor of the vehicle. The wheel that secured the closed door turned. She blanched when her sleep-deprived mind wondered for a moment if this wasn't a trick by the Zoo and that the beasts had found a way to kill her. Too exhausted to think this through, she suppressed a soft whimper as the wheel made one final turn and clunked loudly when the door opened.

Light washed inside. Not much of it, but more than she'd become used to over the past couple of...however long she'd been trapped inside. No monsters waited outside, only two faces hidden behind heavy armor helmets. They were definitely human, though.

The woman offered a hand to help her out and Anja paused only to retrieve the pack Andrej had left behind. It wasn't a small door, but the fact that the vehicle had tipped over meant it was somewhat awkward to get through. She managed it finally and stretched when her feet touched the ground once more.

It wasn't as dark as she'd thought it would be. The windows must have been tinted or something since the spots she'd thought were stars were actually hints of sunlight that seeped through the tree cover. There weren't many of them, but they sure beat the hell out of the darkness she'd lived in.

"So," the man said cautiously and looked first at her and then at the other woman, "do I offer to take her pack? Is it sexist to offer? Is it more sexist not to offer? I'm so confused right now."

His companion chuckled. "Shut up, Jacobs. She's armed, and she has the two of us. She'll be fine." She paused and turned her attention to the hacker. "I'm Kennedy. This blabbering dumbass is Jacobs."

She nodded a greeting. English had been taught as a

second language in primary school and she'd advanced it further during her studies in an IT college in Boston. As a result, her grasp of the language was good, if a little rusty after spending the past five or so years in Russia.

"My name is Anja Petrovitch," she replied and realized there was a crack her voice. Tears tracked down her cheeks and her two rescuers seemed somewhat disconcerted as if uncertain what to make of that.

"What say you we get moving, hm?" Jacobs said with an encouraging smile. "Do you want me to take your pack?"

"I've got it," Anja replied and tried to smile, but the tears persisted as she clutched the pack tighter like a lifeline.

He nodded and hefted the large rifle in his power arm before he glanced at the other woman.

"Let's get this show on the road," Kennedy said. Her suit was bulkier, heavier, and looked more powerful than the one the man wore, and Anja wasn't sure what to make of that. Either way, they both looked like they were able to handle themselves, as had been their reputation. Andrej had told her that before she headed out there. She didn't feel completely safe, but it was nice to not be alone anymore.

It wasn't a short walk out and she knew she slowed their little team. That wasn't entirely surprising. She was dressed in a uniform, while they wore suits of armor that had been designed for this kind of terrain. It made sense that they would maintain a faster pace than she could. She had been dropped off somewhere close to the edge of the Zoo, however, and before too long, vast dunes spread ahead in an endless sea of sand as far as the eye could see. It was close to sunset, which made the shock of seeing the sun and the unobscured sky a little easier as they moved out from the heavy tree cover.

Sal stepped forward once they reached the edge and peered across the dunes.

"He's late," he muttered and shook his head.

"He most likely had trouble finding us," Kennedy replied, shaking her head. "He knew more or less the location, but I could only send coordinates once we were close to the desert. I had a ping from him saying he caught our signal and was headed our way. We won't have to wait long."

She wasn't wrong. The sun hadn't even slid behind the horizon before the sound of a heavy diesel engine could be heard. Soon, the vehicle in question came into view and roared quickly and smoothly over the dunes in their direction.

Anja froze and wondered if she should be afraid of this, but Jacobs waved her fears away quickly.

"This is the guy who organized all this," he explained with a chuckle.

All this, she guessed, meant getting her out of Russia, faking her capture and death, and finally, her rescue from one of the most terrifying places on Earth. She knew she should feel relaxed by that, but all she could come up with was exhausted.

The JLTV, easily distinguishable as American by the more delicate Hammerhead design, stopped a few meters away from them. The door was pushed open and Gregor stepped out. He looked exceptionally tired as well.

"I don't know how you Americans get around in these things," he complained and sounded more than a little frustrated. "So light and nimble, yes, but do you really expect to need that speed and maneuverability out here? I had to stop for repairs twice on the way to meet you."

"We have someone working on that already, Gregor," Sal said. He shook the man's hand with a smile as Kennedy guided Anja into the vehicle. "We really appreciate you doing this for us."

"Hey, you saved my life," the Russian said with a grin. "I thought I owed you at least one."

"And a bar tab," Kennedy reminded him as she shut the door.

"I thought that was only an act," Gregor protested. He slid into his place in the driver's seat as Sal and Kennedy took the passenger seats in the front and back, respectively. "Something to sell the pretense to the others."

"Gregor, you should know me well enough by now that I never joke about alcohol," she said with a grin as she shuffled to find a more comfortable position in her suit. "Now drive. We want to be back at the base before it gets too late."

He slid their Hammerhead into gear, but his expression looked thoughtful. Sal knew what the man wanted to ask. Courtney had been there to help him out of the Zoo and get him to a hospital while Sal and Kennedy stayed out there to do their job. Where was she now?

Sal ground his teeth and shoved the subject from his mind.

"Someone back there isn't buckled in," Gregor called from the front. Sal checked to make sure although he already knew he'd strapped himself in. He wasn't sure how the Russian drove, but all things considered, it was better to be safe than sorry.

To his right, though, Anja leaned back in her seat with eyes closed. Her hands held the pistol she'd refused to let go of all day and her pack had been shoved between her legs. He reached over gently to click the safety on her gun before he pulled the three-point belt over her and snapped it securely.

"Good to go," he called. The woman didn't even stir.

It wasn't often that the real world lived up to its Hollywood equivalent, and this was one area that failed in that category. Where Courtney had expected a metal table and metal chairs in a brightly lit room that had a one-way mirror to it, all she had was the one-way mirror. Four worn office chairs, a faux-wood table that had all kinds of coffee stains on it, and a cheap light bulb were the disappointing reality.

Movies and TV made being a cop look more glamorous than this. Then again, they had to. No one would watch an hour of what she now looked at, plus commercials, every week.

She smirked and leaned back in her seat. That sounded like something Sal would say.

"Is there something amusing about your current situation, Miss Monroe?" one of the detectives across from her asked as he leaned forward.

"The fact that you clowns repeatedly try to get me to

talk without my lawyer is damn amusing, yeah," she said with a chuckle. "And it's Dr. Monroe to you."

"Right, whatever," the second detective retorted, his gaze fixed on his notes.

After a few minutes, the door to the small room opened to admit a woman in an expensive pantsuit in her mid-thirties. She wore gold-rimmed glasses, but that didn't detract from the fact that she rocked the sexy librarian look with her blonde hair tied in a classy yet rigid bun.

Now that sounded like something Madigan would say. She smirked again.

"Alisson Marie, attorney-at-law," she said by way of greeting and shook Courtney's still handcuffed hand before she addressed the two detectives. "Come on, Henry, Frank. You guys tried to grill my client without any legal supervision? Do I have to write you two up for that kind of bullshit again?"

The two detectives looked like they knew this woman. And from the way they straightened hastily and cleared their throats, they didn't much like her, even though they exuded a healthy amount of respect.

"You're my lawyer?" Courtney asked.

"Of course," Marie said with a practiced smile as she took the seat beside her. "Silverton called and told me he had a client who was in something of a bind and needed the best to help her out. I'm the best, and I'm here."

"What are you the best at again?" Frank asked with a surly grimace.

"Making sure you two bozos don't slap a guilty charge on any old person and call it a day," she snapped. Damn, she sounded like a schoolteacher.

"Why isn't Silverton here himself?" Courtney asked curiously.

"Isaac is great at residential and financial law, but his comprehension of criminal law is rather basic," the woman explained, "so he called me in." She had the look of someone who moved fast and wanted to make sure everyone kept up with her.

Monroe nodded and focused her attention on the two detectives.

"The first question is if you're so innocent, how come you need a criminal defense lawyer?" Henry asked and folded his arms.

"Because when in the Zoo, you make sure you have all the weapons you need," she responded tartly. "Given that I'm in a police station and am not delivering coffee and fucking donuts, I think the same principle applies."

"And I would ask that you direct all your questions to me and not my client," Marie interjected sharply.

"Well, you might want to ask your client about this apparent fixation with the Zoo," Frank said. He shook his head and refused to meet the lawyer's eye.

"My client has no need to answer any question regarding any alleged fixations," she said with a small smile. The two detectives were on the defensive. In all fairness, it was three in the morning and neither looked like they enjoyed being dragged out of their beds to deal with this kind of thing.

"Well, perhaps you would rather ask your client about the five men we found dead on her premises," Henry said and pushed four open files containing pictures of the men across the table. "Four of whom were found shot in what some might call an execution-style kill."

"With their own guns," Courtney added with a smirk.

Marie looked sharply at her, and she had the feeling that the woman silently told her there was no need for her to say anything more. She shook her head with a similar sense of defensiveness that she had seen in the two detectives before she leaned back in her seat and folded her arms.

"As fun as all this conjecture is—and believe me, I've seen good movies based on less—I'm afraid conjecture is all it is," the lawyer said with an apologetic smile. "You boys are fishing, and you know it."

"We have two officers who are witnesses to your client shooting one of the men from her second-floor window!" Frank protested.

"From what I read of those two witness statements—and forgive me if I missed something, but I had to read the files on my way over here..." Marie retrieved a couple of files from her briefcase and laid them on the table as if to make a point. "From what I read, the man who was seen shot was the one who opened fire first and subsequently invaded my client's personal property, still shooting, before he was gunned down in self-defense. And, I might add, quite possibly in defense of your two officers as well."

"The fucker ruined my lawn," Courtney pointed out belligerently.

"The fucker is dead," Frank snapped.

"The four men—" Henry began, but Marie cut him off masterfully.

"Wore black tactical equipment and body armor and

were armed when they invaded my client's house," she said. She leaned forward and fixed the detectives with a hard look to maintain the pressure of her cold tone. "Now, if you want to go in front of a grand jury and explain to them that my client should not have defended herself and her property from four heavily armed invaders, be my guest. Especially since this is based solely on the fact that—according to your, shall we call it less than expert analysis—her defense was conducted in a fashion that might be considered by some, to quote your words, an 'execution-style killing.'

"I don't like your odds, though. We might be in the state of California, but we're still in the United States of America, where people tend to get tetchy when the topic is self-defense."

Neither detectives appeared to have anything else to say. They sighed and leaned back in their seats like they were the ones who were under interrogation.

"Now, you boys could still press charges for the five... Well, let's see...oh, aggravated assault, assault with a deadly weapon, two weapons possession charges... Very nice. Five pending arrest warrants between Oregon, Florida, and New York," Marie said as she scanned the files of the dead men. "You'd be able to push a manslaughter charge, at best, since California has no laws regarding the duty to retreat, but if you do that, I'll have to bring up the fact that you interrogated my client before her Miranda rights were read and without waiting for her legal representative to arrive. I'm sure your commissioner would be very interested to hear about what you consider the proper and due course of the investigation."

The two men gulped, and the woman pushed to her feet. She brushed something disdainfully from her gray suit. "On the other hand, you might see these as a homicide committed in self-defense, press no charges, and make sure the crime scene cleaners know that my client's house is a priority. In either case, we're done here. Have a nice evening."

She gestured for the men to undo Courtney's cuffs, and in under a minute, the two of them walked toward the exit of the precinct.

"Here's my card," Marie said and made no effort to slow her pace when Courtney struggled to keep up. "I'll make sure to send my invoice for billable hours to your residence since I couldn't find a work address on your file. Well, I did, but it was in the Sahara Desert and you know I won't pay postage for that."

Courtney smirked, took the card, and studied it. "Holy shit, you're good."

"I take pride in my work," she said with a smirk. "Not as much as you do with yours. I don't know what biology doctorates do out there in the Zoo, but that was some damn fine shooting."

"Son of a bitch," Monroe muttered.

Her companion turned to look at her with a small confused smile.

"My shooting has gotten much better," she explained. "Sal and Madie won't believe this when I tell them."

The smile remained as they reached the revolving doors of the station.

"You're not quite right in the head, are you Dr. Monroe?" the lawyer asked.

Courtney made no effort to hide her confusion at the question.

"Don't worry, no judgments on my end," Marie said as they walked across the parking lot to a Jaguar parked nearby. "I've dealt with far worse than you, I'm happy to say. And in this case, I like your style. Come on, I'll give you a ride home. That'll go into the billable hours too."

Courtney smirked. If she was honest, she rather liked Marie's style as well.

CHAPTER TWENTY-SEVEN

S al examined the power arm that carried his rifle. Their return to the compound had left them with enough time to repair what had been broken and bruised on their last couple of trips. Unfortunately, having someone new in the operation meant additional expenditure for new equipment.

In her defense, Anja had come up with a fairly comprehensive list of what she would need to set up shop with them. She was willing to work with them anyway since they had been there to help her get on her feet after she was hounded out of her country. But they needed something from her too, and that meant she had to be properly equipped to do it.

The downside was that everything on her list was extremely expensive, and even more so to have it shipped all the way to the compound. Their buffer had taken care of the buy problems, but for the shipping to come through, they needed more cash flow.

Which meant Sal and Kennedy once again suited up and headed into the Zoo.

"I fucking hate this place," he all but snarled. "I have literally started to loathe coming in here."

"Give it a week," Kennedy replied.

"What?"

"Give it a week," she repeated. "One week spent lurking in the compound, playing video games, running lab tests or whatever, and you'll be more than ready to come back here. You're an action addict. You'll always complain about things but you'll always come back for more. That's who you are."

"I...no, that's not who I am at all," he protested with a chuckle. "What are you talking about?"

Kennedy raised her hand and Sal bit back his next words. After a few seconds, he also heard what had caught her attention.

"That's a distress signal...bearing northwest of here," she said. "Do you want to check it out?"

"Well, if we've picked the signal up, it can't be that far away, right?" he asked and shrugged. "Let's do it."

They adjusted their direction and walked on with their weapons drawn and primed for a fight. Surprisingly, there was no sign of one. Usually, any fight included a horde of animals screeching and an equal amount of gunfire. Both were conspicuously absent, which meant they were probably way too late to help anyone.

Their focus intensified as they tried to find the source.

"I don't see anything around here," he said, alert for any sign of danger while his gaze roved the underbrush. "Not even any signs that there might have been a fight large enough to warrant setting off an emergency beacon."

"I do." His partner's tone seemed almost a growl and she raised her rifle. He mirrored her battle-ready stance even before he identified the source of her belligerence. No animals could be seen for miles but at least a dozen men, fully decked in military gear and all armed, stood with their rifles aimed directly at the duo.

"Well, well, well," a familiar voice said as one of the men moved closer. "If it isn't the famous and deadly Heavy Metal, out to score some cash that should go to some of the hard-working soldiers in the base."

"Brandon?" Sal leaned in for a better look and to confirm why the man's voice sounded familiar, although he knew his partner had recognized him first. She was the one who had beaten him soundly outside the bar. He had only beaten him in a drinking competition.

"What the fuck are you doing out here?" she asked.

"Telling you two to drop your weapons and come quietly," the corporal instructed as the other men moved shifted closer.

"You know, I don't see that happening," she said evenly.

"Well, it's either a quick death, or...well, yeah, a quick death, so it doesn't really matter what happens," the man said with a chuckle. "Although we might simply shoot you fuckers in the knees and let the creatures out here handle things. I hear they like taking their time with their kills."

"You clearly know nothing about animals," Sal interjected. "And I don't mean Zoo animals, either. Just regular, everyday animals. Otherwise, you'd know there aren't many out there that kill for pleasure and even fewer like to take their time with it."

"Whatever. I'm not a scientist." Brandon laughed.

"Obviously," he muttered under his breath.

"That said, a ton of money has been paid to eliminate the two of you," the corporal continued. He sounded aggravated by their noncompliance. "You've poked into stuff that rich people outside the Zoo would rather remain unpoked. I don't know the details, but the fact remains, they're rich and they want your annoying asses gone. See, I would have done that kind of shit for free, but meeting the two of you out here, all on your lonesome... Hell, getting paid is simply the cherry on the very delicious cake that is my life."

"Wow, you like to hear the sound of your voice, don't you?" Kennedy asked and glanced quickly at her partner. His gaze, however, was pinned on something directly above the dozen or so men who stood in front of them.

"Don't move a muscle," he said softly.

"Now why wouldn't I move?" Brandon demanded. "Are you the ones who have the drop on me, by any chance?"

"I wasn't talking to you," Sal said, his voice low. His motion sensors had picked up activity in the tops of the trees—something that looked vaguely familiar and that came closer in a rush.

She followed his gaze and froze when she recognized it too. Unlike Sal, she lacked the faith that not moving would keep it at bay. Instead, she turned and sprinted away in the same second that a clustered group of vine-like tentacles extended from the darkness. They snatched three of the men and dragged them away while the hapless victims screamed and fired haphazardly.

Sal took advantage of their distraction. He followed Kennedy's lead and raced after her as fast as his legs could carry him. Loud yells and gunfire followed him as the mercenaries involved seemed unsure about whether they were supposed to rescue their comrades or pursue their targets. Brandon bellowed at them to gather their scattered testicles and follow the escapees. The shooting immediately grew more intense toward their direction, even though it seemed like Sal was out of their visual range.

Finally, Kennedy grabbed him by the arm and dragged him behind a tree.

"What do we do?" she asked, out of breath.

"Even with the help of our little friend there, I think they're still too many for us to handle head-on," he said.

"I agree, which is why I asked what we should do. Do you have any bright ideas that might get us out of this situation in an alive enough condition to kick Brandon in his testicles once he gets back?"

He paused and listened to the shouts of the men behind them.

"I have an idea, but I don't think you'll like it," he said finally.

"I'll like it more than getting shot by humans in a place where animals are supposed to be the only danger." She sounded angrier than she ever had before. "Give it a whirl."

"So," he said, "have you ever heard about the two friends and the bear?"

Brandon and his squad rushed into a clearing where the sun poured in over the bushes that grew in the middle. They were all thick and, while less than a meter tall, filled most of the space.

They looked around and a couple stared greedily at the plants. They knew the amount of money that could be made if they cleaned these bushes out. Not as much as they would make if they managed to find the two runners, but it was still a hefty bonus.

"We don't have time for this," the corporal reminded them. "We need to find them. They can't have gone too far."

"Hey, Brandon!" Sal called from the other side of the clearing. "I think you might want to rethink that."

The men circled the bushes and found him crouched beside one of the younger plants. It was still small enough to be tugged free but had five beautiful blue flowers already in bloom. That made it a very profitable but dangerous plant to play with.

"We both know that if I pull this plant out, it's basically a death sentence," he said casually. "Which is why I'm here playing truth or dare with you motherfuckers instead of running off like my friend Kennedy. And that means it's only you lot, me, and the bear. I really don't need to outrun the bear, in this case. I simply need to outrun all of you, and honestly, I like my odds."

Brandon stepped forward. "Don't do it, buddy. If you pull that plant out, you'll end up as dead as the rest of us."

"The way I see it, if I don't do it, you boys will simply shoot me. So, in this case, I have the chance to see you assholes go down with me." Sal tightened his grip. "Get ready to run—"

In that second, he yanked the plant out. There was no way to get used to what came next. A shift rippled through the jungle around them like the trees themselves were pissed off by what he'd done. Roars and screeches from all the animals in every direction erupted as a constant warning that they now came in numbers to reclaim what had been stolen.

"Like I said," he said and stepped into the middle of the group, "I suggest we all run like maniacs."

He paused to gun down the first animals to break into the clearing, a couple of locusts with scorpion tails. A crazy part of him supposed they should count themselves lucky that these creatures hadn't developed the same bullet-stopping carapaces that the centipede monster had. Unfortunately, that was a small mercy since a dozen or so more appeared in quick succession.

"We'll kill each other later," Brandon growled. "Let's get out of here!"

They sprinted away from the clearing and fired as well as they could while they ran. The ten men left of the mercenaries Brandon had brought clearly weren't experienced Zoo runners, which meant that one by one, they went down. One was dragged away screaming as the vine tentacles, even more aggressively than before, whipped out to snag him in mid-stride. Sal pushed his pace and proved his promise that he was able to outrun them all when he remained ahead. He forced himself not to look back with each successive shriek that indicated another man had fallen.

As a panther launched onto one of the men and sank its venomous fangs into him while a pack of hyenas ripped at his legs, Brandon realized that the only men left standing were himself and Sal.

"I'm going to fucking kill you, Jacobs!" the corporal bellowed as he paused to reload his rifle.

"That's the thing about the Zoo, Brandon," he responded calmly. "These monsters don't care who pulled the plant. Only who has it last."

He raised his hand—the one that had plucked the plant out of the ground—and waved goodbye. The man didn't see the sarcastic gesture, though, since his gaze was drawn to the animal that moved slowly out of the tree cover. The monster was enormous with four eyes, a jaw with dozens of teeth as long as knives in its mouth, and an agile tail.

"Fuck!" he shouted as he slapped a new magazine into place and tried to take aim. He was too late. The reptile cleared the distance between them in a single leap and rapier-like claws dug into his chest as it pushed him to the ground.

"See you later, asshole," Sal said, talking to the reptile. It looked at him for a moment and seemed to incline its head in confusion before it turned to its meal, which screamed in pain.

As Sal sprinted away, he winced when the shriek was abruptly cut short.

Resolute, he pushed the thoughts from his head and maintained his pace until he eventually found Kennedy on the trail they'd agreed to follow. She had paused to catch her breath.

"See what I mean?" he asked with a cocky grin. "There's no need to outrun the bear, only your friend."

"And have a shot of blue goop in your medical bag. It

was still too fucking dangerous," she remonstrated as they threaded through the jungle to where they'd left their Hammerhead.

"Does this mean I get thank-you sex when we get back?" he asked as they jogged together at a slow pace.

"Is that why you were so gallant and willing to take the fall like that?" Kennedy asked.

"Well, I manage to run better since I'm not so bow-legged—ow!" he exclaimed as she punched him in the chest. "If you break a rib, you'll carry my sorry ass out of here. Again."

CHAPTER TWENTY-EIGHT

"I'm a little busy here, Jacobs," Amanda said, not looking up from the weld she applied to Kennedy's suit of armor. "Say what you have to say and get the fuck out of my shop."

"Our shop," he reminded her as he slid from the counter he'd perched on to watch her work. "We all work for the same team here, right? That makes it our shop."

"My shop," she said but finally dragged herself away and switched the welder off.

"But if it's in my compound..."

"Our compound," she replied with a grin. "My shop. What can I help you with, boss?"

"When Kennedy and I snooped around in San Francisco, we found some very interesting armor designs." He had made a couple of printouts of what he'd seen there and now placed them on the counter for her to look at. "They're a little advanced and probably won't see market sales for another couple of years—which both of us know might as well be decades out here in the Zoo, right?"

"Right." Amanda narrowed her eyes as she looked at the designs. "Well, I can tell you one thing about the designers of these suits or the guys who are supposed to work on them. They watch a ton of anime. Of the big-titted girls and tentacles variety."

"I— What?" Sal asked, confused.

"Well, technically, the Japanese label anything considered pornographic as hentai," she continued, "and the tentacle stuff was invented to get past their puritanical censorship laws there, so...yeah."

He stared her down for a long moment.

"What? I'm not allowed to have interests?" she asked and shrugged. "My point is, you're driving this shit around. Did you design this?"

"Well, I based it off of some designs, but yeah," Sal admitted.

"It won't work," she said with another shrug. "It's too heavy. The more weight you add to fit bigger hydraulic pumps to move the heavy armor makes more weight, et cetera. It'll end up that anything in that design would be crushed under its own weight."

"Well," he said with a small twinkle in his eye, "what if it weighed about a third of even the lightest titanium alloy?"

She grinned and tilted her head with avid curiosity as she leaned in closer. "I'm listening."

Andressa Covington scowled when her alarm went off. She hated that she actually dreaded what the morning would bring but it wasn't like she could do anything about it.

There was no other option but to get up, drink coffee, and deal with it all like a normal person. While her attempt to eliminate another doctor of the Monroe line hadn't gone according to plan, it wasn't like this was the end of the world. She could fix this.

Still, it wasn't like she would go into work with a smile on her face. People would call for her head on the board of directors. That was inevitable, even though it wasn't that they really wanted her gone. She had enough dirt on all of them and the company besides to make sure they wouldn't send her packing unless they provided a hefty severance package to ensure she didn't have to work another day in her life. After how hard she'd worked to come this far in the world, she didn't intend to lose a grip on that now.

She stretched under her sheets and groaned softly. Both stretch and groan ended abruptly when her hand touched something cold and wet. Her eyes jerked open, then narrowed quickly as she scrambled out of bed and pulled her sheets aside.

Her hands came up to stifle a scream that already tore through her penthouse like a burglar alarm as she took a couple of steps away from the bed. On it—and staining her expensive silk linen—was the head of a cow, crudely and recently chopped judging by the amount of blood that poured over her bed.

On the neck rested a small note written on her company's stationery in bright red letters.

No horses were killed to send this warning. Don't send killers again.

Andressa struggled to hold back another scream, this one of anger. That bitch. That heiress fucking bitch!

"Señora?" said the voice of the maid, who had probably heard the shrieks. "Is everything all ri—oh, Dios Mio!" she wailed and hastily made the sign of the cross over herself.

"Don't mind that," her employer snapped, dropped the note, and headed to the door. "Get on the phone and call my lawyer. Now!"

The maid scowled but rushed off to do as she was told.

The young man frowned over his keyboard and squinted at his screen to assess the data it displayed again. He'd been at it for days now, trapped in this gloomy, semi-dark room that had been provided as a so-called home in the middle of goddammed nowhere.

The least they could have had done was fitted an aircon, he thought gloomily, conscious of the sweat that now seeped through his shirt as the temperature climbed toward midday madness. Still, they paid well—extremely well—and if he played his cards right, he could head home one day with enough stashed for a small IT start-up of his own.

If he didn't get his ass burned before then.

Which, he thought morosely, was entirely possible given the nature of this most recent off-the-books assignment. He needed to offload the information like the proverbial hot potato.

Satisfied that he'd included everything, he saved the data to a USB drive and slid the device into his pocket. That done, he worked rapidly and meticulously to scrub his entire system of every possible trace of his clandestine activity. It might already be too late, of course—there was no way to know exactly what the reverse-trace had uncovered—but he'd been at this long enough to shake them off if he played it right.

He disabled all connections and deleted them. Thankfully, this laptop was reserved only for things non-government, which made his task easier. With his files stashed in various inaccessible cloud locations, it took only a few minutes for him to wipe the entire device clean. A replacement laptop already lay beside it, ready to go once he'd put all the protective parameters and firewalls in place. This one would vanish as soon as he felt it was safe to dispose of it.

The hacker pushed back from the tiny desk and headed to the door, his expression grim. He'd had a bad feeling about this from the beginning, but the client was a man he respected—and one who seldom asked for help. They had sufficient history to make his agreement to assist him an easy one. He knew that if the man asked, there was a good reason.

The bar was fairly busy when he pushed through the door and headed directly toward a small table tucked in an alcove at the back. Good. The colonel was already there, which meant this shouldn't take long at all.

He sat opposite the man and the two exchanged a quick handshake. The waitress arrived and he ordered a beer, not because he really wanted one but because he'd have looked suspicious if he hadn't. His companion nursed his, and judging by the foam still on top, he'd ordered for the sake of appearances as well.

They made small talk until his drink arrived, simply

two men meeting over a cold one to catch up. When they were alone once more, the hacker retrieved the USB and slid it casually across the table beneath the menu neither of them had looked at.

"That was all I could find on Project Bellerophon," he said quietly. "And you were right to be concerned."

The colonel nodded and pretended to look at the menu as he palmed the device.

"There's more, though," the hacker continued. "Much more, but I couldn't dig any deeper. They're already onto me and damn near busted my ass."

Anderson frowned. "Damn near? They didn't identify you then?"

"I don't think so, but it was a close call. Too close. Reverse-tracking is a bitch, but fortunately, I know the signs. I've covered my bases and will work on some redirection in the next day or so. I think I should be in the clear."

"I goddamn hope so," Anderson muttered and looked apologetic. "I'm sorry. I should never have hauled you into this business."

"Someone had to do it." He shrugged. "But I'm done. I can't risk it, even though I'd like to."

"I know, and I appreciate what you've done. Those bastards need to be stopped, but I can't do it with half the information."

"Less than half, probably. This goes deeper than even you suspected. These people are scary powerful, Colonel, and they have contacts right up into the Pentagon. They don't play games, and even from the little on that drive, it's clear they aren't above 'disappearing' people who get in their way."

Anderson thought of the way the test pilots had gunned down the unsuspecting team in the Zoo and scowled. "You're right, kid. And it's time you got the hell out of this. Let me know if you take heat down the line."

"Sure." The hacker slid from his seat. "And you take care, Colonel. I hope you find the help you need."

So do I, kid. So do I. He watched the young man amble through the crowded bar toward the door. The real question, though, was who? The colonel finally took a sip of his beer and grimaced. The damn thing was already warm. He pushed it aside as he considered the future.

He knew this obsession would likely be the end of him, one way or another. Already, he was stuck in this goddamned desert and fully accepted that he might leave in a body bag—if he wasn't simply dumped in the Zoo, of course. Still, it was the right thing to do. And like the kid said, someone had to do it.

Now, all he needed was someone as crazy as he was— maybe a few somebodies. Some IT talent, of course, but also some badass, take no prisoners, do the right thing and fuck the consequences somebodies.

Anderson grinned. The Zoo was Crazy Central after all. The impossible happened there all the time.

JANUARY 23, 2019

THANK YOU for not only reading this story but these *Author Notes* **as well.**

(I think I've been good with always opening with "thank you." If not, I need to edit the other *Author Notes*!)

RANDOM (*sometimes*) THOUGHTS?

Right now, we have book 04 of this story in production and almost completed. We should (hopefully) be publishing the book sometime around March 1ˢᵗ, sooner if we can—but that depends on the publishing schedule.

If you haven't read the *Soldiers of Fame and Fortune* series, the first four have been wrapped into a bundle and it is for sale now at Amazon, here:

Soldiers of Fame and Fortune Boxed Set One

What is the timeline?

Well, the timeline isn't a timeline exactly, but it is a question of "which walls are built" so you know when the stuff happens. I suspect (if I can get my production editor on board) that we will take a stab at an honest to god calendar at some point.

I just think (to myself) "Wall 02 is built, Wall 03 is built and the ZOO has done XYZ…"

At some point in the future, the answer for what is happening with the stories will be, "The aliens are back…"

"Shit."

AROUND THE WORLD IN 80 DAYS

One of the interesting (at least to me) aspects of my life is the ability to work from anywhere and at any time. In the future, I hope to re-read my own *Author Notes* and remember my life as a diary entry.

Phuket, Thailand

This is the last *Author Notes* I will be typing from Thailand (for the foreseeable future. I don't suspect we will come back for a few years.)

I'd love to say the last few days have been relaxing and enjoyable, but that wouldn't be true. Mind you, a sucky day in Phuket still beats an excellent day in the upper Northeast of the United States right now, with the winter weather up there.

Here, I am walking around in thin cotton shorts. There I imagine you need seven different layers of clothes.

Well, at least I would need that many clothes and preferably a portable heater along for the ride.

We leave tomorrow to fly to Bali, stay in a hotel near

the airport for one night, then jump on at least two (2) if not three (3) planes heading back to Los Angeles, California.

During that time, I will be outlining multiple books and working on our efforts to…

As the Brain tells Pinky every show:

"Try to take over the WORLD!"

(Of publishing. Not so much the other parts. I can assure you I believe it would be a ginormous pain in the ass to control the world.)

FAN PRICING

$0.99 Saturdays (new LMBPN stuff) and $0.99 Wednesday (both LMBPN books and friends of LMBPN books). Get great stuff from us and others at tantalizing prices.

Go ahead. *I bet you can't read just one.*

Sign up here: http://lmbpn.com/email/.

HOW TO MARKET FOR BOOKS YOU LOVE

Review them so others have your thoughts, and tell your friends and the dogs of your enemies (because who wants to talk to enemies?)… *Enough said ;-)*

Ad Aeternitatem,

Michael Anderle

CONNECT WITH MICHAEL TODD

Want more?

Find us On Facebook

https://www.facebook.com/Protected-by-the-Damned-193345908061855/

OTHER MICHAEL TODD BOOKS

PROTECTED BY THE DAMNED UNIVERSE

PROTECTED BY THE DAMNED*

8 Book series

WAR OF THE DAMNED*

8 Book series

DAMIAN'S CHRONICLES*

4 Book series

WAR OF THE ANGELS*

8 Book series

ZOO UNIVERSE

BIRTH OF HEAVY METAL*

10 Book series

APOCALYPSE PAUSED*

12 Book series

SOLDIER OF FAME AND FORTUNE*

12 Book series

TEAM SAVAGE *

3 Book series

Dungeon Core TV*

6 Book series

Dungeon Rails*

3 Book series

Hellspawned Chronicles*

3 Book series

The Sheva Chronicles*

6 Book series

Unlikely Bountyhunters*

6 Book series

House Drakonnen

The Accord

The Anchor's Inheritance Saga

* DENOTES COMPLETED SERIES